FACING THE MOB

Doc Cambert called: "Hey, you…Camden!"

The big man yawned in their faces and made no other reply except to shut his strong white teeth with a *click.*

"We've come to give you a runnin' chance! Come out of that there brush and we'll give you a twenty-yard start on the hosses to get back to the hotel. If you make it…you got an hour to get out of town. If you don't make it…"

"Shut up, Doc," cut in Josh Williams. "He don't get no runnin' chance. We've had enough of that devil. We've had too damned much."

"You want me?" Camden said. "Then come and take me!" With that, he stepped forth from the shelter of the trees and began to walk toward the hotel, slowly.

They trooped their horses after him, but no man spoke, no man moved a hand. There was something too formidable about that light-footed bulk—that terribly soft-stepping monster of a man. He seemed capable of leaping at them like a mountain lion. They held their distance until Josh Williams, with a shout as though at a roundup, whirled the noose of his rope and spurred forward.

Other *Leisure* books by Max Brand ®:

SMOKING GUNS
THE LONE RIDER
THE UNTAMED WEST (Anthology)
THE TYRANT
THE WELDING QUIRT
THE BRIGHT FACE OF DANGER
DON DIABLO
THE OUTLAW REDEEMER
THE GOLD TRAIL
THE PERIL TREK
THE MASTERMAN
TIMBER LINE
THE OVERLAND KID
THE HOUSE OF GOLD
THE GERALDI TRAIL
GUNMAN'S GOAL
CHINOOK
IN THE HILLS OF MONTEREY
THE LOST VALLEY
THE FUGITIVE'S MISSION
THE SURVIVAL OF JUAN ORO
THE GAUNTLET
STOLEN GOLD
THE WOLF STRAIN
MEN BEYOND THE LAW
BEYOND THE OUTPOSTS
THE STONE THAT SHINES
THE OATH OF OFFICE
DUST ACROSS THE RANGE/THE CROSS BRAND
THE ROCK OF KIEVER
SOFT METAL
THUNDER MOON AND THE SKY PEOPLE
RED WIND AND THUNDER MOON
THE LEGEND OF THUNDER MOON
THE QUEST OF LEE GARRISON
SAFETY McTEE
TWO SIXES
SIXTEEN IN NOME
THE ABANDONED OUTLAW
SLUMBER MOUNTAIN
THE LIGHTNING WARRIOR
OUTLAWS ALL
THE ONE-WAY TRAIL
THE BELLS OF SAN CARLOS
THE SACKING OF EL DORADO
THE DESERT PILOT/VALLEY OF JEWELS
THE RETURN OF FREE RANGE LANNING
FREE RANGE LANNING
WOODEN GUNS
KING CHARLIE
RED DEVIL OF THE RANGE
PRIDE OF TYSON
DONNEGAN
THE OUTLAW TAMER
BULL HUNTER'S ROMANCE
BULL HUNTER
TIGER MAN
GUN GENTLEMEN
THE MUSTANG HERDER
WESTERN TOMMY

MAX BRAND®

CRUSADER

LEISURE BOOKS  NEW YORK CITY

A LEISURE BOOK®

May 2005

Published by special arrangement with Golden West Literary Agency.

Dorchester Publishing Co., Inc.
200 Madison Avenue
New York, NY 10016

ISBN 0-8439-5441-8

Printed in the United States of America.

Visit us on the web at www.dorchesterpub.com.

CRUSADER

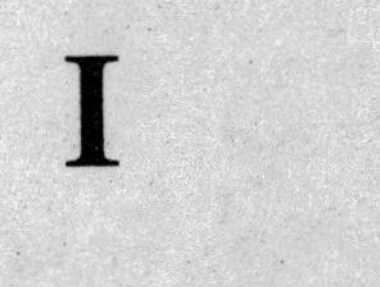

CYCLONE KNOCKED SENSELESS

The distinguishing feature of Sparrow Roberts, among managers of prize fighters, was that he believed in keeping his protégé busy in the ring, even if the purse were small. The result was that when Colonel Joshua Nichols decided to put the town of Juniper on the map and make his own name famous by bringing over the middleweight champion of the world to fight for a great purse, the American middleweight champion refusing to close for moderate terms, the fight was offered to Sparrow Roberts and his protégé, Cyclone Ed Morgan. Pierre Lacoste, the great French fighter, the idol of Europe and the king of his class throughout the world, claimed such a huge purse that even Colonel Nichols, with all of his new millions dug out of Western mountains, was dazed. A quarter of a million in hard cash was a staggering sum. But Colonel Nichols wanted Lacoste and closed with him for that figure. Then he tried to balance the bargain, to a certain extent, by making reasonable terms with some American fighter. When the American champion refused to sign for less than a hundred and fifty thousand, Colonel Nichols paid no more heed to him but cast about for a good second choice and found one almost immediately in the person of Cyclone Ed Morgan.

The Cyclone was a known man. He never had boasted much science, but he carried a devastating punch in either hand and he had never been so much as knocked from his solid feet. He was, first, last, and all the time, a fighter, and Sparrow Roberts had kept him at his work. He had fought for a hundred and fifty dollars a night in small towns throughout the East. He had been in the four-round game in California. He had toured the States far and wide, sometimes battling a dozen times a month with every man who came along. In all of those varied contests he had never been so much as staggered. These experiences, moreover, were well compacted into the short space of six years. Beginning as a welterweight, at the age of eighteen, he had matured to the full middleweight limit, and at the age of twenty-four he was a seasoned veteran.

The whole country knew him. When a sporting writer announced Cyclone Ed Morgan's next engagement, it was always with a little verbal pat on the back. For, much as boxing fans enjoy cleverness, what they like best of all is real fighting. The Cyclone was a warrior of the truest mettle from his head to his heels. A stinging blow to the face, a crushing swing to the wind, instead of sapping his heart or his vitality, made his eyes glisten and brought him dancing and gliding in for more. It was his boast that, wherever he appeared, there was sure to be a good fight—while it lasted. There were few so ignorant and slow that they could not hit him, and there were few who, when he struck in return, could keep on their feet.

Such was Cyclone Morgan when he was signed to meet the famous Pierre Lacoste, the wizard of the prize ring, the genius of the padded gloves, who whiffed strong men into sweet sleep with a touch of his hand, whose dazzling speed made the fastest boxers seem slow, whose chivalrous and carefree nature had made him an international favorite. He looked like a gentleman and spoke like one; he fought like a dozen fiends rolled in one.

No one granted Cyclone much of a chance against Pierre Lacoste. But still, the odds were not high against him, for Lacoste, it was said, had built up a reputation by knocking over the foreign crop of middles and light heavies. However, there was a general feeling in sporting circles that the only good fighters are Americans, or foreigners American trained. There was a feeling that no foreign champion could quite understand the ripping, tearing in-fighting game that flourished on this side of the water until he had been through the mill here. Besides, since the bout was limited to fifteen rounds, it was felt that there was a very excellent chance for Cyclone Ed Morgan at least to last out the limit. All of his backers sent their money to Europe and bet vigorously that the American representative would at least last the full fifteen rounds.

In the meantime, Sparrow Roberts brought his man to the town of Juniper to train there.

Juniper was at a crossroads saloon, at one time. Then Colonel Josh Nichols found gold in the mountains nearby and turned Juniper into a town by his discovery. As he grew rich, Juniper was transformed in a brief six months to a swarm of hundreds of tents and wooden shacks. The gold strike caused a typical gold rush. Other camps leaped into being through the surrounding region, and some of them were very large. But Juniper remained the chief center, the fountainhead of supplies for all the others. Its importance was assured when the enterprising railroad drove a branch line nine miles to the doors of the village. Its population, thereafter, felt that Juniper was definitely on the map. They began to build more permanent structures in place of their old flimsy ones. Presently a thriving little city sat in the throat of Juniper Pass, with the Juniper River washing its feet, and the great mountains lifting their white heads in a circle around it. Like spikes in a spider's web, from Juniper a dozen trails led out toward various of the other nearby camps, and all day long there was never a time when a rolling dust cloud on some quarter of the horizon did not mark the approach or the departure of a group of horsemen or of a number of wagons drawn by long teams of mules. Sometimes, when Colonel Josh Nichols sat on the roof garden of his Spanish house on the outer verge of the town and overlooked all this multiplying activity, he had the sweet content of a child, who had created a toy, and by chance the toy had worked.

He was troubled by one thing only: whenever he mentioned Juniper, he had to tell where it was. No one had the slightest idea that there was a place of such a name, or in what state it might be located. It cost the colonel a good many hours of humiliation, here and there, to explain the location of his home town. That was why he finally decided that he would put Juniper on the map.

The colonel thought of many schemes. He thought of erecting a great hospital among the adjoining mountains and opening it to the free use of tubercular patients who might need the dry, bracing air of those high plateaus. But there is something repulsive about a health resort, to the people who are not sick. The colonel thought of establishing a stock farm in the valley and raising there only blood race horses of the finest quality.

He discarded these ideas, and others. He discarded, among the rest, the thought of creating a fine newspaper, to be known as the Juniper *Times*, which would embody all that meant the most in the mountains and to the mountain people. When the world wished to learn what the Rocky Mountain district felt about a certain topic, it needed only to turn to the Juniper *Times*. But a friend who had had experience in financing a newspaper confided in the ear of the good colonel certain expense items that made his head swim.

The very next idea upon which he hit was the prize fight. Pierre Lacoste was the most brilliant and romantic figure in the ring. Pierre Lacoste had beaten everyone within twenty pounds of his weight in Europe. No one could put up a sufficient purse to induce Pierre to cross the Atlantic and stake his crown. That is to say, no one could be found until the colonel appeared. He offered Pierre, as has been said, a quarter of a million "to fight fifteen rounds with any man in the world weighing not more than one hundred and sixty pounds." So the fight came into being.

The colonel began to reap a reward at once. Every sporting paper in the country got out maps and, failing to find Juniper anywhere upon it, sent special representatives to write up the place. The representatives came and smiled, but remained to pick up what news they could, and found plenty of it. Seven gun duels within a week furnished the reporters with a tidy bit of gossip. They sent out a flock of feature stories that made some millions of people in far-off cities rush to the moving-picture houses and stare at the Western films with a new credence.

On the whole, it took the colonel about a fortnight to put Juniper most decidedly upon the map. It would also cost him three hundred thousand dollars in stakes and expenses, plus two hundred thousand more for the lining of a certain natural amphitheater nearby with seats. He arranged that amphitheater to accommodate thirty thousand people. His average price would be twenty-five dollars. If he sold out the house, he would have a quarter of a million in profit above all of his big expenses. He was reasonably sure that he would sell out the house. Inquiries for tickets floated in from every side. The railroad made Herculean endeavors to improve its lines of communication with Juniper, and all was well. A twenty thousand sale would meet all expenses. But even if there was a deficit, the colonel felt that he had given the place a million in advertising. Men swarmed in from every side. Where the mines had gone short-handed for lack of labor, now the mine owners could cut the wages and still get all the help that they needed.

In every way it looked to the colonel like the best and the cheapest bit of advertising that he had ever undertaken in his life, and he blessed the day when he had first conceived it. The mines prospered more and more. The wide main street of Juniper was paved from the station all the way out to the amphitheater, and that bench-lined hollow was given by some aggressive reporter the title of "Nichols's Coliseum."

Under that title it grew famous. It appeared in Sunday supplements. It was a household word. The colonel had immortalized himself as well as the town that he had created. How could the work have been more complete?

In the meantime, Pierre Lacoste began his training in France, but Cyclone Ed Morgan and his manager and trainer and sparring partners, arrived in Juniper, looked over the place for the site of a training camp, and finally, rejecting all persuasion on the part of those who wished to make them a part of the show properties of the town, they left Juniper's noise and dust far behind them and went out into the open woods to camp and live in a tent until the hour grew near for the opening tap on the gong.

Sparrow Roberts was an outdoor man. He selected the camp wisely. It was not high and exposed, but sat in a shoulder of a mountain, with a considerable view beneath them. A little stream trickled across its face and showered away in a musical cascade below. In the corner of the clearing, Sparrow had the ring erected, built strong and high, so that all who came could see clearly. Then he started Cyclone Ed Morgan to work.

They would hunt through the mountains in the morning. At noon they came back to a square meal, two hours of sleep after it, then some gymnastics, and in the golden cool of the late afternoon some brisk boxing in the ring. Under that regime Cyclone Ed developed rapidly. In a fortnight he was in perfect trim. His wind was right. His muscles were neither too hard nor too soft. His mental condition was perfect. It always was, for Cyclone Ed Morgan was born with the happy conviction that he was invincible in a fight. The only reason that he did not set sail after the heavyweight championship of the world was that his manager would not make the correct engagements. But, in his heart of hearts, Cyclone Ed smiled at the thought that any man in the world could stand up to him in a finish fight.

Then the first crushing blow fell. At the end of the first night, walking by himself through the woods, rifle in hand, Ed Morgan came to the Parker farm and found pretty Jenny Parker in the vegetable garden. As for Jenny, she was quite overwhelmed at meeting with a celebrity. She was agreeably astonished by his appearance. She had imagined all prize fighters as abysmal brutes, but she found Cyclone a fellow with a pair of bold, pleasant blue eyes, and a smile that had not yet been spoiled by the impact of four-ounce gloves. One ear was a trifle thicker than it needed to be, and there was a scar across the bridge of his nose. But these were surely very minor and by no means insurmountable defects.

As for Cyclone Ed, he had been too busy fighting for six years and watching his bankroll multiply to pay much heed to girls. On this day, feeling on top of his game, so to speak, with the sun warming his body and her smile warming his heart, he left the door open and Jenny Parker walked in and took permanent possession. Ten minutes later he kissed her for the first time. Ten minutes after that they confided in each other that this must be love of the purest water. And ten minutes further on they were started for Juniper. They found the minister's house. He arranged all the rest. In the evening, four reporters and half a dozen eminent townsfolk saw Cyclone Ed Morgan take a bride.

When poor Sparrow Roberts heard about it, he turned pale. He was so distressed that he could not even curse Cyclone Ed. He could only express his fury feebly, in good English.

"Look at me," he said to Cyclone Ed. "I've been married twice. What good did it do me? Where are my wives now? But you can't learn from me. You know too much. You'll have to learn from Pierre, too. I hope he . . . I hope he tears your block off . . . you sap!"

Then he went to Colonel Nichols. "Lacoste has won," he said. "Ed got married."

The colonel merely grinned. He had very little interest in the actual outcome of the fight.

"Maybe not," he said. "Maybe it'll be simply a good bit of extra training for the ring."

But Sparrow could not see any humor in the matter. "Nobody can do two things at the same time," he said sadly. "Nobody can be a good husband and a good prize fighter. Ed is done for."

Then he went slowly back up the valley to the training camp. It was the dusk of the evening. Coming up the path, he tripped over a limp figure. He leaned and turned it over. It was Cyclone Ed Morgan, lying senseless upon the ground!

THE BAREFOOTED GENT

The yell of startled Sparrow Roberts brought two burly sparring partners with a rush down the slope. They caught up poor Ed Morgan and carried him hastily to the half shack, half house where they lived. There they doused him with a bucket of water. But even the water brought him only slowly to his senses, and, as he wakened and groaned, they felt him muscle by muscle and bone by bone but could find no injury. There was not a spot or a mark on him, except a long blue welt along the side of his jaw.

"He tripped and fell and hit the rocks," said Sparrow at last. "I was some scared at first. Hey, Ed, how d'you feel? What's wrong? Shake yourself together."

Ed sat up with a sudden ferocity. "Where is he?" he snarled out.

"Who?"

"The bird that soaked me."

"What? Did somebody knock you out, Ed?"

"Knock me out? Not with his hands. He hit me with a club! Or he had a friend that sneaked up behind me and swatted me."

"What happened?"

"I was comin' up from town. I was walkin' slow and easy. I wanted to tell you, Sparrow, that me bein' married didn't make no difference about me trainin' for the fight. . . ."

"Sure it don't," groaned Sparrow. "Take on all the worries of a married man . . . try to box so's your face don't get spoiled for the sake of your wife . . . act up like that . . . and a devil of a mess you'll be when Pierre Lacoste gets ready to tap you on the bean. But lemme hear about this bird that slugged you."

"With a club!" shouted Ed Morgan. "You know that I ain't ever been lifted off'n my feet with a punch. Don't you, Sparrow, old boy?"

There was such a wail of appeal in this voice, that Sparrow blinked and regarded his champion again. This time more closely. "What happened?" he snapped out.

"I was comin' up the path. Had a stone in my hand, and I slung it onto the brush along beside the path. Dog-gone if I didn't hear that stone spat on flesh. There was a snarl that made my hair stand up on end, but what jumped out wasn't no wild animal. It was a gent that was mostly bare, brown like an Indian . . . maybe he was an Indian . . . and a wild pair of eyes, darned if I ever seen amber-lookin' eyes like them, before! He didn't say nothin'. I was too paralyzed to do nothin'."

"And he knocked you flat?"

"Him? His punch wasn't more than a tap. But just as he tapped me, I felt something slug me in the back of the head like. . . ."

Sparrow Roberts fumbled at the back of the head of his fighter with expert fingers. "It feels like that, sometimes," he said to those who were standing around, listening and wondering. "You get rapped on the point and you feel like somebody had soaked you in the back of the head with a club. A doctor, he tried to tell me what made that. I dunno. It's something where the nerves . . . well, Ed, your luck started on your weddin' day. You got knocked out the same. . . ."

Cyclone Ed leaped to his feet and threatened to destroy all who cast such aspersions upon him. He had never been knocked out. He would annihilate everyone who pretended that such a lie was the truth.

To this raving, Sparrow Roberts listened with an impassive face. "This is all pretty smooth, kid," he declared gravely. "But they ain't any lump on the back of your head, and we all can see where you was slugged on the jaw. There's a welt as big as a hen's egg."

"By the heavens . . . !" began Ed Morgan, shouting with wrath.

"Lay low," snarled out Sparrow. "I ain't claimin' that this here was handed you on the level. All the baby had that socked you on the jaw was a pair of brass knuckles, I guess. No bare *fist* ever done that. I've seen 'em all soak. And nobody ever done that! Not with his fist!"

"Brass knuckles, eh?" said Bert Kenny, who did duty as one of the sparring partners. "Then maybe it's the same dirty dog that swiped the punching bag and the punching bag platform. Maybe it's the same sneak thief that swiped the gloves, too, and the weights. . . ."

"There's gettin' to be something wrong about this here camp," said the second sparring partner, Vince Munroe, whose speed had left him, but whose tricks and ring wisdom still made him a dangerous teacher. "The way I figger it. . . ."

"You figger too much," snapped out Sparrow. "Too much thinkin' around this here camp. I'm tired of it. I'll do a little bit more. You all hear me talk? I'll do the thinkin' from now on. To hear you birds chatter, you'd think that there was a jinx on this camp!"

He stamped on into the outer evening, and then came hurrying back again. "Look here, Cyclone," he said, "what was the looks of this crook with the brass knuckles?"

"Sort of young-lookin'. I didn't get a fair look at him. He came so fast! Like a cat that jumps and sinks its teeth into you and then gets away. You know how it is. But it seemed to me that he had a patch of fur around his hips. Outside of that, clothes didn't bother him none. Y'understand? Didn't have a thing on. Maybe he'd been down havin' a swim in the pool."

"How did he hit?" asked Sparrow.

"A straight right with a. . . ."

"A straight right, eh? Brass knuckles or not, that baby can cock, believe me."

"When I get him . . . ," began Cyclone. "Well, that's all that I'm askin' for, another chance to have a whirl with him. I'll do the swatting next time, and he'll do the sleepin'."

"Sure," said Sparrow a little absently. "Sure. They ain't nobody in the world, heavy nor light that can really take you off your feet, kid. I guess you know that."

"I've tried the stuff they sent for six years," answered Cyclone sneeringly. "None of it's fazed me yet."

Thereafter he bade them good night and went forth toward Juniper and his bride of yesterday.

"He's sure a fathead about that iron jaw," said Vince

Munroe. "Damned if I ain't sort of glad that somebody crooked him."

"It'll take him down about where he ought to be," suggested Bert Kenny. "Still, he's got a mighty hard jaw to crack. You got to hand him that."

"Do I hand him that?" Vince Munroe scoffed. "Don't I know him, boob? Ain't I hung 'em on the button with him twenty times? Ain't I bust my hand on that chin of his, and never rung the bell? I know all about his jaw, old son. It's padded. That's all."

"Where's the padding?" asked Sparrow.

"I dunno. He's made that way. That's all."

"It's inside of his head. He don't think that nobody can hurt him. And so they can't. He's a fathead, sure. If *you* was a fathead, Kenny, you'd be a champion inside of a month."

Kenny sighed and shook his head.

"Now listen to me," said Sparrow. "You've heard the kid chatter. You know what he thinks. But I'll tell you the facts. I was just kiddin' him along when I said brass knuckles. Brass knuckles never raised a welt like that. It was just a plain fist, but, if the kid gets it into his head that he's been knocked out, he won't be able to lick even a Chinaman."

"Who could have done it?" they asked.

"I'll show you a part of him," said Sparrow. "I've saved it ever since the day that the punchin' bag was copped."

He led them back through the house to his own small room. There he removed a piece of paper and exhibited to them a strip of shingle upon which was a quantity of mud, and in the mud, deeply printed, was the print of a man's foot.

The others gathered and stared at it.

"What of that?" asked Kenny.

"Take off your shoe," snapped out Sparrow.

Kenny obeyed. He stood up in his bare feet.

"Look at the length of Bert's toes. Then look at the toes of this barefooted gent. He could almost hang onto a stick with 'em!"

The others, more and more interested, gathered closer and began to note different points. Nearly all of the print was of the toes, and the mud had been jammed up into points between them, a certain sign that the heel received almost nothing of the weight of this traveler.

"Where did you get it?"

"Under the tree down near the spring. There were other footmarks, but they'd been wiped out pretty careful. This here one was still there. I sliced it off of the face on the ground. And here it is. We've got the length of his foot, here, down to a pretty small fraction. I guess that'll help when we get him cornered."

"But what sort of a gent is he that goes around barefooted without much clothes except patches?"

"I dunno," said Sparrow. "But when I see him next, I'm gonna try to play tag with him with this here." He drew from his pocket the shining bulk of a new automatic pistol.

SPARROW TAKES A DETOUR

Such was the attitude of Sparrow to the stranger. It was copied instantly by the other men around the camp. But although they got their guns ready and although they were prepared to shoot on sight of a stranger, half naked, with brown skin like an Indian, Sparrow had secret thoughts of his own that he by no means was prepared to divulge to his companions, and among those secret thoughts there was a very definite objection to the destruction of the unknown.

The reason of Sparrow was very definite and on logical grounds, for he said to himself that the hand that had knocked the invincible jaw of Cyclone Ed Morgan into the proverbial cocked hat was also the hand that could floor many another famous name in the American ring. The strong jaw of Ed Morgan had withstood the shocks of some of the strongest men of his weight. But here he had gone down sick and groggy—no, rather smitten by a thunderbolt.

Over this, Sparrow brooded for some time. He tried to get a description of the stranger from Cyclone, and Ed responded as well as he could. But the whole thing had been so swift and strange and it had taken such a violent hold upon the imagination of Morgan that his details of the encounter grew like any green thing in the spring of the year, from day to day. His imaginings put forth leaf and became more and more gorgeous.

He finally arrived at a point where he declared that the stranger who had leaped upon him was a giant of two hundred and fifty or sixty pounds, wild as a demon turned loose in the forest, who had charged at him, snarling like a beast and gnashing his teeth.

This was a little too like a Jack-The-Giant-Killer story, and out of it the manager evolved a story somewhat in the following fashion: The man who had attacked Cyclone had done so simply because the thrown stone had struck him in a tender place as he lurked behind the shrubbery, waiting for the man to pass. Furthermore, he was of great size. This was proven by the very strong evidence of the footprint that he had found in the mud, and allowing for the fact that the foot, if it had slipped a little in the mud, might not be nearly so huge as it appeared in the print, still it was the toe-spread of a very big man. Besides, although Cyclone had undoubtedly exaggerated, yet it must have taken a man little short of a veritable giant to strike tough Ed Morgan so completely senseless. Never in all of Morgan's long career in connection with the ring had Mr. Sparrow Roberts seen a man so completely knocked out. A mighty arm, indeed, must have struck that blow, a big man, with speed, no mere mauler, for a heavy-hitting mauler does not produce unconsciousness with his strokes. He crushes and pains and bruises his antagonists; he beats them gradually to weakness, then he strikes them down and they are unable to rise. But mere size and bulk of brawn could never have produced the complete coma into which Ed Morgan had fallen.

Such a state is induced by a clean-clipping blow, a punch struck with the speed and the sharp decision and the accuracy with which the snapping end of a whip cuts the hide of a horse. That one punch, Sparrow was afraid, reduced his near champion to the ranks of the ham-and fighters. But perhaps, through the effects of that punch, he would be able to attach himself to a still more brilliant warrior who would go on to greater heights of glory than Ed Morgan could ever aspire toward. Perhaps this would result in that dream of dreams—a real heavyweight, perhaps the world's champion of champions—under the management of Sparrow Roberts, the distinguished impresario.

So ran on the mind of Sparrow in his dreams. He confided his thoughts to no one, but he began to make secret inquiry, first of all to find out the name of the man who, in that section near and about Juniper, was considered the finest hunter, the surest hand to unravel a trail. Wherever he went, he was met with only one answer: there were hunters and hunters. There were good men at the trail and good men at the rifle. But the man who was useless on the back of a horse, stupid with revolver or rifle, helpless with a rope, was nevertheless a concentrated genius with traps and in trailing, and this man, they said, was called Knut Rasmussen. He had come in from the North Country, and little was known of him except that, in the spring, he brought in the finest furs that were ever taken out of the mountains. As to his past history and as to his nature, no man could say a word. He had no friends. He communed with no man. The reason was that, when he came down from the North Country, he bore upon his face the ragged, horrible scar of the gun brand.

At this story, when he first heard it, Sparrow innocently asked what the gun brand might be, and he shuddered when he was informed that it was done by dragging the sight of a gun first across the forehead and then down the victim's face over the bridge of the nose, tearing lips and chin down to the throat.

Thus prepared for what he might find, Sparrow went into the hills and found Knut Rasmussen, a big, dark man whose face was crossed by the great, ragged scar. As one talked with Knut, at every pause his fingers absently caressed that mark of torture and shame.

What Sparrow wanted, he said, was someone who could go on the trail of a most dangerous animal—a man. He then told Knut Rasmussen all that he knew of the stranger near the Cyclone Ed Morgan camp. Knut Rasmussen considered the matter for some moments, and then asked what remuneration would be his. As to this, having in mind what trappers made in good season, Sparrow very reasonably offered two hundred dollars for this single bit of work, but Knut Rasmussen merely smiled at him.

"If I get twelve inches of knife rammed through my back while I'm sleepin'," he said, "it won't be so doggone much use havin' *any* money," and he added: "About a thousand will suit me, Mister Roberts."

Sparrow cursed and raged, but he could not avoid the bargain, for an instinct told him that this was the man, and that this was the only man who could avail him ought in the hunt for the hard-hitting stranger. So he met all the terms of Knut. That is to say, he paid ten percent, or a hundred dollars, upon the spot, and he agreed in writing to pay nine hundred dollars more when the stranger of the large footprint was delivered into his hands, bound and helpless.

This contract having been drawn up, Mr. Sparrow Roberts started back through the woods for the camp, and on the way he made a deep detour through the woods, for he had newly purchased a fine pump gun with which he felt that he was the true king of the forest. Thus equipped he hunted eagerly here, there, until, losing his way entirely, he found himself at length in a long, deep ravine, of which the sides were composed of rough boulders, made still more difficult to scale or descend by a dense growth of shrubs and vines. He was passing through the bottom of this ravine when he heard a peculiar rapid sound, echoing out of the mouth of a subterranean tunnel, and he paused to listen and make out the strange disturbance if he could. What it sounded like, he thought, was a number of horses running in the distance over a hard pavement, the sounds blended and confused by the depth of the cave.

He tried in vain to persuade himself that the sounds were probably the effect of water splashing in an underground torrent. There was a perfect steadiness and rhythm about the noise that assured him that it could not be the effect of anything so simple. What else could it be? Something in the back of his mind suggested one very definite explanation, but, being a very reasonable man, he forgot this matter at once and turned his back upon it, so to speak, and absolutely refused to consider it.

Sparrow Roberts ventured into the mouth of the cave. Here the noise was far clearer, and now the character of the rapid and yet regularly irregular pattering was such that the trainer blinked. Certainly it sounded most amazingly like one thing and one thing only—a thing with which he was most familiar.

He hurried down the gloomy tunnel, holding the shotgun at the ready before him, ready, indeed, to let any wild beast have both barrels at the first sign of danger. So he turned a corner of the underground passage and came in full view of the very thing that he had so strongly in mind, but which he dared not believe the sound to issue from. It was a punching bag hanging from the very platform that had been stolen from the camp a week or so before. It was the same bag that had been stolen, too, and it was still swinging on the end of the string in rapid vibrations back and forth. There is nothing, after all, that will develop certain qualities of speed of hand and eye like exercise with a punching bag. But why should it have been brought out to this strange place?

He looked around him and found that he was in a sort of rude room, partly the effect of the natural wideness of the tunnel, and partly increased by an industrious removal of the rocks that had been taken away from the walls wherever they were loose.

But where was the owner of the place? The punching bag still swung. Certainly the last blow that was dealt it must have been a snapping one. It recalled to Sparrow, very vividly, a certain broad purple welt along the side of the jaw of Cyclone Morgan. Yes, this must be the same hand. This was he who had stolen the punching bag and the platform. This was he who had helped himself most liberally to the provisions in the camp, time and again. This was he who had felled Cyclone. This was the giant of the woods!

Instantly Sparrow built a story around the idea. Here was a fellow who had committed some crime, been exiled to the safety of the mountains and a hermit's life, and who had been so passionately fond of boxing in the old days that he could not resist an opportunity to take away even such a cheap and cumbersome prize as this.

Here a whisk in the air, like the flicker of a rapid wing, made Sparrow look up in time to see a flying shadow. He dodged at the last possible moment to avoid a large stone that whirred past his temple and crashed loudly against the side of the cave.

Perhaps Sparrow was a little too excited by what he had seen. At any rate, he did not pause to ask questions, but he sent a charge of fine shot rattling in the direction from which the stone had come. He pumped the old shell out and a new shell into the barrel, at the same time calling out: "Don't be a fool, kid! I'm a friend. I've come here to give you a tip that'll . . . !"

Something glimmered before his eyes. A flying stone clipped him on the side of the head.

"All right," said Sparrow, "I'll make you wish that you was in purgatory for that, you rat! Where are you?"

He crawled forward to a favorable position, the pump gun ready. But as he crouched there, guarding the darkness at the farther end of the cave from which the mischief had proceeded, he heard a grating sound, and the hole in the ground above him through which light descended upon the open space where the punching bag was affixed to the roof of the place, was covered with something which at once shut off all the light and left Sparrow in the deepest darkness.

Filled with a sudden panic, he rushed for the mouth of the cave through which he had just entered. As he hurried, he heard the noise of the crashing fall of a great mass of stone. A scream tore its way up through the throat of Sparrow. It seemed impossible that there could be enough malignance in any mere thief to make him wish to bury another man alive, but that was what was being attempted. He heard out of the distance a peculiar snarling sound like a worried beast at work. He came in view of the mouth of the tunnel in time to see the fall of a second quantity of rock that nearly covered the entire mouth of the cave. With a yell, he sprang forward. He heard a deeper and a louder snarl, most beast-like, less human than before.

Then, thrusting away one heavy stone with his hands, he worked his way out into the open day just as a larger and a longer slide began down the side of the ravine over his head.

Sparrow made no pause. The new and highly prized pump gun was allowed to fall unregarded. He sprinted for safety across the rough floor of the ravine. Behind him came a great crashing. The earth quivered beneath his flying feet. Fragments and smaller pebbles flew about his ears. Then, flinging himself a stride or two up the farther side of the narrow gorge, he turned and looked back, sick with horror, upon that place which he had just left.

Where the mouth of the narrow cave had been, there was now a raw pile of rock debris. Tons and tons of it, loosened from the loose boulders of the cliffside above, had rushed down into the gorge, and it would take a hundred men a hundred days to clear away the heap of the ruin. How long would it have taken poor Sparrow Roberts to dig his way out from such a trap?

As he stared, with the perspiration oozing out beneath his armpits, and with his heart turning sick, something flashed in the sunshine on the farther side of the ravine, and a stone whipped like an arrow's flight past his head.

He picked it up with an exclamation of dismay. It was large enough to have dashed out his brains, and only the hand of a giant could have flung the missile so far and so straight across the ravine. Certainly if this were the man for whose capture he had employed Knut Rasmussen, he must warn Knut that it was apt to be a job that would occupy all the wits and the courage of half a dozen hunters rather than merely one. He must warn Knut of that. In the meantime, he had upon his hands the problem of saving his own hide. The stranger had attempted to bury him alive. Next he had tried to brain him from a distance. What the brute would do next could not be surmised, but, at any rate, Sparrow decided to return to the camp as fast as his best speed of foot could take him.

BAITING THE WILD MAN

Between that spot and the camp, there lay some eight miles of rough country, and Sparrow hit out and ran a stiff half mile for the beginning of the race and in order to shake off the pursuit, if a pursuit there should be. He was a great runner, was Sparrow. A few years before he had been able to run his mile well under four thirty, and his half far below two minutes. He had lost some of the edge from his speed, but he had gained, instead, an even greater ability across country, gained through his roadwork with Cyclone Ed Morgan. He was as proud of his running as Cyclone was proud of his durable jaw. After that first half mile, which he told himself was enough to drop far behind him any clumsy mountain-bred yokel, he settled to a swift, frictionless pace that ate up distance almost as easily as the lope of a wolf.

Just as the climbing of a long slope had brought out the perspiration on his body, and just as he was wondering what excuse he could make to the men in his camp because of the loss of the shotgun of which he had been so proud a few days before, he was struck a resounding *thump* in the middle of the back that pitched him forward upon his face, while the big, thick clod of earth that had landed on him crunched to bits and lay scattered about him.

For a moment he was so stunned and so breathless that he lay flat, without a movement. Then he started to drag himself to his feet, only to feel something leap upon him from behind with a peculiar snarling sound like the noise of an angered beast. Sparrow was seized with hands of iron. He had been a wrestler in his younger day, and upon his body had sunk the burning grip of many a Herculean hand. But it seemed to Sparrow that he had never before been held with such power. Then a bit of dirty fur, like the pelt of a coyote, was wrapped around his head. Half smothered, half choked, he was lifted and carried to the verge of a bank, then cast into the air.

As he fell, the fur slipped from his face. He had a glimpse of a rushing stream beneath him, and a tall, naked body standing on the bank, looking larger than human as Sparrow looked up to him. He had time for that glance only, then he crashed into the flooding water.

He saw no more after that, for he was involved in a tumult of white water that shot him violently, head over heels, down a small cascade. Bruised, dazed, bewildered, it seemed to him that he heard a strong-lunged laughter ringing over him, mocking him in his fall. Perhaps this was the savage's idea of a jest. But to Sparrow it was an excellent close call to death that he had so recently passed through.

He staggered up the bank of the stream and looked down at himself, pouring water from every seam, cut in half a dozen places by the sharp rocks, and still this fiend in the form of a human being was not through with his work. Another big stone shot like a bullet across the water and glanced off the shoulder of Sparrow with force enough to make him yell with pain. Sparrow fled into the underbrush.

The rest of his journey to the camp was a nightmare. Sometimes rocks whirred past his ears. Once he heard a noise overhead and thought that he saw a brown, naked body swing from the end of one great limb into another tree, far off, a feat of aerial courage that would have made a circus performer sick with envy—a feat so astonishing that Sparrow refused to believe his eyes. When at last he was hounded into the confines of the camp and fell exhausted in the house where Bert Kenny and Vince Munroe were playing cards, he could stammer forth to those heroes that he had been through hell, escorted by the devil himself!

When Vince and Bert grasped arms and proffered to go forth and attack the foeman, he assured them that this dexterous fiend would slip through their hands and find a way to come at him. He preferred, by far, to have them with him in the camp in case the brown-skinned savage should attempt further pranks. The more opponents the creature had, the more chance there was of eventually overcoming him.

But they were left undisturbed. It was not until the next morning that the cook found that a hundred weight of the choicest provisions had been stolen from the larder, and on a damp bit of ground near the kitchen door there was printed the sign of the big naked foot.

The whole camp gathered to gaze on this sign, and Knut Rasmussen, when he arrived a little later, was brought to examine the track. This he did for no great length of time, but, after measuring the track carefully and without the slightest mystery in his manner, he set about drumming up the neighborhood of the camp and hunting for further sign of the stranger of the forest. He was not long in unearthing what he wanted, and, with the afternoon of the next day, he was off on his long trail.

They saw nothing more of Knut Rasmussen for three days. Then he came back to the camp, much altered. His fine pack was gone from between his shoulders. His cheerful air had disappeared. His clothes were in rags, as though during the interim he had been to the pole and back again. His face, moreover, was lean and pinched, as only hunger or anxiety, or both combined, can do.

When he arrived, he asked for Sparrow. When he was told that Sparrow was not there, he shrugged his shoulders and sat down to wait. An hour later, when Roberts arrived, he was reached and forewarned on the way by Kenny. Still, when he came to the house, it was something of a shock to see the big trapper leap to his feet and thunder out a violent accusation that Sparrow had taken part in a plot against him—that they knew—that they all must have known—that the brown-skinned stranger was a demon and not a man.

He was fingering his knife before the end of this speech came, and then Sparrow had all that he could do to subdue the woodsman. He reiterated his offer of a thousand dollars. But Knut Rasmussen replied with a growl and faded away into the woods, swearing that he would find his own way and his own day for dealing with the savage and that, when that time came, the other could wish that he had never been born.

So much for the coming and the going of the famous Rasmussen. But there remained the mystery. That very day it invaded the camp again, and, almost under the very eyes of the men, it stole two pairs of the best gloves and a fifty-pound dumbbell with which Cyclone Ed Morgan was very fond of exercising.

Cyclone stormed furiously in the camp after this small tragedy. He had come up from the town to occupy his quarters, which had been newly built for him in the camp. These quarters consisted of a little cottage rudely thrown together, but comfortable enough for camping out. With Jenny, the wife of Ed, came Jenny's best friend, Nan Pearson, to keep Jen company in such a large circle of men only.

In five minutes Nan had the heads of all the men in the place whirling. She was not like Jenny. Jenny was pretty and no more. But Nan was pretty and then there was something stirred into the prettiness, a touch of a new seasoning, a spice of difference, a manner and a way of which the mountain men knew nothing and of which the boxers from far off Manhattan knew even less. She was not beautiful. But she had beautiful ways with her. If her mouth in itself was not lovely, her manner of smiling was enchantment itself. Her eyes were neither the largest nor the deepest in the world, but her way of looking at people steadily, frankly, gently, unsettled the inwards of a man decidedly.

Bert Kenny, when he first saw her, went off for a long walk. He came back looking gloomy and thoughtful. That afternoon, when Vince Munroe paid attentions to Nan, Kenny found means of crossing the path of the other, and after a playful scuff or two they went at it hammer and tongs. Vince had rapped a few hard ones to the wind of Bert, and Bert had jarred the jaw of Munroe, when Sparrow came into view and ripped the pair apart.

Afterward, he consulted with Cyclone Ed. "Ed, old kid," he said, "your wife is all to the good. She's the candy. But. . . ."

"Look here," said Cyclone carefully. "If you aim to take a crack at Jen behind her back while you pretend to. . . ."

"Shut up, kid. Don't try to read my mind. What I want to tell you is that Jen may be all to the good, but one woman is enough in pretty near any camp. It looks like two is more'n enough in this one. Ain't there something that ought to be done back in Nan's own home? Don't the cows need milkin', or some such thing?"

"Look here," said Cyclone. "Loosen up and tell me what's wrong?"

"Bert and Vince have been tryin' to tear each other to bits. And before long, if she keeps on lookin' around her the way she does, I'll begin to want to fight for her! She's got a way with her, that kid has."

"She's straight as a string," the prize fighter said hotly.

"Sure she is," murmured Sparrow. "But she's poison. She'll kill this camp, I tell you."

"If she's poison," growled out Cyclone, "why don't you use her to kill off the wild man? Then we could have some peace."

At this, Sparrow leaped up with a shout. He remained poised upon one foot, alarmed, his eyes blinking as he strove to make the thought fast before it could be forgotten and fly away from him.

"By the heavens," he said, "you ought to get out of

the fightin' game, kid. You know too much. You got too many fine fancy ideas. Use that poison on the wild man? Well, I dunno. I dunno! What sort of a trap could I use?"

"I dunno what you mean," answered the fighter, blinking.

"Bah!" Sparrow said, his eyes glittering more keenly than ever. "You dunno what I mean? The devil, man, the whole idea come out of your head, but you. . . ."

He turned on his heel and went away to find Nan.

TWO MEN DOWN

Poor Nan Pearson had nothing to warn her. She was taken in quite easily. In the first place, when she learned that Sparrow was the brains behind so important a person as Jenny's husband, she was quite willing to believe everything that he said, upon all matters, as the Gospel itself speaking. He showed her a scrap of weed, a peculiar little plant that he said he had found near the camp, and he wanted her to hunt for more of it, combing the woods carefully for the prize. As for its use, he had an old recipe given to him by his mother's distant aunt, a wise and venerable woman, which was of the greatest power in case a man. . . .

Poor Nan Pearson drank in this wild tale with her eyes as wide as they could stare. In the end, she smiled and nodded and took reverently the bit of withered weed in her hands. She was ready to spend all the time that was at her disposal for the sake of locating the strange plant. She would do her best, and she would do even more than her best.

So Sparrow watched her go away, coiling the long pigtail of her hair about her head. For Nan was only sixteen. As she reached the edge of the clearing, she turned back to him and thanked him for having shown so much confidence in her and for having given her the only sample of the rare herb that he possessed. Such was the setting of the trap and the baiting of it.

Then Sparrow waited. He had a tingling dread of what was to come. In the meantime, he decided that the best method was to wait quietly and watch for the developments. Those developments came quickly enough.

The poison, as he called it, having been turned loose in the air, could not fail to begin to kill. First of all, he heard Nan come running hastily into the camp. Kenny and Munroe vied as to who should be the first man to follow her. They rushed like two bulls, side-by-side, and so they came to a spot in the woods where they found a saddle of venison wrapped in the entire deerskin and packed about with fragrant leaves and with cool moss and bound up neatly with stringers and running vines.

This strange find they carried hastily back into the camp, and all observed it with much wonder and with the greatest admiration. That admiration grew as they ate the rich venison steaks that their cook prepared. All wondered how on earth a deer could have been found in a region that had been so thoroughly hunted over as this? Who could have been the hunter? How could he have chanced to bring his prize to such a place as this? Why had it been abandoned there? It was a puzzle, surely.

No one guessed the true explanation except Mr. Sparrow Roberts, and he very wisely said not a word. He waited for the working of time, and, when on the very next day Nan Pearson stumbled over a great skin of a grizzly bear rolled up in her path, the camp began to wake up to the fact that something most peculiar was in the air.

It was the skin of a monster grizzly, newly killed. When they carried it down to Juniper to have it taken care of and cured as a good skin should be, it was at once recognized by certain markings and by its yellow color as the pelt of a famous cattle killer, an old king of the range.

But how had it come so near the camp?

Now Bert Kenny blurted out what was probably the truth. "It's that same Indian . . . that loafer that sneaks around through the trees. You bet that's who it is. He's been seein' Nan Pearson while she's working to get at that fool weed you want, Sparrow. And this is his way of making her presents, I guess. Nan, you better stick close to the camp for a couple of days."

But Nan did not stick close to the camp. She protested with shudders and with such emphasis of stamped feet that it made her tremble—the mere thought of encountering such a strange monster—that his bringing of presents to her was a perfectly ridiculous thing, and yet she saw no reason why she should not go forth—armed, of course.

Munroe and Kenny, very serious, picked out a light .32-caliber revolver for her use. And she could use it! But Sparrow, watching her sally forth, was immensely amused. The idea that such a slim slip of a girl should seriously confront that brown-skinned tiger of the woods for a single moment, was absurd to him. He was hardly less amused when he saw Kenny and Munroe begin to escort her forth on her walks.

She, however, seemed not at all amused by the attendance of Cyclone Ed Morgan's sparring partners. One might have thought that she loved the silent wilderness and all of its monsters, human or beast. But Sparrow, who looked and understood a little of what might be going on in her mind, smiled complacently. This was taking time, but it was working out just as he would have it.

Cyclone Ed Morgan was doing his best with the gloves every day, but he was greatly changed. He had grown serious; he had grown sober. He no longer rushed to the fray with the carefree abandon of a child leaping down into a swimming pool. He advanced sourly and grimly to the fight. His was now flesh of another sort, and not lightly to be risked and battered.

These were the ideas of Cyclone Ed, and in them the manager saw the wreck of all his schemes for a bright pugilistic future for his protégé. Poor Cyclone, in becoming the genesis of a good citizen, had become, also, the genesis of a failure in the ring.

First Vince Munroe discovered that fact when, as Cyclone Ed made a rush, Vince dared to stand up to him and soon discovered that he could block the swinging blows that came toward him, and then that he could return them with at least equal force. He kept up that savage rally until Sparrow beckoned him wildly away, and he broke ground and retreated, like a well-trained sparring partner—as though he had the heart taken out of him by the punches of Cyclone.

Afterward Sparrow had to take both sparring partners to one side.

"Look here," he said. "The Cyclone is a little off, just now. But after a while he'll swing into shape again."

"Good enough shape to get licked!" exclaimed Vince Munroe. "He never was good enough to stand up to Pierre Lacoste. I tell you, I know. I was in London when Lacoste fought Pete Riley. Lacoste is a tiger. Damned if he ain't. He'll swaller this here little hand-raised Cyclone of ours!"

"Well," snapped out Sparrow, "who wouldn't get swallered, if he could come out again with twenty-five thousand dollars? Ain't that worthwhile? And ain't the kid a married man, now?"

After that, the two sparring partners understood perfectly. Sparrow had no hope of Cyclone's winning the fight. He merely wished to keep the poor fellow in sufficient heart to enter the ring. After that, he could sit back and watch Ed Morgan crushed in a miserable round or two. It made no difference. He, Sparrow, would have his share of the fat purse and of the accompanying position in the limelight of publicity.

If the sparring partners thought it was dishonorable business, they did not say so. They merely shrugged their shoulders and decided that they need not put in too much of their attention upon the training of Ed Morgan, who was slipping daily in his work. Instead, they spent most of their time dancing attendance upon pretty Nan Pearson.

They watched over her daily with the most brooding care but were incapable of preventing new presents from showering in upon her. It was most remarkable. The silent man of the forest carried in another saddle of venison every two days, to make sure that his dear was properly fed. He carried in lovely fawn skins, exquisitely dappled in color like the bright sunshine spotting a carpet of brown leaves. He brought in other pelts. There was a mountain lion, a hide that showed no wound, except for a narrow knife slit in the skin of the side over the heart, and which Sparrow and the rest concluded must have been slain by a bullet shot though its eye. There was a lobo's pelt, once, and at another time simply the head of one of those dangerous beasts, cunningly sun dried.

The game went on for a full week, and the camp of Cyclone Ed Morgan was stricken more and more deeply with wonder. But now matters of another nature began to come upon the camp. The escorts of the lady appeared to be less welcome to the silent hunter of the forest than was the lady herself. In the first place he dropped thirty feet out of a tree and struck his knees on the back of Bert Kenny.

Bert was so terribly stunned and bruised that they had to carry him back to the camp, after they had been attracted by the screams of Nan Pearson. But although Nan seemed terribly frightened and terribly concerned for the sake of poor Bert Kenny, yet she insisted upon going forth into the woods the very next day. She no longer seemed to hunt for the weed. At least, she no longer talked about the strange herb. She seemed to love the forest for its own sake.

That next day, Vince Munroe fell behind the girl. She passed on not more than fifty yards. Then she called for Vince, received no answer, and hurried back down the path. She found him, lying crumpled in the path, his face black and swollen with blood, his mouth still gaping for breath. At her cry, they came from the camp and carried Munroe back, also.

When he recovered enough to speak, he told them, faintly, how he had been attacked from behind, and how a sinewy arm had wound around his throat, and how he had been brought to the ground in silence, how he had struggled vainly and briefly, and how the battle had ended in death, as he felt. Certainly all the pangs of death had been his.

COWPUNCHERS ENGAGED

Although two strong men had been struck down by the terrible stranger in the woods, still Nan Pearson continued to go forth every day with the most singular disregard of danger.

"He will carry you away, child!" cried Jenny Morgan in the greatest alarm.

"He won't dare," Nan Pearson said, and tossed her head. "*I* don't think that there's such a person. *I've* never seen any sign of him, at any rate."

"But you've seen the things that he brings to you?"

"Well, that may be a joke. . . ."

Jenny did not pursue the subject. Women have a singular understanding of one another. As for men, they persist, most foolishly, in arguing with the ladies. With one another, women seem to understand that, after a certain point is reached, it will be foolish to continue talking. So Jenny Morgan, staring rather sadly at her friend, changed the subject of their talk.

"Don't you think," said Ed Morgan, "that Nan is sort of interested in what this gent might be like?"

At this Jen grew violently red and stamped her feet. "How can you talk so, Ed?" she cried at him.

As a matter of fact, she agreed with Ed entirely, and that was the cause for her anger. She did not like to see a comrade of the huntress sex tracked down by mere stupid man.

Sparrow was watching the girl like a hawk, and every day he said to himself, as he observed her: "Has she seen him today? Or has she not?" Sometimes he was sure that she had, because she would come into camp with her eyes languid and dreamy and her manner careless, like one who has large and important thoughts to take all of their attention. Sometimes she was a little nervous, secretly worried. About what?

Once she came sadly to Jen Morgan and told her that she must leave the camp. She could not stay there any longer. When Jen pressed her for reasons, she confessed quite freely. She had gone from day to day in the hope of seeing the stranger in the forest. Every day, when she went out through the woods, she knew that he was near her. But she could not see him. He was always like a shadow, breathing at a little distance, a thing guessed among the trees but never discovered. If she sat with a book on the ground, she could be sure that he was crouched somewhere near, listening, waiting, watching. Sometimes, afterward, by hunting through the brush nearby, she could even find some slight traces of where he had been. As for sight or sound of the creature himself, there was never either glimpse or whisper of him.

To all of this Jen listened, fascinated. Her eyes were shining with envy and with fear.

"It might be some monster!" said Jen. "Some man so very ugly that he doesn't dare to show himself for fear that you'll be taken with a horror at the sight of him. Or," she added, "perhaps it's a real wild man, a fellow who's never been with other men. Oh, Nan, d'you think that might be?"

"A great ugly monster of a wild man," sighed Nan Pearson. "I don't know. Sometimes I think that it may be. But . . . I can't tell . . . I don't know. Oh, what a queer thing it is, Jen."

A very queer thing, indeed. The very next day there was a revelation of the stranger to Nan. She had walked far away from the camp and come at last, suddenly, to a blackthroated cave into which she adventured partly from mere curiosity, and partly because a sound of trickling water reached her ears from the heart of the tunnel, and, she was very thirsty. But caves are not always safe to venture into.

She had not gone twenty steps down the cavern when she heard a faint rumbling noise, then the unmistakable noise of a growl. She had no time to turn or to flee. She was frozen in her place, watching two luminous eyes slide toward her along the floor of the cave. At the same moment she was caught from behind and whipped around. Powerful arms lifted her. She heard a quick-taken breath of a man straining at a great weight and running at full speed at the same time. Then she was whisked into the sunlight and dropped down the face of a rock to soft, level sand beneath. As she was dropped, she looked up and had a glimpse of the stranger of the forest.

But so contorted was his face, so purpled and swollen with blood from his effort in sweeping her away from the danger of the cave, that she saw in it simply a glimpse of horror. One thing more, however, she saw without fail, and that was a pair of strange, amber-colored eyes, like the eyes of a beast of prey, at once terribly vacant and terribly filled with fires.

So much she saw. Then, very foolishly and very helplessly, she fainted and lay like dead upon the sand. When she wakened a moment later, it was to hear a terrible snarling from the cave, and then mingled with that snarling was the voice of a man—a shout that was a roar of fury, and then a cry of battle as man and beast closed. There could not be any doubt of that. Since they closed without the sound of a gun discharged, she knew that her rescuer was now attacking the monster of the den—whatever it might be—with no weapon more deadly than knife or club or, perhaps, his bare hands only!

So she crouched by the mouth of the cavern, trembling. Sometimes she started up and made a step or two into the darkness, half determined to rush in and help in the battle. But every time she shrank back again, as though realizing that her strength would be futile in such an encounter. The shouting and snarling increased. There was a shrill screeching. Then silence.

Was that the death cry of the beast? Or was it the cry of triumph? Did the man stand with his foot planted on the warm body of his enemy, or had the man fallen and were the fangs of the destroyer fixed in his flesh?

Such a wave of fear and horror passed over the girl at this thought that she whirled away and ran as fast and as far as she could. Since she was a lithe-limbed mountain girl, that furious burst of running carried her almost to the camp before she was exhausted. She hurried on to the camp, turning all that had happened in her bewildered brain. This much was clear, that the stranger of the forest had entered the cave to attack the beast that sheltered in it simply because she had been for a moment in peril of the brute. At the thought of such wild chivalry, the breath of the girl was taken.

The first person she met was Sparrow, and she told him all that had happened, to which he listened with his scrawny head cocked upon one side.

"Do one thing for me," he said.

She nodded, breathless, her eyes brilliant.

"Stay in the camp. Don't go out of it for a minute till I give you word," said Sparrow, and she agreed.

After that, he went down to Juniper, and in that stirring town he found two cowpunchers that had come to try their luck in the mines. They were quite willing to undertake a more congenial work than the pick and the shovel. The proposition of Sparrow was very liberal. They were to wait near the Ed Morgan shack at the fighter's camp, and, if the wild man approached the place, they were to endeavor to snare him with their ropes. If they succeeded, each would receive a hundred dollars in cash at the moment the stranger was subdued.

They came at once, and that very night they began their vigil. The shack stood a little removed from the clearing that was used as training quarters, and in the brush before it Sparrow and his two ropers took up their position and watched.

Until the gray of the morning they lurked there without hearing a strange sound except the rustling of the wind through the trees. But in the first light of the dawn, Sparrow saw something glimmer behind some nearby bushes. He ground an elbow into the ribs of his nearest companion cowpuncher and made that drowsy fellow raise his head with a jerk. The next instant, out of the trees glided noiselessly the stranger of the forest. But how different from the imaginings of Sparrow! His dream of the champion heavyweight went flickering away into nothingness. Here was a slender boy, not more than eighteen or twenty at the most, naked except for a deerskin that was made into a rude garment and gathered around his waist and held up by a thong that passed over one brown shoulder. Tawny hair crowned his head, rudely sawed off at the nape of the neck. At his waist a narrow strip of belt sustained a knife in a sheath, and under one arm he carried a large, folded pelt.

He stood for a moment in the clearing, turning his head restlessly from side to side, with a frown of suspicion, as though he guessed at the nearness of a danger that he could not see. Then he slipped on toward the house.

He was almost at the door when the first cowpuncher half rose and flicked the noose of his rope forward. At the whisper of the rope in the air, the stranger whirled around. It was only to receive over his head and shoulders the coil of the descending noose.

He made no sound, no outcry, but Sparrow saw his face wrinkle into such an expression of angry malice and fear that it made the blood of the man run cold. The wild man reached for his knife, but at the same instant the rope was jerked taut with a shout, and the pull snapped him forward upon his face. He was up in an instant and charged straight at Sparrow Roberts. As he charged, the rope of the second 'puncher darted through the air, swooped like a bird, and the stranger was knocked to the ground again.

As he attempted to struggle to his feet, the coils of both ropes whipped into action. In a second he was swathed in strong hemp from head to heel. Still ripples of violent effort ran through his body. It was utterly in vain, and after another moment he lay still, breathing hard through lips that curled up, beast-like, from his teeth.

Sparrow stood over his prey.

A BARGAIN IS STRUCK

He could see the secret of the lad's power at once. To be sure, the captive was not huge of thews and sinews, but legs and arms were covered with an inter-twisted network of ropy muscles. Whenever he stirred, the big muscles swelled and seemed about to start through the shining brown skin. A sure sign of the strong man, his neck was large and perfectly symmetrical. So much for the body of the youth. The face was the next concern of Sparrow.

His prisoner was handsome, in a sort of savage way. His nose was cruelly arched; his jaw was square-tipped and broad at the base; his brown cheeks were lean; but all his soul lay in the strange, amber eyes. Once before Sparrow had seen those eyes—in the body of a jaguar that lay crouched behind the bars of a Manhattan zoo. Here they were again, blank, expressionless, with small points of fire forming and dying in their depths.

"Pick him up, boys," said Sparrow, "and take him over to the scales."

They lifted the prostrate form and bore it to the scales. A brief shifting of the weights, and then Sparrow stepped back and looked from the balancing beam at the roped figure.

"A hundred and fifty-five pounds," murmured Sparrow. "A middleweight just the way he stands. A hundred and fifty-five pounds! Now take him over to the big shack, boys."

They lifted him and carried him again to the appointed place. The cook, just beginning his work to prepare breakfast, came clamoring to see the thief of so many of his choicest provisions, but Sparrow sent him sharply about his business. Into his own small, private office he had them take the youth. There he was put into a chair, his hands secured strongly behind his back, and his ankles lashed together. He was quite helpless, and now the pelt that had been under his arm, when he came to the house, was unrolled upon the floor. It was the pelt of a big mountain lion. There was no bullet mark, but, as upon another occasion, only a narrow slit, as of an entering knife, through the skin just over the place that once must have sheltered the heart.

After this, Sparrow sent his 'punchers away. He locked the door in the face of Kenny and Munroe, who had come eagerly with the first rumor of the great event. Then he turned back to his captive.

The latter had composed himself perfectly. Upon his face there was no expression of fear or anger more than on a countenance of stone. The big, somber, amber eyes failed entirely to see Sparrow, but looked straight before him.

"Now, pal," said Sparrow, "you and me are gonna

have a nice, quiet little talk. We'll start off by getting introduced. I'm Sparrow Roberts. What's your name?"

There was not a flicker of light in the amber eyes.

"You can't talk, eh?" asked Sparrow. "Dumb, maybe?"

Still the eyes of the prisoner were blank.

Sparrow went into the big room outside, and there he found Kenny and Munroe, chattering busily with the two 'punchers, getting as close a description as possible of the stranger of the woods.

"They say he ain't so very big," said Kenny.

"He's big enough, kid," answered Sparrow.

"I'd like to get at him," said big Bert.

"Maybe you'll have a chance," answered the manager. "Now I'm gonna go back into that room, and after I get the door closed, I want you to come runnin' up to the door and holler . . . 'Hey, Sparrow, here's Nan Pearson come. . . .' "

"What for?" asked Kenny.

"Put your questions in your pocket, kid, will you? Just do what I tell you to do."

Kenny grunted, and Sparrow hastened back into the room that he had just left. He had hardly locked the door behind him when a heavy footfall approached it and a hand was laid upon the doorknob.

"Hey, Sparrow!" called Kenny. "Here's Nan Pearson. . . ."

Sparrow stared at the eyes of the wild man, and at the sound of the girl's name there was an indescribable change, a softening of the expression.

It was all that Sparrow wanted. "Let Nan wait," he called in response. Then he sat down and drew his chair close in front of the prisoner.

"Look here, kid," he said, "you ain't such a fool. You know how to play a gag pretty well. But it ain't gonna work right this first time. It ain't gonna work at all. I want to hear you open up and do a little talkin'. Understand? First place, what's your moniker? What's your name, blondy?"

Blondy stared curiously at him, then looked through him.

In spite of himself, Sparrow flushed. Just above the knee, there is a deep-seated nerve buried in the leg. Into the flesh of the prisoner, the knuckle of Sparrow ground the nerve against the bone. He looked up into the face of the captive and saw him turn a shade pale. Perspiration started upon his face, and the long muscles of the thigh leaped up and grew hard and rigid as iron.

"Will you talk?" asked Sparrow through his teeth.

Still the youth did not alter his expression. It might be, perhaps, that he was not deaf, but was dumb. But Sparrow was not one to allow any method to remain untried. He bore down wickedly with his knuckles again, the full weight of his body upon them. When he looked up, the captive had set his jaw hard and the nostrils were flaring out in the agony of that trial, while his eyes glanced rapidly from one side of the room to the other, as though seeking for some way of escape. But there was no way. Suddenly the set jaw relaxed.

"I'll talk," said the victim in a voice surprisingly deep and soft for a youth of his years.

Sparrow leaped up from his chair with a sigh of relief. "That's better." There was plenty of iron in his nature, but, nevertheless, he was far from enjoying the part that he had had to play. Besides, it was like tormenting a lion that is bound only for the moment and is sure to be free again a little later.

"We'll have your name first," Sparrow repeated for the third time.

"Camden . . . Harry Camden," said the stranger, and waited.

"How come you to be wanderin' through the woods like this?"

"That's my business," Camden answered.

"Maybe. But it's mine, too, just now. Camden, I want to know."

The blunt jaw of Camden clenched again. "I'll give you some pretty good advice," he said coldly. "Keep shut of things you don't *have* to know."

Sparrow, considering the matter quickly from every angle, decided that this advice was, indeed, thoroughly competent. Far better to infuriate any formidable enemy than to anger this slippery son of mischief.

"Camden," said Sparrow, "what brought you out here in the woods, I'll let go. But there's one thing that I hang onto. You've done a good deal of thievin' around this here camp."

"I've brought you in enough venison and enough skins to more'n pay for what I took," Camden responded calmly.

"Who asked you for venison and skins? Young feller, you stand in a pretty fair way to be sent up for robbery. You busted locks here, one night, to swipe chuck from the kitchen. D'you know how many years in prison the bustin' of locks means?"

The eyes of the other widened a trifle. "Prison?" he echoed.

"Prison!" Sparrow snapped out, following up his point with great energy when he saw that he was winning on this tack. "Bread and water . . . four stone walls around you every day. About fifteen years of livin' in a hole, that's all it would mean to you if I was to turn you over to the law, kid!"

Camden was turned to stone. All the color could not leave his face, as brown was the skin, but he changed to a sort of sickly yellow. Still he said nothing. He was terrified by that thought of imprisonment more than any fear of actual pain. That much was clear.

"But," said Sparrow, "all you got to do is to promise to work for me for a year. You understand? You work for me for a year, and you do everything that I tell you. After that, you go free. But for a year you do what I tell you to do. I promise that you'll have good clothes and plenty to eat. But for a year you're my man. Understand me, Camden?"

Camden nodded slowly. "I guess that I understand," he said huskily. "I turn into a sort of a hoss for a year. Is that it?"

"That's it!"

"How'll you know that I'll stay with you?"

"You'll gimme your word and your honor, and I'll trust to that. Besides, if you try to break away, I'll get you back and turn you over to the law."

A faint smile, the first smile, appeared on the face of Camden. "Could you get me back?" he asked.

That touch of superiority angered Sparrow. "I caught you once, Camden. I'd catch you again."

Camden shook his head sadly. "It was the girl I came to find out about," he said. "The cat scared her. . . ."

He scuffed the big fur of the mountain lion with his bare foot, and Sparrow looked down with a sigh of wonder. This was a sort of desperate manliness on a large scale that he found it hard to comprehend.

"It was the girl that you got hooked with," Sparrow said, angry because the cleverness of his devices was not appreciated. "But who sent the girl out there to be bait in the trap? Who used the girl to hook you, Camden? And what I done before, I'd manage some way to do again." He snapped his bony fingers under the chin of Camden as he spoke.

"*You* sent the girl out!" breathed Camden. "*You* sent Nan Pearson?"

"*I* sent Nan Pearson."

"You hired her?"

"Anyway, I got her to go out. I fixed the trap for you, old son, and you up and walked into it."

A little pause fell between them. During that pause, before the fury in the eyes of the captive and the agony in his face, Sparrow scowled down at the floor.

"Well, kid," he said hurriedly, "all I want is your promise. Look here . . . I got a chance to do big things for the both of us. I got a chance to make a fortune for you, if you do things the way that I want you to do 'em! I got a way for you to make money . . . big money, Camden!"

Camden shrugged his shoulders. "What do I need of money?" he said. Then he added slowly, thoughtfully: "She helped you to catch me?"

"Did you think you'd get her interested?" Sparrow demanded scornfully. "And you without a bean in the world?"

"*She* likes the money, then?" asked Camden, and he turned his big, inscrutable amber eyes upon the other.

"There never was a woman that didn't," responded Sparrow. "A little coin'll sweeten up pretty near any man, as far as the women goes. Now, kid, you hear me talk. One year . . . that's all I want. After that, you won't have to work no more. You can live in the woods and keep a wife in town, if you want." He laughed heartily. "You'll have enough coin to do whatever you like. You hear me, kid?"

"How much money is that? How much money . . . would . . . well, buy a house and keep it runnin'?" Camden asked heavily.

"And a wife inside the house?" snapped out Sparrow, grinning broadly.

Camden turned a dark, dark red.

"Look here! Fifty thousand I'll make for you. Fifty thousand . . . maybe a hundred thousand . . . in a year. In a year! D'you hear me, kid? D'you understand?"

The "kid" regarded Sparrow with unutterable scorn and contempt, with a deeply buried hatred, and yet he was forced to nod.

"Then we'll shake hands on this," said Sparrow. "You make the bargain. You gimme your word of honor?"

"My word of honor," muttered the other.

Sparrow touched the ropes with the edge of his knife. Camden leaped to his feet, free. He made one threatening step toward Sparrow, and the latter, feeling that the man of the woods had doubled in size with the first taste of freedom, stood his ground with fear and trembling—yet he remained without flight, simply because he knew that flight was impossible from the face of this active hunter. Sparrow had already tried it and knew.

AGAINST KENNY AND MUNROE

When a million dollars is put at the command of a lucky man, what does he do with it? He usually sits down and folds his hands and wonders where he will begin with the splurge. So it was with Sparrow. He felt that he had a great treasure given into his keeping for exploitation, and he wanted to use it to the best advantage. But how should he manage that affair?

First of all, was he so absolutely sure that Camden would be formidable in the ring? Might it not be that, dreadful as he was in action in the wilderness, he would be a very tame lion when he stepped into the ring with a tried veteran like Bert Kenny, durable and hard hitting, or a clever fencer with hands like Vince Munroe's?

A perspiration of anxiety started out on the face of Sparrow when he thought of this matter. He hastened to test the thing at once. He brought both of the sparring partners to the ring. It was the dew time of the morning still. The smoke was rising thickly from the chimney above the shack of Cyclone Ed Morgan, and Cyclone himself had not yet put in an appearance. There were only the four of them, and the frightened eyes of the cook in the distance. He made the audience for the fray.

"You've hung around in the trees and watched the boys box?" asked Sparrow.

Camden nodded.

"After you swiped the punching bag, you practiced on it, the way you seen the boys work on the bag?"

Camden assented again.

"Well," said the trainer, "if you've done that enough, you know something about glove work. You go into the ring, there, and take care of yourself."

He tossed a pair of gloves to the man from the woods. Then he went to Bert Kenny, the slugger.

"Look here, Bert," he said, "this bird from the forest thinks that he can knock you cold. You want a chance to put him away. Well, kid, here you are. Knock him dead, Bert!"

Bert smiled cruelly, contentedly. This was a game entirely to his liking.

Camden had been furnished with trunks and with rubber-soled shoes that clung to the rough, padded canvas on the floor of the ring. Those shoes slowed up immensely feet that were accustomed to working without any covering—big feet, spread out by going bare over all sorts of country, and only covered in winter, or for rocky country, with a rudely made sort of moccasin. He tried a few steps about the ring and shook his head.

"Lemme take off the shoes," he suggested to the manager, but Sparrow merely grinned.

"And have somebody put his heel on your toes?" he said.

So Camden, as Bert Kenny slipped through the ropes, put up his hands as he had seen the others do many and many a time as he lurked on the edge of the camp and watched. It was a fascinating game to watch. It was one with which he himself was not entirely out of touch. The giving and taking and dodging of blows are something that all who live wildly must soon understand.

Bert Kenny took his distance and began to measure his enemy with his eye.

"Break when I tell you to break," instructed Sparrow, slipping into the ring as referee. "And no hitting when you break. Mind that, Camden. No hitting when you break!"

This was something that had to be explained, and Camden shook his head over it. Then he stood up to Kenny. The latter feinted with his left. The guard of the youth flew out to meet that feint, and Bert grinned as he stuffed the glove into the face of the wild man. He glanced aside at Sparrow, whose forehead was black with a frown of disappointment, and at Vince Monroe, as though to reassure them that this was the easiest work he had undertaken in a long time.

Camden snorted the scent of the glove from his nostrils and glided away. Kenny followed, looking for an opportunity to close, but still willing to try out his foe a few passes before he struck in earnest. He was sensing his own superiority comfortably. He was working his shoulders, smoothly back and forth, and taking shrewd aim at the youngster.

He feinted again with the left, but, instead of striking with the same hand, he followed with a lightning long drive of the right for the jaw. The feint was a beautiful piece of work; the drive was a joy to behold, and it landed fairly on the side of Camden's jaw with a shock that sent a delicious half-numb tingle all the way to the shoulder of the pugilist. It was his pride that he could take it; it was also his pride that he could give it, and certainly he had given it now. Kenny stepped back hastily to give the man room to fall.

Camden did not fall. He merely passed the tip of his glove, with a curious frown, along the side of his jaw, and then squinted quizzically at his antagonist. There was a joyous yell from Sparrow.

"He took it, Bert! He took it! He soaked up your best!"

"The devil!" said Bert Kenny. "That wasn't nothin'. Wait till I'm through with him. I'll turn you inside out, kid!"

And, forgetting caution, he rushed blindly. He struck the thinnest air. Camden had slipped from his path as the cat slips from beneath the falling shadow. Bert Kenny, recovering himself sharply, whirled and lashed out heavily—a full right-handed swing.

Camden struck inside that swing, a slightly curving left-hand punch, jerking the glove down a trifle at the instant of his glove's impact against the jaw. Against his elbow swayed the swing of Bert Kenny, adding impetus to his own punch.

It was a small thing, that blow. It looked no more than the most simple sort of a jab, but the effect was most remarkable. Bert Kenny's head jerked back as though he had run at full speed into a clothesline. His feet whipped up from the floor, and he fell flat on his back. Neither did he rise, but he lay there with eyes closed and a loose expression upon his face, a faintly thoughtful frown upon his forehead. They picked him up and carried him out of the ring. They doused him with cold spring water. Then he sighed and opened his eyes wearily.

"What happened?" asked Bert.

"You were soaked by the next champion middleweight of the world," said Sparrow through teeth that fairly chattered with the morning chill and with excitement. "You was soaked by the fastest steppin', hardest-hittin' boy I ever seen in that class, and I've seen 'em all . . . I've seen 'em all. If I can only teach him how to block! If I can only teach him how to block!"

He turned to Vince Munroe. "Hop in there, Vince. Stay away from him. Box, box, box! Don't let him put a hand on you!"

So Vince Munroe obediently hopped into the ring. He was the exact opposite of Bert Kenny. In their prime, a few years before, each had been formidable and rising middleweights. But each had gone wrong in a different way. Bert Kenny, learning how to hit a knockout punch, had died on his feet and become too slow to confront a first-rate performer, although he retained all of his original ruggedness. Vince Munroe, originally a fairly hard puncher, had forgotten how to punch but had learned to box with a mystic grace and effectiveness. He could out-point almost anyone; he could outfight hardly a child.

Now he stepped confidently up to Camden. A man whom Bert Kenny could feint out and hit at will would be child's play to him. He could play tag with this fellow all the day long, and call it a game in the end.

He began well. He popped left and right into the face of the wild man and danced away from any return, chuckling. He dipped in again, dexterous as a swallow, and pegged right and left into the body of Camden.

"How is he?" Sparrow called anxiously.

"India rubber!" answered Vince.

"Look out!" called Sparrow. "Here he comes!"

Camden, in fact, had held back from the enemy for a time, striving vainly to block these accurate whiplash blows, not heavy enough to hurt, but delivered with such inescapable speed. Now, angered, he leaped suddenly at Vince Munroe.

Never did Vince box so beautifully as in this crisis. He blocked a driving left and a whipping right, but the sheer force of the punches swept him before the onslaught. He caught a hard punch on the point of his elbow. He picked another out of the air with his gloved hand; he held out a glove to stop another, but the punch crashed home. In spite of his glove, there was force enough to that blow, landing on the side of his head, to knock him sprawling. He staggered to his feet and faced another furious rush, but not a blind rush. Every movement of Camden was planned with the most deliberate care. He struck as a boxer strikes at a punching bag—a shower of blows, but every blow had in it the force of a knockout. The first half dozen were blocked by Vince Munroe, fighting desperately to uphold his boxer's reputation. But the seventh punch was a feint learned from Vince himself, and the eighth slid like a snake through the small opening that the feint had made in the guard of Munroe.

It did not strike him on the jaw. It landed not even on a vulnerable point of the body. But it crashed fairly against the chest of the fighter, lifted him, and flung him against the ropes. The ropes, swinging back, tossed him face down on the canvas, and there he writhed and groaned and gasped for breath, while Sparrow danced around and around the ring in an hysteria of joy.

A LITTLE SCARE

There was no joy of victory in the face of Camden, however, for, as he looked around, he saw Nan Pearson, standing between Cyclone Ed Morgan and Cyclone's wife, with a look of wonder and of horror on her face. A moment later she had fled back to the house as fast as she could run, drawing Jenny beside her.

Camden laid on Sparrow's shoulder a hand that even through the glove was like the touch of iron.

"Why did she run away?" he asked.

"The look of you, man," answered Sparrow. "It would have scared ten men and a boy to see the look of you . . . let alone a snip of a girl like poor Nan."

As Sparrow spoke, Cyclone Ed Morgan came up and surveyed the stranger from head to foot.

"You're him," he said savagely, "that soaked me when I wasn't lookin'?"

"You're him," Camden said with equal venom, "that threw a stone at me?"

Sparrow rushed between them. "You'll get your chance at each other, boys," he said. "But wait a while."

Then, while he was busy talking with Cyclone Ed and with Bert and Vince, the man of the woods found his chance to leave them and retreat through the trees to the side of Ed Morgan's shack. Perhaps no lesson against eavesdropping had ever been read into his early life by another. At any rate, quite shamelessly, quite noiselessly, he slipped up to the side of the house, and there he found a convenient crevice in the loosely constructed wall through which he could both see and hear all that passed inside the house. There was enough to make Camden turn crimson with shame and then white with anger.

For pretty Nan Pearson sat in a corner of the room with Jenny Morgan beside her, alternately laughing and crying.

"Are you still afraid of him?" asked Jenny.

"Afraid? Oh, Jen, I've been thinking him such a big, terrible man . . . and he's only a boy. He's only a boy! And how silly he looked when he saw us."

"When he saw *you* comin', Nan. You was all he could see. Poor boy, he's wild over you, Nan. Ain't it sort of pathetic?"

"I've spent these days and days," Nan said, "fair shiverin' in the woods because I thought he might be near me. And it was only this!"

She laughed again, but poor Camden, listening and quivering under these repeated strokes, stole down from his place and across the camp to where Cyclone Ed Morgan and Sparrow were in close conversation.

"I've tried my best," Cyclone Ed Morgan said within the hearing of young Camden. "And it ain't good enough. I'm slipping, Sparrow. Used to be I didn't think nothin' except to knock the block off of every gent that stood in front of me. I used to want to put my fist right through Bert's body. But lately I ain't had no ambition. Just get to thinkin' of the way Jen looks at me with her head cocked a little to one side, and darned if the punch don't come home and soak me on the point of the jaw. I'm no good, Sparrow. I'm about done for. Besides, I don't care for the game no more. I used to want to be famous that way. Now I been talkin' to Jen about a farmer's life out in her country, and we both figger it would be pretty good. Y'understand I ain't quittin' on you, Sparrow . . . I'll go right along through with this here game and fight it out for you. But I'd rather cut my share of it, if you can manage it. I got only one more good scrap in me, and that's to clean up on that skunk that jumped out of the brush at me and slammed me that way!"

"That," exclaimed Sparrow, "is about the only other fight that I want you to have!" He turned and faced the man of the forest and saw the black thunder on his brow.

"What's wrong, Camden?" he asked.

"Womenfolks," Camden said darkly. "I guess they's too many women in this camp."

Once again Sparrow beamed. But this, in fact, was too good to be true.

"Women?" he said. "I wish they was all in kitchens, and no kitchen nearer to us than Chicago!" He added: "Take it easy, son. I'll have things fixed up around here the way you like 'em."

Ten minutes later, he was on his way to Juniper, and in Juniper he went straight to the office of Colonel Joshua Nichols. The colonel was very busy, selling land to an Eastern investor, but he was never too busy to talk about the great fight that was making the names of Juniper and Nichols famous. Sparrow Roberts, as was his custom, dropped his bomb in the first ten seconds and gave the colonel the rest of the interview in which to recuperate.

"Colonel," he said, "Ed Morgan is slippin', and, if he does the fightin' ag'in' Pierre Lacoste, the fight'll make you and Juniper a joke that'll never be stopped."

At this, the colonel blinked. He was only mildly interested in prize fights, having seen too much fighting of a more serious kind himself—having both seen it and taken part in it. Therefore, he regarded Sparrow with a mere sigh of disappointment until the other idea struck home in his brain—that a poor fight would make him and his town ridiculous. At this he leaped from his chair and exploded in such a burst of mixed Mexican and English cursing as even hardy Sparrow Roberts had never heard before.

"If that fight is a fizzle," said the colonel wildly, in concluding his speech, "I'll have you rode out of town on a rail, Roberts, and the clothes you have on'll be tar and feathers. Damn my eyes if it won't!"

Hearing was believing for Sparrow. He was infinitely glad that he had had this little chat with the colonel before the fiasco took place. He was gladder still that no fiasco, perhaps, would occur.

"Look here," he said, "there's only one way to fix this thing up. I've got the way to do it, and to give Juniper the finest ring fight that it ever saw. But I got to have your backing."

"You got my backing," said the colonel hotly. "And what did I get you and your man they call Cyclone out here for if it wasn't to fight the damned Frenchman?"

"Cyclone," said Sparrow Roberts, "will never lick one side of Lacoste. Not one side, old-timer. He's slippin'."

"What the devil is makin' him slip?" roared the colonel, beating upon the table with his hand.

"A wife," said Sparrow.

At this, the colonel choked, stared again, and then sighed in something like pity. "That's right," he muttered. "I forgot that the young fool stepped out and got married. I forgot all about that. I suppose his wife is makin' trouble for him at home?"

"Worse'n that," said Sparrow.

"How d'you mean?"

"I've known unhappy marriages to be the makin' of a man. Wife so dog-gone mean at home that she'd keep him out workin' late, just for the sake of something to do besides listen to the clack of her tongue. But this here girl, this Jen . . . why, she can't do nothin' but hang around and fold her hands and tell me how dog-gone wonderful her husband is. A woman like that, she sort of melts the heart out of a man and puts a lot of soft soap inside his ribs instead of beef and iron. Eh?"

At this the colonel grinned. "I've done my share of foolish things in my life," he said. "But I never seen the day when I was fool enough to marry. But the main thing here, Roberts, is to get hold of a way of putting pepper into young Ed Morgan. And how can that be done?"

"Put a new man in his place."

"Eh? After we've advertised him as the . . . what do they call it? The typical fighting American, against the brilliant Frenchman, and all that sort of thing? After all, d'you mean to say that we're to get somebody else? I've spent thousands of dollars. Damned if I ain't seen the name of Cyclone Morgan so many times that I got half a mind to go give him a good lickin' myself."

Sparrow grinned. "We'll get all of our crowd here, right enough. But when the last minute comes, we'll tell 'em that Cyclone Ed Morgan has sprained an ankle, or some gag like that, and then we'll put another man inside the ropes. You foller me, Colonel?"

"They'll shoot us full of holes and take their money back," said the colonel tersely. "I know these Western folks, young man."

"We'll offer 'em their money back," said Sparrow. "But after they've seen the fight that I got to offer 'em, they won't want no money."

"You mean," said the colonel, "that you got somebody that can lick Lacoste?" His eyes lighted.

Sparrow, however, merely grinned and shook his head. "Nobody's beatin' Lacoste," he said. "Besides, they's only fifteen rounds to catch Lacoste, and that ain't enough. No, there never was a chance that anybody could beat Lacoste. He's lightning, and, when he strikes, something's got to go down. I've seen him work. Ed Morgan would've been chopped meat for that baby."

"Why in the devil, then, would you have them fight?"

"Because there's nobody better on the market today."

"You swore to me that Cyclone Ed Morgan would give Lacoste the fight of his fightin' life."

"Sure I did, and I told you true. But there ain't nobody that's ever give Lacoste a fight. He's always stepped around the fastest of 'em as if they was tied to a tree. And he's always soaked the hardest of 'em so hard that they didn't come to for half an hour. He's a fightin' fool, this here Lacoste. You write that down, old-timer. They ain't nobody cleanin' up on him."

This information the colonel absorbed, scratching his chin the while. "Well," he said at last, "how d'you know that this new man will be better than Ed Morgan?"

"Why, Colonel, you won't have to take my word for it. I want you to come out and see 'em mix . . . the night before the fight is due with Lacoste. Or you can come out and see 'em mix now, or see one of the boys out at the camp put on the gloves with my new man."

"What's the new man's name?"

"He calls himself Camden."

"How old is he?"

"I dunno. Maybe seventeen. Maybe eighteen."

"And fight Lacoste at that age?"

"Wait till you see him work, Colonel."

It did not take much to rouse the curiosity of the colonel. He was thoroughly excited now, and he joined Sparrow straightway on the trip to the camp of Cyclone Morgan. They talked little on the way, the colonel from expectancy, and Sparrow busy with his own thoughts. So they reached the camp and hurried out into the clearing. The cook met them.

"Where's Camden?" cried Sparrow.

"Gone," said the cook.

FACING THE JOB OF FIGHTING

To such a blow as this, poor Sparrow Roberts could make no reply for a moment except to thrust out his head like a chicken and gape at the cook. Then: "Gone?" he echoed.

"Gone out into the woods," said the cook. "He said that, if you wanted him, all you needed to do was to holler and you'd have him back quick enough."

"Holler what?" Roberts asked angrily.

"He didn't say. What I think . . . this bird, he'll never show up again."

"Damn what you think!" groaned Roberts, and he turned a face purple with humiliation and with anger upon the colonel. "The hound has done me," he said. "He gave me his word."

The colonel was a little amused. "Take a try for him," he said. "Go out and give him a call . . . the way he left word."

"Does he think I'm a fool?" cried poor Roberts. "Well, I've *got* to try him."

He and the colonel passed across the clearing and into the forest that extended down the mountainside. There, among the pines, Sparrow strained his throat with a long *haloo!*

He listened, then shouted again, and again listened. But there was utterly no response except, from the camp, a distant roll of laughter. Sparrow raged with a wild temper.

"He's made a fool of me," he said to the colonel. "This Camden . . . I'll have his heart before I'm through with him."

This burst came from his lips as, rounding a turn in the path, they came unexpectedly upon the form of Camden himself, dressed now like any other civilized mountaineer, roughly but comfortably. Then he stopped short.

"Well?" he said, his anger still hardly more than swallowed in the greatness of his surprise.

"You called," Camden said laconically.

"Is this the man?" murmured the colonel.

"It is. This is the man. But wait till you've seen him work. He don't look much right now, but when he starts movin'. . . ."

"A damned queer pair of eyes," murmured Joshua Nichols. "I'd hate to meet him after dark. Damned if I wouldn't."

"We'll go right back to the camp," said Sparrow. "You'll see what he. . . ."

"I dunno that we need to do that," the colonel said, very thoughtful as he watched the other. "I dunno that we need to do that," he repeated. "I'd take your word that young gent could do . . . about anything."

Although certainly the outlines of the form of Camden were not peculiarly formidable, there was a certain dignity in his manner, and his eyes had an uncanny manner of resting straight upon the eyes of another and never moving.

"You're satisfied?" murmured Sparrow.

"Yes. It'll be a fight . . . while he lasts. He'll be a tiger till he's knocked out."

"Colonel, that's it."

So the colonel left and went back to Juniper. Behind him, Sparrow remained with Camden in the darkening woods.

"Pal," said the trainer, "the way it looks to me, you're hating the whole job around here. You want to be loose and free to get back to the woods. But if you got back to 'em, what would you have? Tell me, old-timer, what the thing is that you want most in the world?"

"Nothing," said the other harshly, "except to be alone!"

Sparrow grinned and cocked his small head upon one side. "That's what you think now," he said, "while you're sour on that girl. But down deep, Camden, what you want is her. Am I right?"

There was silence for an answer.

"Well," said Sparrow, "you let me see what you can do."

He passed on into the camp, and in the shack of Cyclone Ed Morgan he found Jenny and Nan Pearson busy, cooking supper. He took Nan out under the open sky.

"Nan," he said, "what's the thing you want most in the world?"

She answered quietly, smiling up to him in a whimsical way. "Happiness."

"Sure." He chuckled. "That's a pretty good all-round answer, but, getting down to particulars, what d'you want that'll *make* you happy?"

Over this she pondered, but only for a moment. "Something to make Dad settle down."

"That'll make him happy, eh? What's he do now?"

"He traps . . . he and Lew trap. They don't make much money that way, you see, and, not making money, he isn't able to do much for me, and that makes him unhappy, and, being unhappy, he can't work very well at the trapping. You see it works around in a circle. It all starts with being unhappy."

"Of course," murmured Sparrow. "It all starts with that. A fellow can do anything, if he's happy about it. This Camden, if he was happy and had his heart in it . . . he might have a chance even with. . . ." He paused.

"I don't like him!" said the girl with a little shudder.

"Why not?"

"Because he's so fierce. I saw him fight. It was like . . . an animal fighting."

Sparrow broke in: "What does your dad want to do in the line of settling down?"

"He's always wanted a farm. But that takes money."

"How much?"

"I've heard him say that he needs ten thousand dollars, to really start right."

"Ten thousand! He wants to start pretty fine, Nan. Suppose he had that ten thousand. What would you do for it?"

"To see Dad happy . . . and Lew happy and doing something worthwhile? Oh, I'd do about anything!" cried the girl.

"Maybe you think so. Maybe you think so now. But just how much would you do? Would you marry a guy that could give you that much?"

She looked up at him, frightened, and blushing.

"Not me," said Sparrow, grinning, "I ain't that way. But I know a guy that is. He likes you."

"Is he rich?" asked the girl, frowning.

"Not a cent! But if he knew he could have you for ten thousand, maybe he'd get rich. He'd try it, anyway. Nan, would you marry a man that brought you ten thousand in cash? Would you give me your word?"

"Somebody that I didn't. . . ."

"You'd get to like him, wouldn't you, if his money made your folks happy?"

Tears came into her eyes. "Of course. I *would* marry him."

"That's your promise?"

"That's my promise."

"Shake on it, Nan."

They shook hands, he eagerly, and she with a sort of excited resignation.

Straight back to gloomy Camden he went. "Well, kid," he began, "it's fixed up. First place . . . you know what sort of a job you got ahead of you?"

"Fighting," Camden said sullenly. "For you."

"And Pierre Lacoste is the man. If you beat him, Camden, your work with me is done. You're free."

"Bring me to him!" cried the other with a savage enthusiasm.

"And get you chopped to bits? Camden, you're strong and you're fast. Right now you could beat even a gent like Ed Morgan. But you couldn't stand up to Pierre Lacoste for a round. That means three minutes.

That fight comes in six weeks. Can I teach you to take a little care of yourself in six weeks?"

"Maybe you can. This Lacoste . . . is he such a great man?"

"He's a burnin' fire, kid. He's made up of steel and fire. That's him!" He added: "And if you can learn enough to beat Lacoste . . . mind you, to knock him out . . . to lick him cold . . . Camden, I'd give you ten thousand dollars, and set you free from the contract . . . if you was darned enough fool to want to be free."

"A fool?" muttered Camden.

"Because, with me running things, that ten thousand would be just the beginning. I'd make you rich in a year, boy. And now lemme tell you what ten thousand dollars means. It means Nan Pearson."

"Could she be bought for that much money?" asked Camden, wondering. "I didn't know she *could* be bought."

Sparrow was staggered. For an instant he hesitated between shouting and laughter. Then he changed his mind and settled to the problem before him. This boy was utterly without experience of people. He knew nothing. Anything could be made of him.

"Everybody has a price, I guess," said Sparrow. "This girl . . . she's mighty cheap at that price."

"Why don't everybody come to buy her, then?" asked Camden.

"They ain't in on the secret. But I tell you, Camden, if you had ten thousand dollars, you could walk right up to her now and count out the money and walk away with her for your wife."

He said it with such utter conviction that Camden made no instant return, but remained for a moment dreaming upon distant spaces.

At last he said slowly: "I'll fight this Pierre Lacoste. If I must beat him, I'll beat him. If I must kill him, I'll kill him."

"Damned if I don't think that you almost would!" exclaimed Sparrow. "Half this game is believin' in yourself."

CAN LACOSTE HIT?

Pierre Lacoste arrived in Juniper for the great bout only two weeks before it was scheduled. Two weeks was enough for the great Pierre, who was always in a very fair condition. He needed a little severe exercise, a few runs on the road, a little boxing, and then he was ready for a contest of any length. To gratify the public, he established his training quarters in the town of Juniper itself, and opened his camp to the people, free. From the instant of his arrival, it was plain that he would be the popular favorite as well as the favorite with the betting public.

As for Cyclone Ed Morgan, working industriously, plodding in his camp in the mountains, only handfuls of visitors went out to him from time to time. They watched him go through his paces. They observed him struggling around the ring with Bert Kenny or Vincent Munroe, and they shook their heads. Here was no good specimen to uphold the United States against the

Frenchman. Yet thousands of people, who had not a chance to observe the two in action, clung to their belief that Cyclone would win, for the very ample good reason that it was unpatriotic to dream for a moment that any foreigner could beat an American.

So thousands and thousands began to stream into Juniper. The hotels were gorged. The houses of the town charged what price they pleased for the guests they were willing to pile on their verandahs or even in their yards. Tents were thrown up. Juniper began to look like an army camp—a very disorganized one.

There was only one thing to think about—the fight. There was only one thing to do—wait for the sound of the opening gong.

Now and again the colonel called in Sparrow to learn how matters were progressing with his newest protégé. On these occasions Sparrow was rarely cheerful.

"Lacoste is too good," he would say. "I went down and saw him work the other day. They let me right in and give me a ringside seat. They didn't care what I saw or how much I saw. Why? Because they knew that Lacoste has so damned much to show that I couldn't get it all if I tried with four eyes, instead of with two. And they're right. No trick about Lacoste. He doesn't need 'em. He never moves faster than he has to when he wants to beat the other guy to the punch. He never steps back except far enough to make the other guy miss him by a hair. He works on a narrow margin, that bird, but he's sure of himself. I'd rather try to chase a ghost than Lacoste. I never saw anything like it."

"But can he hit?" the colonel asked one day.

Sparrow threw both hands into the air. "Can a fish swim?" he countered. "Can a bird fly? Can Lacoste hit?

He's a thunderbolt. You put your coin on that baby, because he ain't never gonna be stopped . . . not till he's an old man."

At this, the colonel went back to the camp of Pierre Lacoste. It seemed very simple, when one saw the famous Pierre in action. He stepped about the ring smoothly, without show, blocking the punches of his sparring partners, ducking or dodging their punches by so close a margin that he always seemed a little lucky to have escaped, and punching in return just hard enough to stop their rushes or to straighten them out when they were inclined to work too much inside.

He liked the open work, standing at long range, plying with both hands to head and body. That was the type of boxing that appealed to Pierre Lacoste, just as it appealed to every follower of the game. But, at long range or at short, he was the perfect master of himself and his opponent, no matter who that opponent might be.

The colonel watched Lacoste long enough to wonder what there was to him. Then he asked a famous boxing critic on a Manhattan paper—one who had traveled across the continent to report the training period as well as the fight itself.

"This baby is under wraps," said the boxing critic, without shifting his eyes from the moving form of Pierre Lacoste. "But ain't he a sweet thing to watch? Did you see him sift that right cross through? Look at them feet work across the canvas. Like he had wheels under him. Where did he learn to punch, and where does he get it? He ain't a middleweight! He's the champion heavyweight of the world!"

Such was the rhapsody that the colonel had to listen to after he asked his question. Then he went out and about his other business. He only delayed long enough to try to place a bet on Lacoste. But he failed. The odds were three and a half to one in favor of the Frenchman and rising every minute.

Sparrow returned to the camp. But here he gave only a summary inspection to the work of Ed Morgan. It was all a bluff now. Ed Morgan had agreed to go along with his training up to the day of the fight, and then to disappear or feign illness, so that his place could be taken in the ring at the last moment by a substitute. It was with the substitute that the trainer spent his long hours of work.

Up among the mountains, a half hour's walk from the Morgan camp, he had established the headquarters of the man from the forest. There was a scene of such activity as Sparrow had never known before. For two hours in the center of the day, Camden slept. But the rest of the time, from morning until night, he was feverishly busy with his gloves, or shadowboxing, or practicing footwork—that difficult mystery of the prize ring—how to advance smoothly, swiftly, easily, and yet with the body well planted on both feet at all times for the delivery of punches. But how terribly much there was to learn!

To begin with, there was such a matter as that of the straight left. Sparrow worked over his pupil steadily, patiently, but at last in despair, for there was no possibility of teaching the man of the woods that punch. All of its beauties were demonstrated by Sparrow. In vain he vowed that there never was a good fighter who did not have a good left. In vain he swore that the straight left was to boxing, what the foundation stones are to a house. It is the punch that erects a wall against the attacks of the foe. It is the opening wedge through which finishing punches may be slipped. It should be delivered with the head and shoulders and hip and heel and knee all on one straight line, true driving, the whole body stiffening behind the blow. These are the things that the straight left can be and should be, but to teach it to Camden was impossible. After struggling for a time, Sparrow gave it up. For when the other hit, there was always a natural hook at the end of every punch. His wrist and fist snapped up or sideways or down as the case might be, and that whiplash finish marked every blow that he used.

It was a grave waste of his time and effort and space, but Camden could not be cured. That was his one great defect. Everything else he learned with amazing speed. Footwork was his easiest problem, because, on his feet, he moved with a natural and frictionless adroitness. He learned something about boxing—an immense lot for a period of a mere six weeks of training—but still it was not enough. Yet Sparrow watched him develop in blocking and ducking and dodging from day to day until the time came, before the end, when Sparrow himself, swift though he was with his fists, could not make an impression upon the defense of his client.

"Still it ain't good enough!" Sparrow would say. "If I had another month . . . if I had another month. Oh, kid, if I had another month or two to put you into shape, I'd stack you ag'in' the best in the land! But it don't make no difference, for you still got a fighting chance."

To these remarks, Camden made no replies. Criticism could not discourage him, it seemed. While he worked at his training, he had a grim and dogged look as of a purpose far away that will be striven for endlessly, perhaps hopelessly.

Sparrow, watching him, knew that he was thinking of the girl. Not that he ever mentioned her. Her name was not once on his lips. Indeed, during all of those six weeks, he rarely spoke. Sometimes, as Sparrow labored over him, cursed him hysterically, praised, blamed, scorned, mocked and honored him, he went the whole day without speaking in reply. Only his amber eyes made acknowledgment, and the speed with which his hands and his feet moved. Hit straight he could not, but God had given him a natural hook, which is the next best thing.

So the day came for the fight; the hour came for the fight. In the dressing quarters that the colonel had erected near his natural amphitheater, Sparrow sat beside the man on whom his hopes were centered, while, through the big amphitheater he heard a sudden, sullen roar from the crowd.

He knew what it meant. Already half cooked in the heat of the afternoon sun, the crowd had been maddened by the sudden sting of disappointment when it heard that, after all, one of the pair that so many of them had come literally thousands of miles to see had disappeared, or at least was unable to step into the ring.

A hurried step, a beat on the door, and there stood the colonel, white of face, before them.

"For heaven's sake, get your man out here!" he shouted to Sparrow. "They've nearly mobbed me. They want blood, that crowd. I've had the announcer tell 'em that they can have their money back if they don't like the show that we put on. But they won't listen. They're in there bellowin' like steers. They'll plumb raise the devil with me and all Juniper if. . . ."

Sparrow was usually a mild little man, particularly when he stood before a millionaire, but his temper was set on a hair-trigger on this day of days. He yelled at the colonel: "You long-legged tramp, get out! I ain't to be bothered. I'll bring my lad up to the mark. Now shut up and get out!"

The colonel got.

"Now, kid," said Sparrow, "you're in there to make your coin and get a name for yourself and then go out and collect a wife. You'll fight for yourself. But you're gonna fight for me, too! After you climb into that ring, I'm gonna bet money . . . real money, kid . . . that you last the whole fifteen rounds even if you got the great Lacoste in the same ring."

Camden said not a word, but he sighed a little and rose from his chair. For a moment the trainer stared at that lean brown face with a speechless anxiety.

"They're gonna yell. They're gonna rave when they see you . . . because you look sort of skinny . . . particular at a distance where they can't see the way you're put together and the make of your muscles. But don't listen. They ain't nothin' in the world for you. They ain't nothin' you're gonna fear . . . nothin' but my voice out of the corner tellin' you what to do!"

AT IT, HAMMER AND TONGS

Pierre Lacoste was making a speech, and, under cover of that speech, Sparrow and Harry Camden entered the amphitheater, where thousands of men, their faces black with anger, were muttering like a storm, and looking for something on which they could wreak their vengeance for this disappointment. Surely a prize fight had never been planned in a stranger setting, with the huge mountains—blue and brown in the distance—and far away the muffled booming of the "shells" where the miners were still busily at work. For the treasure hunters could not pause even for the sake of seeing the matchless Pierre Lacoste in action.

Lacoste told the hushed and respectful audience in badly broken English, with many bows and gestures, that he was covered with sorrow for their disappointment, that, if there were a fraud, he, at least, was no party to it, and that to show his good will and fulfill the terms of his engagement, he was willing to fight any man in the crowd, regardless of weight, instead of the substitute who, it was said, the colonel had prepared to take the place of Cyclone Ed Morgan.

This speech brought a furor of applause and many yells that "Frenchy" was all right. In the midst of that racket, Sparrow slipped into the ring and with him went Harry Camden. There was a little pause.

"Stand up and toss off that bathrobe," Sparrow said with a snarl. "Let 'em see the worst of it right away, damn 'em!"

The man from the wilderness obeyed. There had been a little silence upon the entrance of the substitute, but the crowd needed only one glance to convince itself that here was a rank imposture. Here was a boy, with a boy's slender body—sun-browned although it was. Yonder stood Pierre Lacoste, short, stocky, but looking speed, every inch of him, and with long arms of a reach equal to a heavyweight's. The contrast was too great. They saw Pierre Lacoste flash one keen appraising glance at his foe to be, and then look down at the floor and shake his head dubiously, as though silently protesting against that imposture. This was enough to loose the floodgates of the wrath of the mob. They leaped up and roared their fury. Then they came in a great wave with hands brandished. The colonel, who stood in a corner of the ring, nervously chewing a long cigar, nearly swallowed a portion of it that he now bit off, and turned a sickly yellow. It was Sparrow who rose to meet the onslaught. He rose not with words, but with a thing more eloquent than words. In his hands, swung high above his head, was a thick bunch of greenbacks.

There grew around him enough curious silence to give him a chance to yell: "I'm this bird's backer! I'll go two thousand in cold cash . . . my own money . . . that he stays the whole fifteen rounds with Lacoste. Who'll take me on that? Who'll take me, boys?"

Money talks. It has a deep, strong voice of its own. The ugly earnest face of Sparrow carried conviction. The offer was repeated. It passed on in a counter wave that washed out most of the noise in its path, and left Sparrow shouting furiously.

"Who'll take me? Who'll put up or shut up, here?"

A man rose. "That's a good bluff, son. I'll give you three to one that your kid don't stay the fifteen rounds. Lacoste'll eat him up!"

Other voices broke in, protesting. They wanted some of the easy money. What were odds of three to one, when they were willing to give five and six? And bets were suddenly placed, right and left. After that, the crowd was half willing to settle back, suspicious still, cursing the colonel under its breath, ready to see a cheat, but, nonetheless, very interested to see whether Sparrow Roberts would lose his money and how soon.

"Five hundred to you, Lacoste, if you knock him cockeyed in five rounds!"

Lacoste turned and smiled. There was only one interruption of that smile. Lacoste was a modest man, as modest as he was brave and skillful. But to oppose a boy to him—that was really too much.

"Roberts, you dog, you've ruined me!" the colonel snarled out at the ear of Sparrow.

"Shut up," groaned Sparrow, growing a little sick at heart as he compared the Frenchman with his own untried boxer. "I've put my own coin into this. Let's see what comes out of it."

The referee was in the ring now. He was a gray-haired ex-pugilist, his face still wearing a battered, lop-sided look, but his eyes were bright and intelligent. He laid a hand on the shoulder of each of the two fighters and bowed above them, for he was a strapping six-footer and more. He seemed to be muttering instructions, but what he was saying was: "Boys, is this here on the level?"

"So help me God, sir!" cried honest Lacoste.

"Well?" the referee said to Camden.

The latter said not a word; he merely fixed his amber, dull eyes on those of Lacoste.

"I think he wants to hypnotize me, *monsieur*," murmured the Frenchman.

The referee stepped back. They were in their corners—Lacoste methodically pawing at the resin, Camden standing idly, his hands dangling at his side. The gong sounded. Lacoste leaped to the center of the ring, and a wail of rage and mirth rose as Camden did not stir.

"Go at him!" barked Sparrow.

Camden went with a leap that cut the noise short, and, as he leaped, he was met in the air with a straight left that traveled as true and hard as a rifle ball. It knocked Camden flat on his back on the canvas with a thudding spat that sounded over the entire amphitheater. The groan of sympathy and derision began again—to be cut short once more as Camden, like a rubber ball, leaped to his feet and closed.

It all happened so quickly—that engagement and disengagement—that most of the spectators did not know what was happening. But those close to the ring saw several things of importance. The first was that Lacoste landed three heavy, short punches as the brown-bodied youngster stepped in, and yet those punches to head and body did not seem to jar the supple frame of the unknown. They saw, moreover, that, when they closed, the younger man caught Lacoste with a left arm behind his back and hugged him. Only an instant, but Lacoste turned white and gasped. Then he tugged himself free and danced away, but with his hands low—looking as if he had fought ten rounds already.

The wise ones looked at one another in amaze. "The kid has something!" they agreed.

"Not much," was the instant answer, for as Camden followed up, he was met with a volley of long-range punches that literally lifted him and drove him before them. Here was a man who boxed with a speed that would have blinded even Vince Munroe, and who struck with a power that made the sledge-hammer blows of Kenny seem like love taps.

Camden sprang back from the deadly shower and shook his head vigorously to clear it.

"He's got enough!" yelled someone. "He's showing yellow like a. . . ."

Here the brown man whipped in again, and Lacoste, striking with both hands, carelessly, left himself wide open. Camden struck. It was not much of a blow. He seemed to reach out casually and drop his gloved right hand on the point of Lacoste's jaw with a little flick of the wrist at the end of the punch. But the results were amazing. As though a pile driver had descended upon his head, Pierre Lacoste sank to the floor and sat there, gazing through a stupid mist at his foe, while Sparrow, from his corner, began a wild song and dance lost in the deafening uproar of the crowd.

This was unbelievable! And here was the referee, with a startled face, tolling forth the seconds. "Six . . . seven . . . eight. . . ." The stricken man gathered his feet beneath him. "Nine!" He was resting on his hands. "Ten!" He was on his feet.

Swaying, like one drunk, his gloved hands extended automatically before him, obviously blinded, stupid from that terrible blow. And Camden? In that precious moment, he stood back with his hands at his sides, the screaming voice of Sparrow drowned by the bellowing of the mob. Once he stepped toward Pierre Lacoste and raised a hand to strike, but as Lacoste staggered away, the conqueror shook his head and dropped his gloves to his sides, as though unwilling to take such an advantage. Here he looked to Sparrow for definite instruction. Sparrow was black in the face with furious anxiety.

"Kill Lacoste! Get him!" he shrieked.

Camden went in to win. It was too late now, however. The brain of Pierre Lacoste had cleared sufficiently for him to block a shower of blows and fall into a clinch. A moment later the bell rang for the end of the round, and they went back to their corners with the amphitheater in a bedlam.

Sparrow made no effort to use a towel to fan his man, for Camden was not even breathing. Instead, the trainer gripped his pupil by both shoulders.

"You fool!" he yelled. "Soak that bird and put him away. D'you think he'd back up if he had you going?"

He clambered down out of the ring as the bell sounded for the second round.

White, drawn face, and staring eyes of anxiety followed Pierre Lacoste as the latter, dripping with water, stepped out for the second round. But it was instantly plain that his brain had by now cleared entirely from the shock of that stunning blow. Yet he had his lesson. He danced around Harry Camden at long range, whipping in accurately timed punches, never taking a chance, or, when he had to close, tying up the arms of the other with wonderful skill.

Round after round, he boxed like a master. Round after round, the man from the forest rushed like a tiger, and was met with an insoluble wall of gloves. Those punches of Lacoste, strong enough to have knocked out an ordinary man, were raising great purple welts on the body of Camden.

Still he came on ceaselessly, striving for a second solid punch. Many a time he struck, but the blows were glancing ones. From the side of the head, from the cheekbones, the breast or the ribs of Lacoste, those man-killing blows caromed away, but, even as they glanced, there was power in them that often shook Lacoste from head to heel.

In the eighth round he complained to the referee as he lay gasping in his corner: "This Camden has something in his gloves. No man could hit like that!"

So the referee went to Harry Camden and thumbed his gloves thoroughly. There was nothing beneath the leather except the padding and the hard hand below. The ninth round was called, and the slaughter began again.

"Knock him out! We've bet on you to win in ten rounds!" his chief second had said to Lacoste, and he went in willingly.

To mix with this brown-skinned tiger was excessively dangerous, however. They had hardly closed in the first rally when a lifting uppercut plowed through the arms of Lacoste, glanced off his chest, and struck his chin. He staggered away the full length of the ring, and, bouncing off the ropes, he fell into a clinch.

After that, there were no more chances to be taken. This was something like playing with a thunderbolt, and Pierre Lacoste had no liking for the work. He stayed away safely, from that point on. When he had to close, he was content to tie up the arms of his enemy. He preferred to dance away at arm's length. The tenth round closed. The eleventh round dragged through.

"You'll last it out!" gasped out Sparrow.

"I've got to win," Camden panted, and his amber eyes, now looking forth through slits at the face of the other, measured Lacoste hungrily up and down.

The referee leaned above him. "Kid," he said with a rough sympathy, "you've done well. But there's no use breakin' your heart. You can't catch Frenchy. He's on wheels. That last round was good enough to end the fight. The crowd has had its money's worth."

"Send him away," Camden said to Sparrow, and rose from his chair at the sound of the gong.

He rose slowly, however, for an idea had formed itself in his mind. What does a bird do when it wishes to lure the dog away from the rest? It flutters away with sagging wings, pretends to be lamed.

So, at the first blow that collided with his chin, Camden allowed his knees to sag, and crumpled to the floor. The referee cast a sharp glance at Sparrow as though to say: "I told you what would happen." Then he began the count.

Camden, acting exactly as he remembered Pierre Lacoste had acted, gathered himself at the count of seven, swaying, and rose at nine, with arms half down. He looked up beneath his swollen brows and saw Lacoste, his face contorted with ferocity, plunge in for the finishing punch. It landed high on Camden's cheek with a shock that cast a splintering of red across his vision.

He reeled far back, letting his knees go limp, letting his head sag far to one side, as Lacoste had done in that wild first round. Yet all the while his heart was swelling with fury and with a sense of power as he saw the Frenchman rush in with a white glint of teeth behind his straining lips. In and in came Lacoste. His left glove was down—his right was swinging wildly.

Then Camden straightened like a sapling released from a weight. He stood suddenly firm on both feet. It was in front of his left that the opening lay, and with his left he struck, the full length of his arm, the full sway of his body, with a chopping little hook at the end of the stroke.

It was not accurately landed. At the last instant, Lacoste saw the trick and strove to cover himself. He was too late for that, but he managed to sway his head a little so that Camden's glove landed on the forehead of his rival, instead of on the chin. Otherwise, so Sparrow swore afterward, the neck of Lacoste would have been broken.

As it was, he fell loosely on the floor of the ring.

No one needed to wait for the count.

As for the referee, he waved Camden to his corner and, picking up the fallen king, began to drag him toward his seconds.

Down on the press bench, reporters, agape, were scribbling as fast as pencils could make notes. The crowd opened its heart with joy, for it had seen the great Lacoste go down at last. It opened its heart, it opened its throat, and it yelled its joy in a key that made the sky ring.

NO WORLD CHAMPIONSHIP FOR HIM

Three weeks later the parting came between Camden and Sparrow. The wounds of Camden were healed, and the patience of Sparrow was finally exhausted.

On a day he stood up in the tent that sheltered them and smote his hands together.

"You're the world's champion, kid. Are you gonna tell me that you'll give it up?"

Camden took him out of the tent. On a long, flat shoulder of the hill a colony of prairie dogs was chattering.

"Listen," Camden declared, "that's your world. Why should I want to be champion of it?"

Sparrow could not utter a single word. Instead, he dug down into his coat and tugged out a thick sheaf of bills.

"I'm done!" he cried, trembling with passion. "And when you've spent this wad, maybe you'll get some sense. Go take that coin and blow it on the fool girl. When it's gone, you'll want to find more of the same stuff. Oh, I'll hear from you again, right enough." He cast the money at Camden. "Ten thousand!" he shouted. "That's what you get for your little outing!"

What he, as the most astute of managers, made out of the transaction was thus left undisclosed, and Sparrow stormed out of the camp and hurried away with a heart swelling with disgust. For here was a gold mine that refused to be mined, a man who refused to make himself great and famous.

Camden went down from the mountains in his own way. That is to say, he covered more miles than a hard-ridden horse for five consecutive days, and so he came at last, into the country of Nan Pearson. He reached it at noon, slept on a bed of pine needles until the evening, and hurried down from the mountains into the lowlands through the dusk. He knew the country. The house, having been described, he went straight to it. It was barely dark. Inside the window of one room, he saw a cloud of smoke. Men must be there. Peering through another, he found himself staring into a small kitchen, and at the sink was Nan Pearson, laughing at her work and rattling the dishes as she washed them.

The hand of Camden closed hard around the package of money, and a lump came in his throat. Then he stepped to the kitchen door and opened it. At that, she called over her shoulder: "Is that you, Lew?"

When he did not answer, she turned, still laughing, and saw him. The laughter was struck from her face. She grew a little white and stood there, staring.

For a moment she fumbled automatically, drying her hands on the apron, still staring at him and his burning amber eyes, and the flare of his nostrils, and the purple blotches that were the only marks of the fight remaining on his face. He saw her fear as clearly as he saw her beauty, and it sickened him.

"Mister Roberts . . . he wrote and said that you was coming," she said. "But . . . when I told him a long time ago . . . I didn't mean. . . ." She began to tremble. "I'll get Dad," she whispered. "He'll . . . he'll know better how to talk to you."

He caught her shoulder and stopped her as she fled for the inner door. How soft was the touch of her flesh beneath his hard fingertips.

"Wait," he said. "Roberts told you that I was bringing down money?"

"He said. . . ."

"It's a loan," Camden said. "Someday, later on . . . maybe I'll come to ask for it back."

He laid the packet of money on the table, without looking at it. Then he backed to the door. "You hate me, I guess," he whispered.

As he stood there with a great sorrow in those wild yellow eyes, and with a great grief making his breast swell, a great warm wave of relenting swept through the girl.

She would have spoken and called him back, but she could not. Fear and this new emotion were too close to one another still. So, without a word spoken, she saw him fade away into the night. She ran to the door after him. But he was already gone.

She hurried out into the night, with an ache of regret already forming in her heart, and then, over the ridge of the low hills, she saw a tall form, looking gigantic from that low angle, appear for an instant against the stars and then dip down behind the close horizon and disappear.

She waited there so long and so still that the gray two-year-old filly came to the fence to stare at her through the darkness, and a great winged owl swooped over her head with whispering wings and passed on. After that, awakening, she went slowly back to the kitchen and found the money and began to count it mechanically, without knowing what she did.

CAMDEN IN TOWN

Through the sun-brimmed world of yellow morning light, when the rose of dawn was as yet hardly out of the sky, rolled a great, deep voice:

All day long on the prairies I ride,
Not even a dog to trot by my side.
My fire I kindle with chips gathered 'round,
My coffee I boil without being ground.

Camden wakened with the roar of the last note in his ears. He pitched his feet off the bed and swung into a sitting posture, his head in his palms, his fingers thrust into the deep, woolly tangle of his hair. Like hammer blows upon his brain, thickened with the tequila that he had drunk the night before, the words beat ceaselessly:

All day long on the prairies I ride,
Not even a dog. . . .

Camden swayed to his feet and felt his way across the room. His legs were weak and uncertain. His knees sagged and wobbled. Of his feet he was only dimly aware that they were in his way, but his arms were as powerful as ever; liquor could not affect them or his mighty hands. So he steadied himself down the wall and along the foot of the bed until his grip was on the sill of the window and he looked out.

The breath of the morning air was so unspeakably delicious to him that for the moment he forgot the malice that was surging in that dulled mind of his. He gulped that air; he drank it with a grin of fierce delight. He tore open his shirt until the wind could touch his hot breast. All the knotted muscles of his body, all the knotted muscles of his thought began to relax. He heard the wailing song more clearly, but more in the distance so far as volume was concerned.

My fire I kindle with chips gath. . . .

The grin of Camden was a wolfish lifting of his lip that exposed white teeth strong enough to have snapped at a bone and crushed it.

"I'm more'n half drunk," he said to himself. "I must have been on a beaut' last night."

He turned from the window. The warmth and the darkness of the room rolled oppressively against his face, and the fumes struck heavily upward to the seat of reason and of self-control.

"I'm gonna get sober!" Camden announced.

It was a stirring thing to see him use his will; as another man might wrestle against a physical enemy, so stood Camden, his legs well braced, half reeling, his big arms extended before him, his big hands half clenched so that the fingers were as rigid as stone. Thought was impossible to him, it seemed, without physical contortion.

"I'm gonna get sober!" he said again aloud.

All at once he stood erect easily on his legs; his eyes cleared; his brow smoothed; and his very breathing grew less rapid and harsh. In one in whose presence so much of the brute was visible, such an effort of the will seemed doubly amazing. Now that he had smoothed his face, it was possible to see him more clearly.

His ugliness was extraordinary. He had a pugilist's wide, short jaw, a cruelly arched nose, and big, cold amber eyes, like the eyes of a beast of prey. Listing his features one by one, they were not unattractive. It was his expression that made him repulsive.

Now he crossed the room, bearing his two hundred pounds with a step of lightness. He lowered his head over the washbowl and inverted the pitcher above it. The rush of cold water cleared his brain like magic. Five minutes later he left his room and went down to the dining room of the hotel.

He was early for breakfast. He had to sit beside a window and wait, staring out across the desert beyond the town to the brown, burned mountains whose distant summits turned blue and melted in the sky. The proprietor came in and greeted him with a nervous smile.

"How you feelin', Camden?" he asked.

"Fine," he replied with a growl.

The proprietor rested his hands on the back of a chair so that it swayed slowly back and forth, and, pressing upon a nail in the floor, it gave forth a steady, subdued squeaking. That noise was the most exquisite torture to Harry Camden, but he took his tormented nerves in hand and checked them. He raised his head a little and forced a smile upon his lips. It was one of the great moments of his life. It was not to honor the proprietor or to conciliate his friendship. It was simply because he was getting a gruesome enjoyment out of this battle with his nerves that protested in a shuddering agony.

"After last night," said the proprietor, winking broadly, "I figgered that you'd be restin' your head a little today."

"I ain't one of them that need rest," Camden replied. "But I . . . ,"—he paused. The loud singer wailed again.

> All day long the prairies I ride,
> Not even a dog to trot by my side.
> My fire I kindle with chips. . . .

"Who might that be, that's singin'?" Camden asked gently.

"You've been noticin' him, have you?" asked the proprietor.

"I been noticin' him," answered Camden, more quietly than ever.

"That's Steve Arnot. Got a fine voice, I guess."

"A mighty good loud voice."

"Yep, they's some say that he'd ought to be on the stage. I dunno but what he ought. He's got talent, that gent."

"He's got talents," Camden agreed softly. "Maybe the cook's got something in yonder for me to eat?"

The proprietor hastened to find out. In the kitchen he said to the old one-eyed cook: "Hurry up with them flapjacks. We got Harry Camden in yonder, and dog-gone me if he ain't plumb good-natured. Darned if he ain't smilin'. The first I ever seen on his face!"

How little can even the keenly observant tell what passes in the mind of a strong man. For in Camden there was only one strong desire, and that was to wreck the hotel, touch a match to its remains, strangle the singer who was "good enough to be on the stage," and throw his body into the flames.

These thoughts he turned slowly, deliberately in his brain. Then food was brought before him, a vast stack of hotcakes, ham, eggs, coffee impenetrably black, thick molasses, butter. Once more he took himself grimly in hand. Had he turned weakling that the very presence of food revolted him? He began to eat methodically, forcing down every mouthful with an individual effort. Perspiration stood on his forehead. A black mist of disgust swirled before his eyes. But he continued to eat. The proprietor came back and rocked the creaking chair once more, and Harry Camden forced himself to finish his meal and chat with the other pleasantly at the same time.

What an effort every smile cost him, no one in the mountains could have calculated. But he persisted to the last. He listened to a long story; he finished the last bite of his food; then he sauntered forth onto the verandah and slumped into a chair. There he rolled a cigarette.

> My fire I kindle with chips gathered 'round,
> My coffee I boil without. . . .

The cigarette tasted like the fume of metal filings, but he forced himself to finish it to the smallest sort of a butt. He smoked it so small that it singed his fingertips before he dropped it, and every breath he inhaled to the bottom of his lungs. Then he snapped the butt away. He was half sick, and he was in a cold frenzy. Still the song droned on, the same stanza over and over again:

> All day long on the prairie. . . .

The proprietor followed him onto the verandah. It was not often that one found terrible Harry Camden in such obviously good humor. Here was a chance for talk. Here was a chance to learn, perhaps, certain stories or hints of stories, which no one in the world knew, for the past of Camden was a dark abyss, hiding unknown things. So the proprietor came out, swinging a thick stick stout enough to have brained a wolf.

"What was that yarn about you comin' down to Withero last year?" he asked frankly.

"I dunno," said Camden. "Lemme see that stick." He took it in his mighty fingers. This was a weapon with which he could crush skulls. How he would like to use it for that very purpose!

"There was some said . . . ," began the proprietor, but then he was drowned by the huge, wailing voice of the singer on the farther side of the hotel.

> All day long on the prairie I ride,
> Not even a dog to trot. . . .

The thick cudgel snapped between the hands of Camden and left two short butts ending in a brush of splinters. He stood up.

"What's the matter?" asked the owner of the hotel.

"This here wood is rotten," Camden declared, and

gave the proprietor another smile. But a gate had opened, and the man of the hotel glimpsed a hell inside his guest. He remained behind to gape at this thing that he had half seen, half guessed at.

Camden sprang down from the verandah and found the singer seated on a stump, repairing a broken bridle, his fingers busy, his eyes half closed with the ecstasy of his song.

"Who are you?" asked Camden.

The artist finished the next long-drawn note, and then broke off his music with regret. "I'm Steve Arnot."

"Arnot, you sing like a brayin' mule."

"Me?" gasped out the songster.

"I'm tellin' you."

"Why, damn your soul. . . ." Then he broke off and leaped up, stiffening as he saw what was coming, and then made a convulsive movement for his gun.

He had not even a ghost of a chance. The flung end of the broken cudgel struck him on the shoulder, and the gun fell from his limp fingers. Then Camden reached him with a leap, as a lion springs on a bullock, and Arnot, after one fierce struggle, screamed like a man whose flesh the claws of a beast are tearing. Then he collapsed.

"COME AND TAKE ME"

Camden went off among the trees, and there he found an opening among the scrubby pines—an out guard, a far-flung outpost of the forest trees, still dwindling in the hot embrace of the desert, but yet existing, a testimony to those first settlers who had come to the place with ideals and had planted those trees when they might have been herding cattle.

There Camden kicked together a bedding of pine needles, and he lay upon it face down, his head pillowed on the cushioning muscles of his arms, the rest of his body stretched at large in the heat of the sun. He slept long and well. It was the middle of the afternoon when something wakened him. He hardly knew what it was, but as warnings come to the sleeping beast, so they came to Camden. He sat suddenly erect.

There was no fog in his brain. The effect of the debauch had been worn away by slumber—just as an animal will sleep away wounds, fatigue, sickness. So it was with Camden. He needed to have rest, to be close to the soil where nature took care of him. Other men wakened with dull eyes, clogged ears, only half conscious. His wakening was like the rousing of a wild wolf. He sat up, bristling, and looked around him. No stretching, no yawning. There was no time for luxuries like that, for in his sleep he had had an alarm. An eye had fallen upon him.

A beast of prey might have learned by uncanny sharpness of hearing or by scent; Camden was guided by something almost as accurate and a thousand times more delicate—an extra sense that had roused him even from profound slumber to tell him that something living had been near him, a sense that gave him now a vague idea of the direction in which the peril stood.

For a peril it must be. All beasts were his enemies, of course, and among men he had no friends. No human being could ever see the devil rise up in the depths of those cold amber eyes and approach him without a shudder of dread. That thing which had paralyzed Steve Arnot had paralyzed other men before him. It was something hard to define, yet easily recognizable.

He stood up. All the lumbering clumsiness that had been noticeable about him before his sleep was gone now. He was light on his feet as a cat is light, and like a hunting cat's was his stride, so silken smooth, so noiseless, so dainty, so terrible. He became a picture of swift grace, vanishing like a shadow into the thick of the copse.

There he crouched in the first covert, and waited. Only a moment, but in that moment he was able to distinguish a dozen things—the noise of a squirrel's teeth gnawing bark in the distance, the stir of the wind in the tip-tops of the tree, the *creak* of a far-off bough against another, and, closer at hand, something stirring in the brush.

He faded back through the thicket. How could he move so fast through such a place and yet without a murmur of noise? It was a mystery. But he faded through a dense hedge as though it had been a wraith and came out on the farther side. He made a quick semicircle and found himself, at last, behind the disturbing presence. He came up just as it was slipping in behind a tree—thinking, it seemed, that he was still before it.

Then Camden saw, and what he saw was a mere boy, a stripling with bare brown legs, a slingshot in his hands, mischief in his eyes, lurking and stealing through the little copse.

His size did not make a great difference to Camden, any more than the size of a coyote keeps the grizzly from closing its paws over the back of the little beast—if he can catch it. But in Camden there was no doubt about catching. He could give the trained athlete a ten-yard start and catch him in fifty strides. It was only what he would do with the adventuring boy.

He picked up a broken branch, that, flung as he could fling it, would drop the youngster. It might break a leg—or a few ribs, but it would teach the boy a lesson. Lessons were good things to learn, and the younger the better. So reasoned Camden. Still, something held him back. He could think of a better thing than force. Force, after all, is what animals use; a grizzly has force, for instance. But Camden was man, also, and had that thing which is given by Mother Nature for the infliction of pain upon others—a brain.

He conned the matter for a moment to himself, the flame in those amber eyes, but he made up his mind swiftly, always, and he determined quickly now. He merely slid from his hiding place and stood behind the boy, making himself still. To make oneself still, the very thought must be controlled, for thought is electric and springs great gaps to give warnings—such warnings as Camden had received a moment before. He knew all about such matters. He could make himself so still that a fawn would come up and nibble his hand. He could make himself so still that even a mother grizzly would come to examine him—downwind!

So he stilled himself now. The boy, crouching behind a tree and peering forth on either side with nervous little movements of his head like a pecking bird, studied what lay before him and squinted through the brush until a shadow began to fall across them—not a thing that he could see, but upon his mind—a shadow that was cold dread.

Camden, making himself still, saw and understood the cessation of the boy's eager peering movements, the quiet that came upon him, the stiffening of this young body, and then—how clearly Camden heard it—his quickening breath.

The horror grew. The youthful hunter stood erect now, his hands clenched at his sides. Behind him stood—what? A snake coiled to strike? A great bear with paw ready to batter the life from him at a blow?

Still the terror grew. The boy could not turn his head, dared not turn it. Camden, observing, drew in his own breath noiselessly, drinking that horror like a precious wine. But the bare drawing of his breath seemed enough to break the spell. The boy whirled about with a scream and struck out—even a cornered rat will fight!

The rubber of the slingshot cut across the face of Camden. That face was iron and scarcely felt the blow. Across the mouth, too, and there he felt it. His thick arm shot out, his great hand fastened on the nape of the boy's neck. He was a sturdy, well-compacted boy, but Camden held him at arm's length, as though he had been a bird.

"You . . . brat!" he snarled out. He threw all the fury of his nature into the expression of a face that was formidable even in repose, but now became terrific.

The boy cast an arm before his eyes to shut out the vision, and shrieked again. Then Camden flung him away. He landed in some stiff brush, crashed through it as though hurled from a great engine, tumbled to his feet, and raced away.

After that Camden sat down to think the matter over. It was a small adventure, but, what there was of it, perfect and satisfying. He felt, on that afterthought, that he could not have improved upon what he had done. All was well. He tasted the thing from beginning to end with relish.

Meanwhile, as a jack rabbit streaks away from the cry of the hounds, so the boy raced for the nearest house, which happened, naturally enough, to be the hotel. On the verandah of the hotel, still naturally enough, he found a dozen men gathered around the form of Steve Arnot. They had carried him here and had bedded him down. The doctor felt that it would not be well to move him again until night, for he was badly battered. A leg was broken—a rib was bashed in—and, above all, he had received a mental shock that was much worse than any physical injuries. To that ready audience, the boy told his story.

What he had to tell he hardly knew, except that a horror had been upon him. The men sensed it, as dogs sense that a wolf has been near one of their mates. They gathered the horror from his eyes and were ready to believe anything when he screamed to them: "Help! Help!"

"What's wrong, kid?" they growled out at him.

"Camden!" he gasped out.

Their eyes sought the prostrate form of Arnot who had groaned even in his delirium at the sound of that dreadful name.

"What's Camden tried to do to you?"

"He tried . . . to kill me!"

They looked to one another. When the blackest fury comes over men, they are not noisy. Such was the silence of this group. They found out where Camden had last been seen, then they acted, as though they had received orders from one commander. They climbed on their horses, unlimbered their guns, and looked to their ropes, and then started for the place.

They found Harry Camden seated with his back against a tree. He had heard them coming. He had guessed that danger was in their arrival, but, being innocent, he decided to brave them out. What he had done today seemed to him only strictly virtuous. Steve Arnot deserved all that had come to him for being a public nuisance. As for the boy, had a hair of his head been injured, saving for a few scratches in the brush? Besides, it was upon danger that the big man fed daily. He sought it wherever he could find it.

They paused, ranged in a loose semicircle before him, like hounds before a grizzly at bay.

"He thinks that we're scared to tackle him," said Doc Lambert.

A growl answered him, and, feeling the backing of the others, he called: "Hey, you . . . Camden!"

The big man yawned in their faces and made no other reply except to shut his strong white teeth with a *click*.

"You . . . Camden! We've come to give you a runnin' chance! Come out of that there brush and we'll give you a twenty-yards start on the hosses to get back to the hotel. If you make it . . . you got an hour to get out of town. If you don't make it. . . ."

"Shut up, Doc," cut in Josh Williams. "He don't get no runnin' chance. We've had enough of that devil. We've had too damned much." Josh Williams was the father of the boy in the case, and, having seen the expression on the face of his son, he was ready to kill. The others, however, were not yet worked up to such a point. They proffered the big man another chance. Then he spoke.

"You want me? Then come and take me!" With that, he stepped forth from the shelter of the trees and began to walk toward the hotel, slowly.

They trooped their horses after him, but no man spoke, no man moved a hand. There was something too formidable about that light-footed bulk—that terribly soft-stepping monster of a man. He seemed capable of leaping at them like a mountain lion. They held their distance until Josh Williams, with a shout as though at a roundup, whirled the noose of his rope and spurred forward.

THE HORSEWHIPPING

Camden slid to the side without turning his head. The noose dropped against his shoulder, and then, as Josh Williams went past, Camden plucked him from his horse. The others saw Josh Williams double up; they heard his scream of agony; they saw him pitch face downward upon the ground. His had been the fate of many advance guards. But now the rest of the men came in one resistless whirl. One rope was dodged, and two. The third gripped Camden about the shoulders. He shot the noose over his head with a shrug of those same shoulders and a wave of the arms. A fourth rope landed while his arms were high. A fifth fell. Suddenly he was swathed from head to foot and lay helpless on the ground.

Two men picked up poor Josh Williams and carried him, groaning, to the hotel. Three riders dragged Camden at the end of the ropes not toward the hotel, but toward the trees. They wanted to be alone, instinctively, for the work that was coming.

Doc Lambert, a just man, a good citizen, took charge. He sat down beside the helpless captive.

"What'd you do to the kid?" he asked. "What call did you have to do anything to him?"

Camden did not answer. He merely looked into the face of Doc Lambert with his amber eyes, and Doc shivered.

"Will you talk?" asked Doc.

There was no response.

A blind fury came over the others. They had seen the result of one bit of this man's handicap after it was finished. A moment before they had seen him at work on Josh Williams, their familiar, their friend. When they looked down at him, they encountered the blank eyes of a beast. It was too much. All humanity was suddenly stripped from them, and they became as beasts.

They tied Camden to a limb of a tree, suspended by both arms. They tore the shirt from his back. Three men took quirts with long, cutting lashes, like miniature black snakes, and these they whirled at Camden. Those lashes, in their practiced hands, could slice through the skin of a mule. They sliced through the skin of Camden. They raised long white welts. They sliced through the welts.

They would never have done such a thing to any other man; not one of them would have been capable of such brutality. But they were not one. They were a mob, and a mob is either divine or demoniac. This mob was possessed of the devil. No matter if blood flowed; it was not a man they tortured, but a beast, so the cruel little whips still played and with every stroke they shouted: "Will you talk now?"

They got no answer. Then Doc Lambert—this was after a long, long time—walked around in front of the victim and looked at his face. What he saw turned him as white as a sheet. He cried suddenly—"That's enough, boys!"—and with his knife he slashed the two ropes. They were good ropes, perfectly fit for working cattle, well tested and tried. A cow waddie loves his own rope that his hand is familiar with. But when Camden fell inert from the limb of the tree, they forgot the damage to the ropes. They looked first at one another, seeking for consolation and getting none, for each was remembering that this was not an animal, after all, but a fellow human being.

Camden stumbled to his feet, but the agony had numbed every limb or, perhaps, the loss of blood had told on him. He stumbled. The arms that he cast out to break the fall were numbed to the shoulders by the long strain of hanging from the limb. They crumpled under him, and he lurched heavily upon his face.

He struggled to get up, but fell heavily on that lacerated back while the others shuddered with instinctive sympathy. Then, seeing his face, they understood what Doc Lambert had done, for it was a colorless countenance, the teeth locked over a hundred groans, the eyes glaring, and such a contorted expression as a man might wear in the midst of a raging fire.

"That'll teach you . . . ," someone began to say. But every head was turned toward the speaker, and he subsided.

Doc Lambert approached the fallen victim. His voice shook like that of a nervous child. "Camden," he said, "we went too far. We forgot . . . we . . . we want to do what we can for you. . . ."

There was no answer, and Lambert stepped back as though he had been struck.

"Leave him alone . . . leave him be," someone said.

They took that unsatisfactory advice. They herded back toward the hotel in a close cluster, no one speaking until they reached the hotel.

Then a voice among them said: "We forgot that we was a dozen to one . . . and no matter what Camden did, he fought man to man, always. And the kid . . . where was the kid hurt?"

This was reason coming a long distance to lag behind passion. They scattered at once, not singly, but in pairs.

"You stay by me, Jerry, till he's out in the country, or . . . out of the way. We ain't heard the last of this here thing . . . not by a damn' sight."

So they made their bonds between them to stand by one another until the peril had passed, not realizing for a moment the nature of him with whom they had to deal. For he had harbored not the slightest malice against one of them, as individuals. Only, in his heart of hearts, a great rage was born that would be long in dying, for it embraced a hatred of the whole race, of his human brothers.

He lay among the trees until the night came. Then his strength recovered, and he started on a long march for the uplands. He would strike back—of that the world could rest assured—but he would not strike until his strength clothed him perfectly again. There was no blind rashness, no reckless impetuosity, in the composition of Camden.

Between dusk and morning he covered thirty miles

and reached the cool uplands and the forests that clothed them. In the morning light he blew off the heads of three squirrels, shooting them out of the branches of trees. Another would have been proud of that feat, but Camden was not proud, no more than any beast of prey that kills to eat. He roasted the kill and ate it, half raw. Then he slept.

So for a fortnight he lived. The wounds on his back closed with marvelous speed, and his strength returned to him. He moved to a richer upland. There he spent another fortnight, and after that he was his old self, or more than his old self, perhaps. For hatred is like any other passion—it gives strength.

In that month he did not see a human voice, he did not think, it might be said, a human thought. In the future, he told himself blindly, there lay a great revenge, but he did not brood upon it. For the present, he was contented if he could live and regain his power, live and regain his pride. For pride is part of the strength of any man, of any beast. So it was with Camden. What the men of the plains had done to him had been painful to the body, but to the spirit it had been a living death.

So he waited until all was well within him. On a morning, when the sun grew hot, he went down the creek to a point at which it pitched over a cliff and broadened below the cascade into a series of still waters, miniature lakes. In one of these, where the roar of the cascade was softened and dulled in the distance and because the ravine had made an elbow turn below the falls, he plunged for a swim, having stripped off his clothes.

To swim for the sake of swimming was one of his dearest pleasures. In that element which was not his own, he felt his powers as he felt them in no other surrounding. With a single stroke of his arms and thrust of his legs to make his body leap through the water, to dive from the bank and feel the ripples close around his toes, to slide up to the surface again on the farther side of the pool and, looking back, discover that where he had dived the water was already calm, to swim a great distance under the surface, until his lungs were nearly bursting, to clutch at the arrow-like fish as they darted beneath him, to float on his face and mark the gold of the sun on the sandy bottom, furrowed across with tiny ripple shadows, to float on his back and watch the way of the breeze among the trees—all of these were an exquisite pleasure to him. No other man could feel them in the same degree, for no other man was so nearly beast. No beast could feel them, for no other beast was so much a man.

These things he knew. He did not know enough to waste his life over a book. He did not know so little that he needed to sleep away the cold winter as the wise grizzly was forced to do. His intelligence lay in between these two. His intelligence, such as it was, seemed to Camden perfect and efficient. If someone had told him that there were other possibilities in his nature, he would only have assured the informant that he had all he wished. Nothing more could be desired.

On this morning he idled in the pool for half an hour. A quarter of that time in the snow water would have frozen another man, but the thickly muscled body of Camden, warmed with exercise, defied the chill of the stream. Then he went out to the bank and climbed a tree, after a squirrel—not in the hope of catching it, but for the sake of the exercise that would warm him. He was dry and panting when he reached the ground again. Then he put on his clothes, but, as he put them on, he touched his back with his hand and made a long pause. There were little ridges along the soft skin, the manifold scars of the whips. He had touched them a thousand times as they formed and healed, and he knew all that patterning. Now he was content to study them and think—not of those who had laid the torture upon him; that was not at all in his brain—but he thought of all the cities of men and of all the lonely dwellers in the mountains. Any of these were his prey. If a grizzly could make havoc, what could a man do?

The time had come.

The rest of that day he spent oiling and cleaning his guns, crooning a soft, monotonous tune over them—a song that no man could ever have taught him. Then he ate a light supper; only fools eat heavily when they have far to journey the next day. After this, he went to sleep before the twilight had barely gathered. He slept solidly until the dawn. A draught of cold water was his breakfast. Then, in the red of the morning, he set out.

CAMDEN STRIKES

There are ways and ways of travel through the mountains. Some go with a pair of pack mules, ponderous Dutch ovens, sacks of canned goods, a guide to show the way, a companion for company, a servant to do the work, with tents, bedding—yes, a great wagon drawn by four horses is not enough to contain all the camp equipment that some people need. They travel in the morning. The whole afternoon is required for the pitching of the camp and the preparation of the evening meal! They turn themselves into an army. There are others who venture forth with only moderate equipment packed behind the saddle and in the saddlebags of their riding horse. They take along, perhaps, only a little flour, salt, baking powder, a coffee pot and frying pan, and a little bacon and a few other details dictated by the personal tastes of the rider. Few will venture upon a long journey with smaller provisions.

As for Harry Camden, he set forth with a cartridge

belt half filled with bullets, a .45 caliber Colt revolver in the holster at his right hip, and a little salt in a pouch. His tent was his skin, his baggage train was his brain. He wanted for nothing. He had no particular direction to travel when he started. Of course, he would have liked to get back to the same town at which the outrage had been practiced upon him. But this was far back in the plains. A grizzly bear likes to stay near rough country; so do foxes and wolves. So did Camden.

He came out, at last, over a long headland of timbered hills thrust like a spur into the rolling cow country. From the end of that spur, lying flat on his belly, resting, his arms folded, his chin resting upon his arms, he stared out over the landscape. He was consumed with hunger, but hunger did not make him impatient; it simply brought his wits to a keener edge.

Camden had covered two hundred miles of rough mountains in four days, and he was still capable of greater efforts. But, nonetheless, that tremendous march had worn him down. He had lost ten pounds, and his body was dried to sheer muscle and bone. His cheeks were hollow; his eyes were sunken a little in his head. His belt was drawn to an absurdly small circle. However, a lean wolf runs farther and faster than a fat one, and its teeth are as sharp and its bite as powerful. Camden lay half the afternoon on that high point, studying the landscape. He was in no haste. He needed to study the country. He had been there before; now he charted it again, little by little, in his brain.

A river swerved down among the hills, reached green plains, and wound away into a yellow-gray desert. Low hills flanked it upon either side. Farther east the plains ran on to the mists of the horizon; south was the great desert; north lay the taller mountains out of which he had descended. The ranch houses were spotted beneath him, drawn close together by the great distance.

In the coming of dusk, a lobo gave deep tongue from a far-off hilltop, a coyote answered with a quavering yell, then Camden went down to find his evening meal. The wind held due east, so he marched straight against it. Twice he passed clusters of cattle, but they grazed in the open and tossed their horns at him, and he gave them a comfortably wide berth, for a range cow that will run from a mounted man is as apt as not to take after a man on foot. When the centaur splits into two parts, the range bull fears neither half. When they scented Camden as he ranged at his swift, shambling trot across the country, their heads went a little higher and their eyes flashed a little wilder in token that they scented in him man and something more awful than man, if there be a creature more awful.

He jogged on. Indians run as he ran, frictionlessly, ceaselessly—the Indian runners who never cease their trot across the sunburned uplands of Mexico until they have covered their hundred miles or more. So went Camden, his head high, his body light with hunger, and the God-given consciousness of might breathing in him.

Due ahead of him, in the face of the wind, he glimpsed a snaky tail whisked in the dusk behind a boulder. Camden stopped running and began to stalk with long gliding strides. At the corner of the great boulder he stood, breathless as a shadow, and peered around it.

There lay a great range bull. His flanks, silken with good feeding and sheathed with glorious strength, were scarred by the wounds of a dozen combats with his kind in which he had emerged victorious and proved himself a king of the hills. Now, his head proudly reared, he was resting after the heat of the day and staring across at the herd that was his.

At Camden's right hip hung the gun. At his left hip was the knife. He drew it now—a long, ponderous blade, whetted razor-sharp. On this he fastened his grip; it was his favorite weapon—the fang with which he preferred to kill. With that in his hand, he shouted. For where is the danger in slaying a prostrate foe? And where is the glory?

The bull lurched to its feet. Not until it was firm on all four, but before it could wheel, the man leaped. He touched his hand to the sleek hips, he vaulted onto the back, and drove the knife home to the haft. The bull dropped with a single groan and over him stood Camden, exultant.

By the river he built his fire. There he spitted the meat on a stick and turned it in the blaze, while the long yellow lights floated on the stream. There he feasted. There, too, he curled himself up and slept a full hour. After that, he wakened, drank, and went on his way again.

The mountains were black in the west. He was in that gently rolling country upon which he had looked from the height that afternoon, and now he felt a sharp need—a horse beneath him. His mount was far south in the hotel stable; he had not paused for the horse when he began his retreat, his brain clouded with pain and his back raw from the whips. In the rough mountains he could get on very well without the help of another animal to carry him, but in this open country it was a different matter. He needed wings beneath him if he were to be safe in his depredations here, and, to begin with, what choicer blow could he strike against his world of rivals then to take the finest horse from this range?

Where should he find the finest horse? The richest man would have the best mounts, and the richest man would have the largest house. That largest house, framed about with wide-flung outlying buildings, he had well marked from the look-out place that day. Toward it he directed his path now, sweeping over the miles with his matchless stride.

The place lay in a broad hollow through which the river ran with a wide, hushed current. Camden crossed the bridge, passed the house, went through the maze of hay and straw stacks, barns, sheds, corrals, on a ceaseless hunt. In a five-acre paddock he found what he wanted. There could be no doubt.

A big barn adjoined the paddock, but only one door from the barn opened into it, and that door communicated with a large, roomy box stall. The paddock was empty, but through the open door of the stall Camden looked in, and among the dark shadows he saw a darker form, purest black from head to heels, without a white hair to mar, and where the starlight passed through a gaping crack in the wall the silk flanks of the monster glistened. Two great bright eyes looked forth at Camden.

Then, with a snort, the horse burst through the door and rushed across the paddock. There he stood, quivering with excitement and fear, sixteen hands and two inches of magnificent horseflesh, muscled like Goliath, but tapering symmetrically to slender legs and round, black hoofs. By the great arch of his neck, by the courage of his eye, by the mighty swell of his haunches, and the flare of his nostrils, he was to be known—a stallion, a king of horses.

Camden squatted in the shadow near the fence and observed. He did not need more than a glance to tell him that this was what he wanted. The loss of this animal would drive the owner half mad with vexation and grief. Therefore, it was just good enough to bear the cumbersome weight of Harry Camden. Now, in the starlight, he went on to read the features of the animal, one by one, as it danced back and forth through the corral, sometimes approaching him fiercely as though to beat him into the earth—then warned by his scent—man and more than man.

When he had looked his fill, Camden went to the barn. From the box stall he passed into another room, filled with equipment for a horse. There were little pad saddles that might have been used to exercise the monster stallion. There were bridles of a dozen makes. There were larger, heavier saddles. There were cruel bits, with all manner of Spanish inventions to bring a jaw-crushing leverage against the mouth of a refractory animal. Plainly the black horse was not a lamb.

But what Harry Camden took was a lariat, a plain bridle with a straight bit, a surcingle, and a blanket. In the corner of the corral he noosed the big horse with the rope. At least the animal was rope broken, for at the touch of the hemp it stopped short on braced legs. Then Camden went up the rope to the head of the monster. It sounds simple—as a matter of fact, it took half an hour to get to the head of the horse. But once there, Camden seemed in no haste whatever. He spent another hour talking to the stallion and stroking its nose. Then he slid the blanket on its back and cinched up the surcingle. The black horse stood as patiently as a family horse could ever have done waiting for a mistress to mount. After that, Camden slipped himself on the back of the great stallion. At the first grip of his knees and the touch of the reins in his hands, he knew that even his fondest hopes were surpassed. He had twice as much horse beneath him as he had expected!

The great animal trembled and tossed its head. The voice of the rider, murmuring and low, subdued it. He loosed the reins a trifle, and the big horse took a few steps forward, perfectly in control. Then chance struck against Camden. For an owl, sweeping low, had swooped after a scurrying rabbit, and the rabbit had streaked for the shelter of the fence and the barn.

Just under the nose of the stallion darted a streak of white, and, when it threw up its nose, shadowy wings beat about its head with a soft *whishing*. Then rabbit and owl were gone. In the farther corner of the corral the steel talons of the owl crunched home in the body of the fugitive and soared away. In the meantime, maddened with fear, the stallion neighed and broke for the first shelter—his box stall.

MOUNTED ON THE WIND

The door of that stall was low, but Camden avoided the peril by swinging along the side of the stallion, with only his right leg hooked over the back of the horse. So he was shot into the close comfort of the box stall. Before he could straighten out the frightened horse and get it through the door again, voices of three men hurried toward him, and the crossing lights of two lanterns.

"That was Crusader. I know his voice," said one. "I knew they'd be after him. If you see anything, we'll shoot now and ask questions afterward. He's worth the lives of a dozen horse-stealing curs!"

Camden did not pause. Under such conditions, it was folly to delay. Given certain circumstances, he would not have hesitated to face three men, but like any wild thing he preferred, always, to retreat before overwhelming numbers. Here was his retreat at hand—a ladder ran straight up the side of the stallion's box stall and through a trap door, probably leading into a loft above.

At least Camden was ready to try it, and, when he tried, he found it exactly as he had expected. In a moment more he was crouched in the hay, listening to their voices as they hurried to and fro. One fired a gun. Other men came hurrying. They looked into the stall first of all.

"Here he is!" shouted the first speaker. "They've put a surcingle on him and a bridle. They have him ready for the run! Who *could* have fixed him up like this? Nobody but Tracy! Somebody find me Tracy! Bring me Joe Tracy. The rest of you scatter and hunt for some sign of a trail."

Camden, in the hayloft, grinned to himself. Presently another voice sounded.

"By the heavens, Colonel Dinsmore, it wasn't me! Where would I *take* Crusader to if I should steal him? Besides, would I or anybody else try to ride that black devil with nothin' but a surcingle? I leave it to you, Colonel Dinsmore."

After that thin, wailing voice of protestation, the voice of the colonel sounded exceedingly deep and bass.

"There's something in that, Tracy. Yet, who, but you, could have managed to handle him enough to get the surcingle on?"

Joe Tracy must have been stunned by this idea. He could make no answer whatever for a moment, and before he could find a word, there was a burst of clamor in the corral, and two men came running to announce that blood had been found in the corner of the corral—only a few drops, but certainly it was blood. The stallion was unhurt. Find a man recently cut and bleeding, and they would have the thief.

Camden had seen the owl strike the rabbit, and he smiled again with infinite enjoyment. He felt an almost irresistible desire to see the colonel; it proved resistless, indeed, and, lifting the trap door a small crack, he stared down at the animated scene below.

He beheld a tall, white-headed, white-mustached and bearded man of the true "Kentucky Colonel" type. He was a lean, angular person with enough dignity to have fitted forth a whole dozen of judges. He bore his person with a military erectness; his habitual expression was a frown that he wore not because he was at all stern, but because he felt that it gave him an imposing appearance. The only cruel things he had ever done in his life and the only unjust things had been executed in a hopeless effort to live up to the sternness of that face.

As a matter of fact, he was a simple soul with a heart of gold—a nature veritably flowing with the milk of human kindness. But Camden could not discover this with a glance. His schooling of experience had taught him to perceive all the faults and the brutalities of his fellow men; it had not schooled him in the ready understanding of their virtues. So he beheld the colonel as a grim fellow, and he hated him accordingly with all his heart. If Crusader had not already been attractive to him, he would have stolen the horse anyway for the sake of breaking the heart of the colonel. It seemed, from what he learned now, that the colonel could hardly have survived the blow, so deep was his affection for the big stallion.

The colonel had sent twenty men scurrying in a wide circle around the corral, cutting eagerly for sign, some on horseback, some on foot. Lanterns flashed everywhere. Little glints and gleams of light broke through the crevices of the barn walls and startled across the eyes of Camden. He paid no attention to these things. The turmoil he had raised gave him a warm sense of satisfaction; his heart was more fixed than ever on the great black stallion at whose head now stood a withered little man of thirty who looked a full fifteen years older. That was Joe Tracy. He was soothing the big animal with little mutterings. The colonel and a dapper youth who had just entered the stall spoke well above this quieting undertone.

"I hoped to wait until morning before you saw Crusader," the colonel was saying. "But even by lamplight there's enough of him to be worth looking at. Here he is, Mister Mervin. He speaks for himself."

Mr. Mervin stood back a little. "A sad thing," he said at last, "that such a horse should be off the turf."

"His damnable disposition," said the colonel. "No one but Tracy can back the brute. No one but Tracy can come near him. That's why I picked him up dirt-cheap. They couldn't get Tracy from me. Any other person would have had to pay fifty thousand for that horse, even to use him as a stud only. But what good would he be without Tracy?"

Camden, in his covert, grinned.

"So," continued the colonel, "I bid him in for a mere twenty thousand. Dirt-cheap, I say."

"Dirt-cheap, indeed," said Mervin. "I remember him in the Derby. Kentucky never saw a finer horse than Crusader, sir."

"I dare say," said the colonel, forgetting his frown of dignity and smiling like a child. "I dare say that Kentucky has not. No Thoroughbred ever walked on four better legs. He'll raise the standard of the horseflesh on my ranch, I presume."

"Your cowpunchers will all be riding stake horses in three seasons," said the complimentary Mr. Mervin.

"Hardly that! Hardly that!" chuckled the colonel. "Back go his ears! What an ugly devil is in the heart of that brute."

Harry Camden, in his hiding place, drew in his breath softly. A fifty-thousand-dollar horse! He might search half a lifetime before he found another opportunity of doing such harm as was put within his grasp on this day. Fifty thousand dollars at a stroke.

"Lock him in, Joe," said the colonel. "No, I imagine there's no end of locking the door. The scoundrel who tried to ride the horse away will probably not be in a hurry to repeat his attempt to ride Crusader, eh?"

Joe Tracy smiled sourly.

"If that blood in the corral is any evidence," suggested Charles Mervin, "the thief was bucked off for his pains."

"The only mystery is, how he could have managed to get the surcingle on the animal."

"Well," said Charles Mervin, "I have seen men who have a way with dogs and horses. Very odd. Someone of that cut must have tried his hand."

"His hypnotism failed him when he was on the back of Crusader, then," said the colonel, and they went out.

No one thought of searching through the loft of the barn. They scoured the country around the corral. There was no sign of blood on any trail. Then they swarmed back where Joe Tracy, having closed the stallion into the dark, warm stall, met them and told them to go back to the bunkhouse, for the colonel did not propose to conduct a wild-goose trail during the night.

In another ten minutes, all was quiet, and Camden, opening the door, slipped quietly down and stood beside the stallion, the man-killer. That white magic of which Mervin had spoken was his in the most ample share. At his whisper, Crusader turned his head and rested his inquiring muzzle in the broad palm of Camden's hand. There could be no greater proof of trust than this.

It set Camden scowling blackly in the shadows. It started something of an insistent ache in his heart, and he could not be rid of it. It closed his throat; it made him breathe hard. Nothing could relieve that pain except to stroke the sleek neck of the stallion and whisper in his ear words of no meaning whatever, yet they were words that brought a murmuring little whinny from the horse.

A step sounded nearby, softly. Camden shrank into a corner as Joe Tracy pulled the door open and stood there a moment with a glimmer of something in his hand.

"By the heavens," he said to himself rather than aloud, "I almost thought I heard. . . ."

He closed the door again, muttering, and Camden set about the bridling of Crusader again. He found the same light bridle. He slipped the straight bit between the teeth of the horse. Upon his back he bound the blanket once more. Other men might want saddles, but saddles meant weight, care, slowness in saddling. Indians had been content to ride bareback. To Camden even the surcingle was a luxury.

So prepared for the theft, he pushed open the door softly. There was an instant challenge.

"Who's there?" came the snarling voice of Joe Tracy.

Apparently the little ex-jockey was determined to watch half the night over his precious charge. In place of answering, Camden slipped onto the back of the horse, and, bending far to one side to avoid the low door, he sent the great stallion out into the corral.

"Hello!" shouted Tracy, hurrying toward them. "What the devil . . . stop there, or I'll shoot . . . !"

Shoot so near to a fifty-thousand-dollar horse? Something told Camden that could never be. He laughed as he cantered the horse across the paddock, kicked open the staple that fastened the gate, and then rushed away into the night. Behind him, the jockey was screaming with grief and furious helplessness, and shooting into the air. Behind him, the swirl of answering voices took up the alarm.

He heeded them not. He was mounted on the wind. Camden had teeth that could slay near or far. He had wits that could serve him. Now the last necessity was added. He had at his command, matchless speed. Now let the world match him if it could!

LOOKING FOR MISCHIEF

Nothing that runs upon four feet can match the speed of a Thoroughbred race horse. Of all other running things an antelope is the speediest. It can turn off a mile in a minute and fifty seconds. But a race horse, with even the handicap of a man on its back, has covered the same distance in a minute and thirty-four seconds, or a little more—a sixteen-second advantage, plus the weight of the rider.

No jockey, of course, even weighed what Camden's bulk of muscle and bone amounted to. But he had other advantages. What a jockey has to learn by years of experience, having been born for his work in the first place, big Harry Camden knew by instinct. He was not on the horse; he was an integral part of it. His reins were loose. They were an almost needless luxury. He had other methods of telegraphing his will to the brain of his mount. The sway of his body seemed enough.

And Crusader? He had learned in the days of his childhood that men are creatures who insist on being burdens to the back and tyrants over the minds of horses. But here was one who merely accented his freedom, whose will seemed merely a pleasant part of his own desire. If the sheer weight of the rider were great, yet it was lightened by the marvelous skill of the rider.

Such was the way of Camden with his horse. He let Crusader rush across a hollow like the wind; he charged the fine animal up a hill straight at the round yellow moon that rested on the crest. This was not riding—this was to be gifted with wings. On the crest of the hill with a word and a touch on the reins, he checked the horse and surveyed the country beneath him. By tomorrow the countryside would be swarming with pursuers. But, in the meantime, he had a night of absolute freedom. Then, across the brow of the next hill, he saw a ghostly pale form gliding.

He knew that outline of old. It was a timber wolf, a great gray lobo that had come down to hunt in the lowlands, some grizzled veteran of a cattle killer, no doubt. By day they are never seen, for by day they know that the guns of men can reach them. But by night the guns of men are charmed to helplessness, and that is the time when they dare to come down even to the campfires.

They are slow runners, these gray wolves. They have been roped by cowpunchers on range ponies. They have one stupid habit, among all of their wisdom, that makes them an easier prey for hunters: when they run, they run in a straight line. It is only their exquisite knowledge of a countryside, together with their ways of using rough terrain to embarrass a pursuer, that keeps more of them from being sighted and captured in the same way. Now there was only dull moonshine in which Camden could follow that elusive creature. But he had no doubts.

He called to Crusader, and they were off down the slope like mad. Up the farther slope they went with a lurch that took the breath of the rider. There from the crest he saw the great wolf again—not a hundred yards away—a magnificent specimen of a full six score pounds.

He had taken the alarm before this, getting on the edge of the wind the scent of a horse, which was pleasant—of man, which was disgusting—and of iron and powder, which was terrible. Now he was running hard, the loose mane along his neck ruffling forward and bristling until his forequarters seemed each time he landed heavily to be twice the weight of the rear. He was running hard, but, compared with the terrific gait of the stake horse, he seemed to be standing still. With rough rocks to course through or running among thick bracken, the chances might still have favored the lobo, but this was a rolling plateau tableland, and Crusader clipped off six yards a second from the distance between him and the wolf.

It was not the sort of a race he was accustomed to, this plunge through the night. Crusader was used to oval tracks of dirt or turf, a lightweight jockey on his back like a flashing flower of many colors, beside him the straining, shining bodies of other Thoroughbreds—in the distance the grandstands, smudged with humanity and their beast-like mumblings. Such were the races he knew. But here he was required to run full-tilt at a creature that every sense and every instinct told him was a deadly foe and a murderous one.

Had he been by himself, he would never have dared so much as to face it from a distance of half a mile, but this man on his back had changed him. This mighty intelligence that now ruled him could gather him together and sweep him along into the fight and through it. It was the only man that Crusader had not tried to measure. Other men he had felt ridiculously puny and disgusting in their efforts to control him. Joe Tracy he endured on his back and at his head for the sake of long familiarity, but he despised the ex-jockey. In Camden, Crusader met something else. It was not strength of hand or sting of whip that imposed upon the great stallion. It was an inexplicable thing that the stallion had felt when first the strange man came into his paddock—a fierce spirit as wild and as untamable as his own.

A horse does not need to be raised in the wilderness in order that it may recognize the danger that lies in the tawny, supple body of a cougar. Neither did Crusader need more than a glance and a sniff to guess at something in this man that was different from all other men. When Camden, with a shout, struck the flank of the horse with the flat of his hand, Crusader did not resent a blow that would have made him pitch any other human in the world over his head. Instead, he leaped away with a final grand effort, and swooped on the gray wolf like a hawk dropping out of the air.

Grappling the straining body of the horse with his legs, one hand twisted into the mane, Camden swung himself low, and, as the wolf swerved from the trampling hoofs of Crusader, Camden's bright knife flashed, and its light went out in the body of the loafer wolf. It still had strength to vault straight into the sky at the moon with a wild yell that died suddenly, in mid-air. Camden, as he shot past, heard the loose *thud* of the body as it struck the ground again and did not need to use his eyes to know that his stroke had killed.

He went back to the slaughter and skinned it. The ripping of a hide from a lobo is not the work of an instant, but in the powerful fingers of Camden that labor was a trifle. He plucked the pelt away, and, as he cleaned it, he noticed with a touch of horror that Crusader had come close to the bleeding body from which other horses would have bolted in mad flight. He sniffed with ears flattened to his neck. Once he struck the red body with a fore hoof until Camden drove him away with a shout. Then, with the pelt rolled into a secure bundle, he struck away for the upper mountains. In his first invasion he felt that he had done enough. Other things might be accomplished later on when the pursuit began.

He had ridden across a gully and was jogging Crusader up the farther slope when he caught the scent of frying bacon, and he drew Crusader to a halt. There is an appeal in that fragrance that never fails to touch a hungry man. Camden was not hungry. He had eaten his fill that night with roasted flesh, and one meal a day was all that he needed for strength and happiness. But the fragrance of the cooking bacon wakened a new appetite. It was like a voice calling to him in the heart of the wilderness, and he turned the head of Crusader up the wind.

After all, it was not so much the desire for the bacon; it was the hungry hope that this trail might lead him to new mischief before the night was over, and in that hope he hurried on. He came on the place at once, an unpretentious little shack in a hollow, with a shed behind it, housing a few plows and harrows. Nearby he saw the black face of plowed ground and scowled at it. When men came to herd their cows and their flocks, it was bad enough, but when they came to plow the ground, it was a certain sign that the wilderness was at the end of its tether. After that came towns springing up, many roads, and presently the iron hand of the law had the district by the throat. What had been mischievous curiosity changed to settled and destructive anger in the heart of Camden. By the size of the house and the shed, he judged that this was some poverty-stricken settler, but his poverty hardly served to soften the heart of Camden. All those who pushed the frontiers of civilization deeper into the mountains were his personal enemies, with whom he was at the bitterest feud.

He tethered Crusader in a cluster of lodgepole pines nearby. Then he stole to the house on foot. The first lighted window through which he looked was a small living-dining room with two men at a table. But there was food before the younger of the pair only—set forth on the oilcloth cover whose dazzling whiteness was certain proof to the judicious eye of Camden that there was a woman in the house. He curled himself up beside the low window to wait and to watch, for here were men, he told himself, worthy of his steel. They were burly giants, wide-shouldered, tall. Their hands were as large as the hands of two. The elder, and from their facial resemblance he was probably the father, was perhaps in his fiftieth year, but time seemed to have hardened and perhaps slowed his strength rather than snapped it. His square jaw was set and his eyes glistening as he watched the younger man talking.

The woman came whirling in from the kitchen, bringing a coffeepot. Camden could not see her face, at first, but he had sight of a slender, round, brown wrist as she poured out the coffee into the great tin cup. She poured it with that careless dexterity that amazed Camden. For his own part, the opposite sex had interested him only once. In men, there was often enough strength to make a respectable fight if they were attacked. But in women there was neither courage nor coolness or adroitness, to say nothing of sheer power of hand. They only excelled in this useless jugglery around the house. So Camden watched the coffee poured and saw her rest her hands on the top of the table and lean forward toward the youth. She was his wife, without doubt.

Now he took up the thread of a story that seemed to have been interrupted. Camden lost his contemptuous unconcern at once, and in the very act of rising to go to the kitchen—whose larder he could plunder now that the girl was gone from the room—two or three gestures of the narrator showed plainly that he was telling a story of the trail. Camden squatted again and listened with a light in his clouded amber eyes, until, at the climax, the son of the house leaped from his chair so heedlessly that his stool fell with a clatter behind him upon the floor, while he jerked open a roll that he had brought with him and exposed to the eyes of the family, and to the eyes of Camden where he watched from the outer night, the pelt of a silver fox.

MIDNIGHT DEPREDATION

That peerless fur, what a beauty it was! The legs were richest black, watered with highlights as though the surface were silk. The head was black, also, but all the body of the fur was frosted over with white tippings of the hairs. Even the stolid father of the house started up at the sight. As for the girl, she clasped her hands at her breast and turned at the pelt with tears of joy in her eyes. For Camden could see her face plainly now. No, she was not the wife of the youth—she was his sister, for the family likeness was printed plainly on every face. Not that her features were bold and bluff like theirs, but everything that appeared in them in the rough appeared in her, also, drawn with a more precise and delicate pencil.

Then Camden saw a gracious thing for so primitive a settler's family. He saw the youth put the fur in the hands of the girl—saw him kiss her, and make her the present with a smiling gesture. And she? She sat in a chair with the treasure on her knees, rocking back and forth over it, laughing back at her brother in a full-hearted ecstasy. But Camden sneered at the pleasant picture. First, he wanted a side of that same bacon that he had smelled from the stove where it fried. Then he wanted that same frosted beauty of a fur. He prepared to get it.

It was plain that it would be some time before the talk ended and the family went to bed. The great prize that had brought the hunter down from his traps in the upper mountains so late in the night would be sufficient to keep them all awake for some time longer. But Camden was not prepared to waste his moments. He made a thrifty disposal of his time, always. When he was not busy, he slept. He prepared to sleep now.

In the lodgepole pine thicket, where Crusader was tethered, he lay down. The night was turning sharp and cold, but that made no difference to Camden. The chill in the air would simply make him sleep lightly, and that was what he wanted, for when the ray from the distant window no longer struck across his face, he wished to waken.

He had no sooner laid down than he was asleep; out of that sleep he wakened suddenly and glanced across the hollow. As he had expected, the light was out and the house was a squat, black shadow in the moonlight.

It was a three-room shack. He had made sure of that before leaving the place. The kitchen was one apartment. In corners of the living-dining room were bunks for the two men. At the side of this was a tiny room where the girl slept. To that went Camden, and, standing beside the open window, he peered into the thick blackness of the chamber. He waited there until he made sure of the hushed breathing of the girl, quite inaudible to normal human ears, but clear as spoken words to him. With this fact determined, he went around to the kitchen and there located the bacon he wanted at once. There was half a side. It would be enough. There were other food supplies, in some quantity, but Camden wanted that one article and no other.

This prize, when he returned to the girl's room, he left outside. Then he climbed through the window with no precaution whatever, it seemed, so swift were his movements, but swift though they were, he made not a sound, not even of cloth rubbing against cloth, and stepped noiselessly at last to the side of the sleeper's bed.

Even his keen eyes could make out nothing but shapeless mounds of shadows in this deep night. Sense of touch must supply the lack of light. His hands became exquisitely delicate instruments at once. His fingertips strolled over the bedding—even touched an exposed hand. But it was a touch as light as the touch of a dry leaf when it falls without wind to the ground, thin as spider silk. Such was the touch of Camden until, at last, under the pillow of the sleeper, he reached the fur. He could tell it by the rich, deep silk into which his hand fell. It was the silver fox!

He had a problem now that taxed even his matchless skill of hand. He had to raise the pillow together with the head of the girl resting upon it, raise them the necessary trifle so that he could slip the fur noiselessly forth. To do this, he must hush his own breathing, still the very action of his brain, and listen for a stir from the girl as the mother wolf listens when it hears the puma prowling near the cave.

Once she sighed. The fur was then half withdrawn,

and he checked the motion, waiting. He had hardly begun again when she moaned in her sleep, and, obeying an instinctive impulse, that great hand of his flew out and hovered in the black of the night above her face. One crunch of those fingers and there would be an end of trouble from her. But something held him back—the memory, perhaps, of the soft curves of that young throat, so brown, so warm, so pulsing with happiness when he had last seen it. So, frowning, wondering at himself, he lowered the hand again, waited until the sleeper was stilled again, and then began to draw the fur softly forth.

At length it was free in his hand. At the same moment the girl sat bolt erect in the bed and, fumbling in the dark beneath the pillow, touched instead the hard hand of Camden. He felt the jump of her own hand, heard the catch of her breath. With a gesture he found both her hands and caught them fast in one of his.

"No talkin' . . . no yellin'," Camden said in a voice lower than a whisper, "or I'll crack you in two so's they'll never put you together again."

Her answer was in the same tone, but, instead of trembling and hysterical terror, he was astonished to hear burning anger only.

"Jed Buttrick, you coward, you've come to steal what Ned beat you in getting."

He waited a moment, recovering the wits that had been scattered by this retort, scattering, at the same time, all of his long-prized prepossessions concerning women. A woman, to him, was a thing that fainted at the sight of blood and screamed at the sight of a mouse. A woman, indeed, was so far beneath contempt that she was almost a mystery. This, however, was shockingly different.

"Leave go my hand," went on the fierce whisper in the dark of the night. "Or I'll holler."

His free hand slipped up and set itself about her throat. "You wouldn't yip more'n once," he said almost thoughtfully.

"You daren't do it," she defied him.

He tested himself, pressing his thumb against the hollow of her throat, and all the warmth of her young life flowed up his arm to his stern heart, and melted it. Dizzily, bewildered, he realized that she was right, and that, indeed, he dared not do this thing. Yet how very simple it was!

"If I holler, Dad and Ned'll be here in a jiffy. They'll blow you to bits, Jed Buttrick, you yaller coward, and you know it. Now gimme back that there fur and get out . . . before I get tired of havin' you so close to me. And keep your hands off'n me. It makes me sick, just the touch of 'em. Bah!"

All of this was in a discreetly whispering voice. He began to see that there was some artifice in this very great assumption of courage.

"You ain't scared?" he asked faintly.

"Of you, Jed?" she sneered.

"I ain't Jed."

"You can't lie out of it!" she asserted. "I give you till I count ten to get through that window."

"Before you holler?"

"Before I call them."

He waited a moment. New warm waves were passing through him—from the touch of her hands, imprisoned in his, from the sensation of her breath that fanned his face softly, from a pure small fragrance that came from her and entered his mind like the scent of the pine woods, but striking deeper, more resistless.

"I'm countin'," she said through her teeth.

"Don't holler," he said.

"Will you gimme back that fur and get out?"

"If you was to holler," he said judiciously, "I'll tell you what'd happen. I'd tear your pa to bits. And I'd smash the young gent to bits."

"Ah," breathed the girl. "All cowards brag."

"I don't brag," Camden replied slowly. "I don't ever brag. What I say . . . them are the facts."

"You . . . ," began the girl, and then her voice died. His grip had slackened a little on her wrists, and now he could feel a quickened pulse and the beginning of a tremor. If her courage had been sweet to him, her fear was strangely sweeter. He was stuffing the fur, automatically, with quick motions, inside his belt.

Then she said, with the terror beginning to creep into her voice as well: "What . . . what d'you mean to do . . . ?"

"With what?"

"With . . . me."

"I dunno. If I let you go, you'll holler the minute I get away from you. Them two fool men of yours might sink a slug in me, by accident. They look like they'd shoot straight. Would you tell me, maybe, that you wouldn't yell?"

"You wouldn't believe me if I told you that?"

"I dunno. I'll see. Come over here to the window, will you?"

He half lifted her from the bed by her hands as he spoke, and she followed whether she would or no. In a moment she stood before him in the dull glow of the moonshine that shaved down the side of the house and made the window sill brilliant as metal. In her bare feet, she was very small before him, and her hair, in two long, dark braids, ran shimmering over each shoulder and flowed before her to her waist. Above the brown throat was her face, rather guessed at than seen, except for the light in her great eyes.

"I dunno," Camden said slowly, "I dunno . . . I guess that I might trust you if you was to promise. . . ."

"That I won't call?"

"Yes."

"I'll promise," she gasped out. "Now go, quick!"

"You're sort of weakenin'," he said. "You ain't so chipper right now. Not the same's you was. Are you scared?"

"Will you go?" she breathed. "Or I. . . ."

"What?"

"Let me go!" pleaded her whisper with a desperate sob in it, and suddenly she flung her whole weight back from him.

As well have flung herself back against shackles of steel. But in the effort she slumped to the floor, and now, plainly, he felt the trembling of her hands, as she cowered. Panic seemed to be overwhelming her more and more.

"Don't touch me," she moaned. "For heaven's sake, don't come near me."

Camden listened, amazed. That strange warm joy that had been rising in him stopped and ebbed away. He stared gloomily down at her for a moment, then, muttering, he flung her hands roughly from him.

She made no effort to raise an alarm as he slipped through the window; he heard only one sound from her—the whimper of unnerving terror. It stabbed and chilled the very soul of Camden. It roused a frantic anger in him, too. But he felt that it was hardly so much a passion directed against her as it was a fury at something else. It surely could not be himself.

But he had remained there long enough. He picked up the fallen bacon and shot off around the house and away at full speed, and his speed was that of an Indian running for life. He had reached the pine trees before the house wakened, a light fluttered from a window, and voices rolled dimly toward him. But he gave no heed to them. What were they and what mattered their pursuit compared with the speed of Crusader?

He loosed the great stallion. For five minutes the rush of wind, the gradual sweep of the hills past him, was an intoxicating joy that blotted out everything else. But a little later he found himself letting the stallion fall to a walk, while the rider was frowning blankly at the ground beneath him.

THE LONG TOOTH OF THE WASTES

Camden lay flat on his back in the forest; it was a favorite diversion of his. His arms were thrown wide, and his body relaxed. Nothing about him lived except his eyes, and they, very soon, were sure to find plenty to occupy them. For when a man walks through the woods, the warning runs before him. The sentinel birds call, the path is cleared, and he goes through a belt of silence. But Camden, turning himself into a log of wood, so to speak, ceased to be a factor in the forest. Every wild thing gave him a glance, cocked an ear toward him, and then decided that, while he must be watched, he might, after all, be merely an inanimate thing. Moreover, from this particular place, where he lay, he could look through the trees toward the glistening black body of Crusader, grazing in the sunshine in a patch of nutritious grama grass. He assured himself of the well-being of the horse. Letting the same glances run down the long funnel between the hills, he assured himself, also, that horsemen were not working themselves into the mountains in that direction. For the rest, his attention was occupied by the teeming life in the upper branches.

It was not crowded. Wild things almost never crowd, if they can possibly avoid it, except those animals in which the social instinct is immensely developed, like the bison. But there was a constant procession of life before the eyes of the motionless Camden. Sometimes he picked out an individual as, for instance, a little gray squirrel that was crying her love call from the side of a great pine and being answered from afar by one voice, and then another. Now they came, the two suitors. They frisked their tails and glared at each other from the base of the pine, as though demanding whether each had come on the same errand that brought the other. Then up the tree they darted—to the very side of the lady squirrel, that ran out on a long branch. They did not follow at once. Instead, they clinched in murderous battle, writhed and twisted in their struggle for a moment, and then tumbled from the branch into space.

A fall to death? No, for they separated at once, and each fluffed out its great tail. This is one reason for tails, then—those gorgeous, burled tails of squirrels. They turn the little animals into astronauts. Down they sail, with the bristling tails cutting so much wind that that force is taken from the fall. Now on the ground they whisked back to the tree again and raced up the trunk to where madam had posted herself, able to watch all the fighting that was in her honor.

Once more they dove for her. She ran to the very tip end of the branch, the vixen, and dove through air toward the neighboring monarch of the forest, gained a heavily tufted branch, and was presently in view, scurrying up a great shaft of naked pine trunk high above. The males had leaped after her, gained the same precarious foothold, and now they raced toward her again.

That race was never finished. There came a dark streak through the sky, a flash of striking talons, and a great hen hawk shot at the lady, missed her by a hair's breadth, whirled with beating wings, and leaped back through the air again with talons and cruel beak presented—a treble threat. She whipped around to the farther side of the tree just in time to escape that terrible danger and just in time, also, to run into the teeth of a horror fully as great. For the hawk hunted with its partner that lagged a little behind to view the game before it took part in the deadly play. Now it came with a rush. One clip of the strong talons caught the squirrel and killed it in the same stroke. Then away they sailed together, triumphant.

A full five minutes—then two frightened little gray squirrels scampered down the tree and made away, each in a different direction.

Here was the path of true love laid bare to the eyes of Camden. He observed it with a grunt of satisfaction. Bloodshed was ever to his liking, and to see those monarchs of the sky sweep out of the blue, make a prize, and away again, pleased him mightily. He had only one regret—that a rifle had not been at hand so that he might have given still another turn to the tragic story.

After that, a growing unrest possessed the mind of Camden. He watched the sun shimmering brilliantly on that beautiful and wicked gossip of the woods, the blue jay; he saw a terrible weasel, tinier than a squirrel, but infinitely more dreadful as a warrior, go rippling up the trunk of a tree in search of young life to destroy. Anything living would satisfy that voracious savage, that fearless and wily fighter. Camden was an old admirer of the weasel and of all his tribe. But now he regarded the hunter with only a side glance. His mind was elsewhere.

He sat up and frowned at the long, smooth outlines of the hills as they spilled away down the valley. For that which was in him was very like one of those stirring premonitions of evil that many a time during his wilderness life had warned him of approaching danger in the very nick of time. The unrest grew so great in him that at last he stood up and cut away through the forest in search of the danger that he breathed out of the air. But there was no sign to be found. He found where a broken-clawed grizzly had raked the trunk of a tree—a new grizzly, and therefore a young one, hunting out a different home in a new range, no doubt. He found the four-pointed track of a whitetail deer. But still he went on and discovered nothing that he need regard. No mere animal presence could account for this uneasy feeling in his breast.

It was like homesickness, but, having never known a home, Camden could not know what that meant. He climbed a tree, at length, a huge, high-towering monster on the edge of the forest, working up its thick trunk with a skill that even a squirrel need not have scorned. Propped on his legs, which were twisted around the trunk, with one hand fixed on a small, brittle branch above his head, he looked anxiously around the landscape. Behind him, the dark pine forest went back among the mountains. Beneath him, toward three cardinal points of the compass, and more, the hills rolled away to the green lowlands and to the gray-yellow desert beyond. Somewhere beyond the haze of the atmosphere, among those softly outlined lowlands, it seemed to Camden that the forest, that was his ordinary home, grew empty and filled with a threatening spirit of desolation.

He descended from the tree, frowning and in thought. This falling of the heart, he ascribed to the approach of some terrible danger against which even his strength would be as nothing. It was unlike anything he had ever known. For, instead of counseling him to flee, that same instinct warned him that miles would make no difference—he could never escape from the sorrow that was within him.

Squatting on the ground at the base of the tree that he had just descended, he took out for the hundredth time the priceless pelt of the silver fox that he had stolen from the girl. For the hundredth time, he closed his eyes and ran his exquisitely sensitive fingers through the silk of the fur. At this, the ache in his heart became an outrageous pain. He could not understand it. He opened his eyes again and examined the fur. Once he was tempted to hurl the thing away from him, since its possession gave him so much pain. Out of his strange childhood he could remember much talk and many warnings about hoodoos, evil eyes, and such matters. He was half inclined to feel that there was some mysterious power wrapped up in the pelt of the silver fox. He banished that thought from his mind with a grunt. Even in his youngest childhood there had been present in his mind something that pointed a finger of doubt at the superstitions of the Indians. Now he forced himself to fold up the skin once more, against his will.

As he did so, he thought again of the anguish that must have fallen upon the home of the girl and the two men when that loss was made known. For the price of the fur must have meant to them new seed for the land, new horses to plow it, new blood in the ranch work. It had been a capital stroke, the winning of that fur. The loss of it was a bitter thrust, indeed.

Considering this, Camden tried to force back into his heart the original thrill of happiness in such mischief. But the joy would not return.

When a man is tormented by the unknown, he has an irresistible desire to go back on his trail and examine the mystery, face to face. There swept over Camden, now, a vast urge to return to the house and to see the man who lived in it. He called the stallion with a whistle—a signal that was already agreed upon between them, and, after lingering for an instant to bite a tough bunch of grama close to the root, Crusader made up for this delay by coming at a round gallop. Around and around the master he frolicked when he arrived, flicking his heels high in the air with force enough driven from the thighs to have shattered stone images, then rearing and beating the air with his forehoofs, or ripping the throat of an imaginary enemy with a lunge of his wicked teeth.

After this, suddenly, he came to a pause just in front of his new master with head raised, with one ear cocked forward and the other sloped back, as though to say: "I have worked some of the deviltry out of my system. Now, if you please, what can we do for sport together?"

Camden clapped blanket and surcingle on the stallion and on him dropped down out of the hills. It would have taken three hours for ordinary riders to have covered what Camden and his horse covered in one. They drove straightaway. When they came to a cliff-faced hill, he whisked off the back of Crusader, and the good horse found a clever way to the bottom of the hill face with the master clambering down by himself, nimble as a mountain sheep. They climbed other and equally steep impediments in the same fashion—the horse working his own way up, the man working his own, and even pausing in his labors to cheer on Crusader over some special difficulty. Indeed, he never sat on the back of the stallion while Crusader had difficult country to go through. Up and down hill the stallion had only his own weight to carry. When they worked through badly broken land, full of twists and chopped with rocks and with brush, Camden ran into the lead, and he picked the way along which the big horse followed with the least friction. Only when the hills smoothed away to a procession of easy hummocks, and when the rough land grew more level, then did he leap onto the back of Crusader, lightly, without forcing the horse to break its stride, and they flew away like the wind. This was the reason that Camden and Crusader moved as the bird flies, straight across country, laughing at gorges, scoffing at broken woods and thickets.

They came swiftly, too swiftly from the mountains to suit with the plan of Camden, which was never to be near the habitations of men except during the dusk, the gray dawn, or the black of night. He waited, now, at the edge of a thicket until the dusk had thickened. By that time he was hungry. At that time a whitetail buck, young, supple, sleek as a tawny puma, came gliding out into the open and looked about him.

Before he was aware of the slightest danger, for the wind was blowing strongly from him and to the man, a black bolt shot out of the woods carrying a man on his back, and the buck had barely time to swerve away before the first rush carried the horse past it.

But even a deer could hardly dodge Crusader. He had been in hunts enough, by this time, to know the will of the master. Such was his confidence in the long tooth that the master struck with, or the still more terrible death which spoke from his hand, that he would have charged straight at a couchant lion, with no doubt of what the outcome might be. He loved the hunt, this great, fierce horse, and, loving the hunt, he was eager for the death.

He doubled back on the buck that was scattering for the open with the speed of a winged shadow. Not fast enough for Crusader, however. The down-pitch of the slope gave length to his leaps. In the heart of the hollow he dashed beside the fugitive again, the knife flashed with that sinister speed, and went out.

That evening Camden ate venison.

THE FOX SKIN RETURNED

He reached the rim of the hollow, but there he paused with Crusader, for he found that his excitement was increased to such a point that he was afraid. He was blind and deaf with a furious tide of happiness. It was like the joy that comes to the traveler who sees the green promise of water not far away. It was like the joy of the first view of home to the homesick. Yet it was more, and far more, than any of these. So, little by little, wondering at himself, half sick, and weak with joy, he let the stallion go up the slope until he saw the shack beyond and one starry eye of light looking forth from a window.

A horse was tethered at the hitching rack before it. Camden, leaving Crusader in the pine trees as before, went down to investigate.

They were in the living room of the house. The father sat in a corner, his chin resting on his sun-blackened fist, his face grown old since Camden looked in on him. His daughter faced him while she talked. The person with whom she talked was none other than that dapper, handsome young youth whom Camden had seen before in the box stall of Crusader. It was Mr. Charles Mervin, clad in whipcord riding breeches, and wearing an old-fashioned, high white stock that gave him an 18th-Century look. That air was accentuated by the long, lean, aristocratic face of Charles Mervin, and a certain half weary, half naïve arch of the brows of that gentleman. Even Jake Manners, the father of the house, was able to recognize something of another century in the presence of Charles Mervin. He reminded Manners of "somebody else . . . I dunno . . . Washington or something like that, if you know what I mean. I mean he looks like he didn't care much about nothin'."

This was the feeble expression of a thing after which Charles Mervin had been striving for a long time. He knew himself, it might be said, by heart. He knew exactly how his face would look, no matter from what angle it was viewed. An actor could not have been more practically aware of himself. But neither could an actor have been more totally without essential vanity. Mr. Mervin was proud of the rôle that he had created. He was not proud of himself.

The same creator who had furnished him with that lean, Old-World, lost-century face, had furnished him, also, with a very wide-awake 20th-Century set of muscles. He could ride across country with any man, play an excellent game of tennis, and drive a golf ball three hundred and twenty yards, to say nothing of undoubted talents at poker and bridge, and a willingness to bet everything he inherited from his father on the turn of a card. In a word, under the exterior of an archaic face and a casual manner, he was as alert a youth as one could find in a thousand-mile search.

He was conducting the conversation, at the present moment, with the older man and the girl as listeners. The father of the house was his apparent object, but it was at the girl, now and again, that he cast certain penetrating side glances that made Camden wince and set his teeth, although why such a small thing should irritate him he could not tell.

The window was wide open. Camden could hear every word.

"It is a matter, after all, of the sheerest inference," he said. "The trail led here, do you see?"

Jake Manners raised his troubled face, seemed about to speak, and then looked down again with a shake of his head, as though he realized that words were of very little practical value at such a time as this.

"Why must it have been Ned?" asked the girl. "Would Ned have brought a hoss like that straight home? And left such a trail behind him? He would of known that Crusader would be followed!"

The father raised his head again and eyed the youth expectantly.

"You see," explained Charles Mervin, "people want to know how it came about that Ned Manners happened to be at home when he was supposed to be up in the mountains trapping."

"Because he'd caught a silver fox, and he wanted to bring the pelt home to us. I guess that's enough reason to suit almost anybody."

"If they could see the fur . . . yes!" said Mervin.

"It was stole by the same man that stole the hoss, I guess!" cried the girl. "I told you how he managed it."

Charles Mervin looked fixedly at her for a moment.

It seemed to the accurate eye of Camden that there was a shadowy smile about the corners of his mouth.

"People have heard that story, too," he said. "Of course, you understand that I credit every syllable you have spoken. But other people don't. They seem to be a hardheaded lot in this neighborhood. Especially the sheriff. He declares that it's incredible that you should have been so frightened that you were unable to make even an outcry until such a long time after he left that your father and brother couldn't get trace of him as he. . . ."

"What do they know?" the girl stated hotly. "They didn't see him. They didn't feel the grip in his hands. It was like iron. I almost . . . I almost thought he was going to tear me to pieces!"

Camden glowered in the darkness as he heard this description of himself. For though there was enough in her words, there was a thousand times more in her manner of speaking and the shudder with which she mentioned him.

"He wasn't like a man. He was like a bear!" she gasped out.

"Steady, Ruth!" called the father suddenly. "It ain't any use arguin', because. . . ."

"Why," broke in Mervin, "of course, I believe every syllable of what has been said. I'm simply telling you the manner in which the sheriff looks at this thing. The matter of the silver fox skin is the point at which they all seem to stick. It seems very odd, they all say, that such a fine horse and such a fine pelt should have been stolen on the same night by the same man."

"Sure it's queer," declared the father of the house grimly, "and when they've got my boy Ned locked up in prison . . . I'll take the trail of the thief and run him down. I'll. . . ." His voice died away. His fierce eyes said the rest as he stared straight before him, looking, as it chanced, full at the window outside of which the true thief stood.

"In the meantime," said Charles Mervin in a business-like fashion, "I'm very happy to do whatever I can to be of service to you. I have engaged a lawyer who. . . ."

"Hold on a minute, young man," Jake Manners said, lifting a great blunt hand. "I ain't told you I could afford a fancy lawyer. And the good ones come high, by what I've heard tell about 'em. Them that can make a judge and a jury think what they want 'em to think, costs like a gold mine."

"My dear Mister Manners," protested the youth gently, "I hope you will not take offense when I tell you that I have grown so much interested in this case, and at the dangerous . . . er . . . injustice that seems in danger of being done to your son, who now sits in jail, that I . . . in fact, I have been bold to engage the lawyer personally and request him to do what he can for your son at my expense."

He said this so suavely, so smoothly, that it would have been difficult to take any exception to it. Only gradually the farmer understood the full meaning, and then a brick red glowed in his face.

"I've never took charity," he said. "I dunno that I'm ready to begin using it for my own boy, Mister Mervin," and he added slowly: "Ned would be pretty mad if he heard about that, I guess."

"Ned will have a long time to think about the whole affair in prison if he is not helped and helped strongly at the present moment," Mervin responded sharply. "As for your pride, I assure you that I respect you greatly for your attitude. But I am thinking of Ned himself, and of how a prison term would ruin his life. Things go rather badly for an ex-convict in these uncharitable times, Mister Manners."

Jake Manners settled back in his chair, silent, beaten, but unwilling to admit it and writhing at the thought of accepting aid from a stranger. Camden, all of this time, had not been regarding Jake with more than a glance or two. His chief attention was centered upon the girl and the youth, and he found enough passing between them to reward all of his observations.

Those occasional flicking glances of young Mervin had whipped the bright blood up into the face of the girl and set a glow in her cheeks. Again the anger of Camden waxed, he knew not why. But he felt the necessity of action on his own part, and action at once.

He did not wait to hear the end of the interview between Charles Mervin and the Manners. He rounded the house to the girl's room, and through the window he tossed the pelt of the silver fox. He saw it land on the bed. Then he went back to Crusader among the pines.

AMENDS ARE MADE

The county jail in the town of Twin Creeks was behind the courthouse. The courthouse was a rambling, wooden affair, the jail a neat little modern structure with concrete walls and cells protected with tool-proof steel in thick bars.

Such was the place before which Harry Camden stood. All was dark except for the rectangle of a window shade lighted from the room within, the shade half drawn and the window half open. To that window went Camden and saw, within, the guard seated, tilted far back in his chair, with his heels dropped upon the varnished top of the desk. A sawed-off shotgun rested, also, upon that same desk. Camden regarded this with a peculiar interest. There is this point of interest about a sawed-off shotgun. One does not need to aim with any particular accuracy. One may turn the muzzle of a gun of that nature toward the mark as confidently as one turns the nozzle of a hose toward a rosebush, confident that at least one drop will strike the mark. One drop of lead will be sufficient to splash out the life of the victim. Such a weapon has the obvious disadvantage of having no effective range beyond an immediate and point-blank volley. His eye was still upon the shotgun when Camden spoke.

"Hello!" he called.

The guard lurched forward in the chair and rocked to his feet.

"Hello!" answered the guard.

"I've come along from the sheriff."

"The devil you have!" said the guard. He came to the window, knocked it fully up, and, with the shotgun tucked under one arm, he rested the other hand upon the sill. With the light behind him, he looked a monster leaning there above Camden.

"The sheriff left here about five minutes ago!" he exclaimed, staring at the stranger.

"Sure," answered Camden. "I know about that. He was tellin' me."

"Who might you be?"

"I guess you dunno me. I used to know the sheriff about fifteen years back."

"You did. When he was over in Roscoe County, maybe?"

"That was it."

"Well, what happened to him that he couldn't come here himself and had to send you, stranger?"

"Dog-goned if he didn't slip in the street and drop his knee on a point of a rock. It laid him up pretty bad."

"Them rocks in front of the Gregory place?"

"That's it."

The guard began to laugh. "For different kinds of lying," he said, "I've heard some of the dog-goned smoothest and slickest that they is in the world, and I guess that I've heard some of the worst, too. But takin' 'em, by and large, I got to admit that you lay it over anybody I ever seen for plain bad lyin'. Look here, young feller, I've knowed Sheriff Tom Younger runnin' on to twenty-two year, ever since one day we give each other black eyes in school. Well, sir, far as I know, he never was in Roscoe County . . . but fifteen year back he was down in Mexico. And them rocks in front of the Gregory place . . . why, stranger, lemme tell you that the Gregory place is away off along the south creek."

He laughed again uproariously. His amusement over the baffling of the stranger, and his appreciation of his own cleverness in thwarting Camden, had put him into the most perfect good humor.

"Maybe," he continued, "you was comin' to ask me in on a little game of shootin' craps, me holdin' the dice and you holdin' the guns? Or maybe," he went on, still chuckling, "you want to ask me for the keys to the jail, or any little old thing like that!"

He laughed again. He had put himself into a high state of humor. As for Camden, in the dark of the night he had snarled at the first hint that he was exposed to the ridicule of the other, for ridicule was the one thing that cut him to the quick. But the guard talked too long, as triumphant men are apt to do. He talked long enough, in fact, to allow Camden to rally his native wits again.

When the guard ended, Camden said simply: "Well, partner, I guess that you're a little too smart for me. I was aimin' . . . well, it wasn't no go."

"I wasn't born yesterday," said the guard complacently. "Who might you be, stranger?"

"My name's Petrie."

"Petrie, what's your game, if I may ask you?"

"Something you could make a little money out of, partner."

"Tryin' bribery, now."

"Maybe you're too rich to want money?" Camden asked.

"I dunno that I am. Lemme hear what you got to say, anyway."

It was such a palpable lure to draw out whatever criminal purpose might be in the mind of Camden that he could not help smiling a little. "Lean down a mite," he said, "I ain't gonna holler this out so's the whole town can hear me."

"All right, kid, whisper it, then."

"Ain't there nobody in the room behind you, there?"

"D'you think that I have to have help to keep this here jail safe? I guess not, old son, I guess not." Again he chuckled.

"This is the way of it," began Camden, stepping closer, and, as he stepped in, his long right arm shot out. It was a trick that Cyclone Ed Morgan and Sparrow Roberts had taught him, years before. Once learned, it could never be forgotten. His fist chopped down at the end of the punch on the very tip of the guard's jaw. It seemed hardly more than a grazing punch. The head of the guard bobbed far back on his shoulders, loosely, and Camden was bringing a crushing left across to finish the work that the first punch had started, when the guard collapsed and slid down through the window, head first. He was caught in the arms of Camden and cradled there, lightly as a child.

Camden looked around him. The only people were two men who lounged at a distant corner, talking and laughing. Their laughter had not ceased, which meant that they had not heard or seen anything to arouse their suspicions. His maneuver had escaped their notice.

Around the corner of the jail, and out of sight, Camden bore the guard. He placed him on the plot of shaven grass that was kept around the county buildings, and, by the time the man of the law revived, Camden had found the bunch of keys in his pocket and drawn them forth. The awakening guard he confronted with the tickling point of his knife in the ribs.

"I'll have young Manners out," he announced.

The other took stock of things stupidly, but then his brain cleared with a jerk. The tickling edge of the knife was a quick restorer of scattered thoughts.

"All right," he said. "But lemme find out where you hid the club that you soaked me with. I didn't see nothing but your hand comin'."

"I'll tell you later," said Camden. "Now lemme have Manners."

They went in through the side door of the jail, the guard handling the keys. Straight to the dimly lighted corridor between the cells he led the way, and then to Manners himself. That hardy youth lay face downward on his bunk, but it needed only the sound of a step to waken him from his fast sleep. He started to his feet, and, when the door was opened, he walked out as one dazed.

"What's this for?" he asked. "What deviltry have you gents got up your sleeve for me now?" Puzzled yet defiant, he looked about him.

"We got a silver fox for you," said Camden.

At this the other winced and turned a dark red.

"You lead us out," Camden said to the guard. The latter, obediently, led forth from the jail to the outer air once more.

"You got a stable near here?" asked Camden.

"Right yonder."

"Is they anybody there?"

"I dunno. Not at this time of the night, I guess."

"Any hosses in there?"

"Sure. Half a dozen."

"Take me in there."

A single lantern hung in the stable. By its light they clearly saw a dappled gray in the first stall, a bright pinto adjoining.

"Look 'em over," Camden said gruffly to young Manners. "Pick out the one that looks good to you."

Ned Manners had marched ahead, without orders, at the side of the guard, as if he took it for granted that this was an escort arranged to guard him. Now he saw that the revolver that the stranger had drawn was leveled at the guard only, and the light began to break on his brain. He leaped down the row of horses. In another moment he was dragging a saddle from the peg.

"Here's my own hoss . . . here's Fanny," he said, "and I guess that she's good enough for me." He saddled her quickly and led her back to the door. "Where's your hoss?" he asked.

"I'll show you later," Camden replied. He turned on the gloomy guard. "You was askin' about that club that I used?" he queried.

"It was quick work," said the guard. "The boys'll make life hard for me, soon as they find out what's happened. But show me how you did it."

"Like this," Camden said calmly, and struck the poor fellow senseless at his feet.

It was an act of such horribly cold-blooded brutality that young Manners gasped. Harry Camden, however, turned on his heel as though he had brushed a gnat from the air—no more.

"Climb onto your hoss," Camden ordered.

Manners, bewildered, but with the fire of hope in his eyes and the first taste of liberty to rejoice his heart, swung into the saddle. "Your own hoss . . . ," he began.

But as he spoke, Camden raised a shrill, short whistle, thrice repeated, and out of the night came the rhythmic beat of galloping hoofs. A glimmering black monster of a horse drew up beside Camden. In another moment they were off together, and galloping hard for the open country.

A STRANGE REQUEST

Fanny was a queen of the range. There was no dash of Thoroughbred blood in her veins, but although she was pure mustang she was a throwback to that early type from which all American mustangs sprang—the purebred Barb and Arabian horses that many of the *conquistadores* brought to Mexico for the conquest. Slender-limbed, close-coupled, with eyes of a deer and grace of a cat, she could run like a racer and endure like iron. The pride of Ned Manners was in her, but although he loosed the reins and let her flash away across the hills from Twin Creeks, in two miles of running he found her breathing hard and some of the spring gone from her gallop; yet the black monster that ranged beside her was still flaunting along with his head high as though the work had been mere play to him.

At this Ned Manners marveled, but he marveled still more at the rider of the stallion. It was Crusader. There could be no doubt of that. In all the world there could not possibly be two animals with so many points in common. The rider, therefore, must be he who had stolen the famous stallion from Colonel Dinsmore and who then had chosen to imperil his own safety in order to liberate another man who was wrongfully accused of that crime. Here was a combination of virtue and of vice that appealed powerfully to the heart and to the brain of Ned.

So, as they rode, and as he found that his mare could not draw away from her traveling companion, he stole many a side glance at big Harry Camden. In sheer inches and pounds there was little to choose between them, but there was an air about Camden that suggested incredible power of hand. There was a lordly carelessness that young Manners, like any good hunter, had marked in the grizzly when no scent of man was near, a lion-like mastery of creation. Besides, he could not help remarking and remembering most vividly the singular ease with which the stranger had knocked down the guard. That guard was no fragile youngster, but a fellow of brain and brawn. Yet he had gone down like nothing. The more Manners regarded his companion the more he was assured that he had beside him a man in a million.

He watched, too, the fashion in which Camden managed the horse. Who was there in the countryside who had not heard much of the manners of the stallion? Who was there that did not know of his tigerish ferocity, his cruelty, his treacherous cunning, his unnatural love of blood? But behold! The great black stallion ranged along freely, with slack reins along his neck, with no saddle to brace and support his rider—rather as if the will of the man were its own will. Manners, knowing men and knowing horses, also, blinked at this sight, it was something, indeed, to remember. This was a story that would not be believed, beginning with that point when he would tell how with a whistle the stranger had conjured the stallion in out of the night.

A thousand questions rushed to his lips and were pressed back from them again. Something like a raised hand warned him not to speak, and speak he did not. As for the direction of their flight, this was established by the big stranger. They held on like a pair of arrows through the darkness, until, rounding over a hill, they saw the shack of Jake Manners in the hollow beneath them, and then Camden drew rein.

"Partner," said Ned Manners, speaking very gently, "I been thinkin' over what I could say to you. But doggone me if I find the right sort of words."

The other turned a leonine head toward him, and Ned Manners felt more helplessly juvenile than ever before.

"That's black Crusader," Manners said humbly. "And you're the gent that took him from Colonel Dinsmore. Ain't that right?"

"That's tolerable correct."

"I figger that you know my name. Might I ask after yours?"

"I'm Harry Camden."

It was a good deal of a shock to the other. He had been conning over the list of the celebrated men of the mountains, outlaws, scorners of danger, demigods in their heroic actions, but there had been none who exactly fitted with the description of the man beside him. This totally unknown name made him start.

"Maybe you've heard of me?" asked Camden.

"Not before tonight."

"And what you've heard tonight, if I was you, I'd start right in tryin' to forget."

There was no doubt concerning the thinly veiled threat in this speech, but Manners, although he flushed hotly, swallowed the implied insult.

"I'd like to tell Dad and my sister," he said simply. "I'd like for them to know what you've done for me and what the name of the gent is that's done it. I'll be off to the hills tomorrow. With a good runnin' start like this here, darned if they'll ever catch me."

This brought about an exclamation from Camden. "What call is they for you to keep on runnin'?" he asked tersely.

"Hoss stealin'," said the young trapper and farmer, "ain't particular popular around these parts." He chuckled. With Fanny beneath him once more, and the dark of the night before his face, and the well-known mountains above him, he felt that he could never be caught. He even looked forward with a sort of grim anticipation to the ensuing struggle.

"Hoss stealin'?" echoed the other. "Who'll lay that up to you?"

"Mostly everybody."

"What hoss?"

"Why, Crusader, of course."

"Crusader? Hell and fire, man, ain't *I* got Crusader?"

"Who'll know that?"

There was a little pause, and by the bended head of the big man young Ned Manners knew that he was deep in thought.

"They'll know before the mornin'," he said. "They'll know dog-gone sure before mornin'!"

"How?" Manners asked, astonished.

"I'll let 'em see me and the hoss together. I'll let the sheriff see us together."

"Good heavens, partner, and let 'em bag you?"

"I dunno if that follows on after the seein'."

There was a grim note in this speech that forbade further questioning on the part of Ned. He could only gape at the other through the night. Here was a wealth of benevolence that took his breath.

"Camden," he said at last, "damn my heart if you ain't the whitest man that ever I met. And the squarest and the most. . . ."

"Talk," Camden said crisply, "is cheap."

"Tell me what I can do for you," Ned asked enthusiastically. "Lemme have a chance to show you. . . ."

"Wait a minute. I'm figgerin' on something that'll pay me back."

Ned Manners waited, hushed, expectant, turning a hundred possibilities in his mind. This fellow was no fool. He had done this heroic thing and planned on still another act of self-sacrifice for the sake of a reward, of course. What could the thing be?

"You're gonna go down yonder to your dad's house?"

"Of course."

"Go in and tell your sister to take a lamp and come and open the back door."

"You want to talk to her? You want to tell her something?"

"I've told you what to tell her," Camden answered, and turned his head away.

There was no mistaking this signal of dismissal. With his brain in a whirl of vain conjectures, Ned Manners rode down to his father's house, threw the reins of Fanny, and hurried in. He found them gathered in the dining room, with young Charles Mervin rising to take his leave. There was a general outcry at the sight of him, and then Ruth, clinging to him, crying: "Ned, you ain't broke out of jail?"

"I was taken out," he said in great excitement. "I was taken out and didn't raise my hand. You might say I was taken out at the point of a gun. Now, Sis, you got to do something for me. Don't ask no questions, because I can't answer 'em. Take a lamp and go to the kitchen door and stand there with the door open."

"Ned, what in the world . . . ?"

"I told you that questions wouldn't do no good, and I mean it. Will you go along?"

There were two lamps in the room. One of these she raised without a word, because it was not the first time in her life that she had obeyed, without answer, a strange command. In her frontiersman life she had come to feel that men have the right to command. She gave one glance to her father. But he remained motionless. It was too staggeringly unusual for him to have a word to say on the subject. Then she went to the kitchen door and opened it slowly, expecting to see she knew not what. But there was nothing before her—only the thick black of the night. She shaded her eyes from the lamp. Now, away from its dazzling glow, she could make out the stars in the sky, the black line of the hills against them, and in the hollow, not far away, the form of a rider on a tall, shadowy figure of a horse. It startled her, that quiet form in the night. But now the stranger in the night turned away. The side view enabled her all the better to estimate the gigantic proportions of horse and man. They seemed to tower above the squat hills in the distance.

The great horse broke into a long-striding gallop; in

another moment it was lost among the shadows of the trees. Then she turned and came back into the dining room with a face white with excitement.

The first question came from her brother. "What did he say?" he cried. "What did he say, Sis?"

"Who?" she asked.

"Cam . . . I mean, him . . . I mean . . . good heavens, Sis, didn't you see anyone?"

"Nobody," she answered. "I saw a rider on a big black hoss. I couldn't make out much about him, except that he was big. But he didn't say a word. He just turned his hoss away and rode off."

Ned Manners gaped at her. "I dunno what it is," he said slowly. "Dog-gone me if it ain't queer. Maybe . . . maybe his head is a little wrong. Maybe . . . he's a bit crazy."

"Who?" they clamored in a chorus.

"The squarest gent that ever lived," Ned said, and said no more.

PURSUIT

The picture in the yellow glow of the lamplight had filled the brain and filled the heart of Harry Camden. Yet there had come a moment, quickly, when he could gaze no more, but hurried away on Crusader. On the rim of the first hill he turned and looked back. The door had been closed, and the light and the girl were gone. But not gone from his memory.

As for the work that lay before him, it seemed a trifle now. He went straight back to Twin Creeks. On the edge of town he met a youngster, whistling down the road, and, in spite of the late hour, driving a pair of cows before him.

"Hello, son!" called Camden.

The boy called back to him cheerily.

"Where's the sheriff's house?" asked Camden.

"He ain't there, most likely. Something's wrong. Or have you just come in to help run down the gent that busted into the jail?"

"I've come to give the sheriff some news."

"Some say that he ain't gonna start on the trail till the mornin'. That's his house over yonder. The big one with the tower-lookin' thing on the side of it."

Toward the house with the "tower-lookin' " steeple Camden went, where he dismounted, left Crusader in the street with the perfect assurance that the savage monster would let no other man approach it, and rapped at the front door of the building.

It was opened by a little wisp of an old woman, her back deformed by long, hard labor.

"Is the sheriff home?"

"He's here. Step right in, young man. He's havin' a bite before he gets into the saddle. They ain't no rest for. . . ."

"Send him out here," interrupted Camden. "I got some news for him. Send him right out here. I got some news that he'll be mighty surprised to hear."

She blinked at him and then hastened down the hall, up which the heavy stride of a big man presently advanced, and a tall, thin-faced man appeared, working his sombrero deep down upon his head and wriggling his hands into gloves.

"Well, stranger?" he said at the door.

"Close the door," said Camden, "and come along out here. I got to say something that ain't to be overheard by nobody."

The sheriff favored him with a sharp scrutiny that was rendered in vain by the blanketing dark, thicker to the sheriff because he had just come out from brightest lamplight. He strode out onto the verandah and slammed the door behind him. "I'll give you thirty seconds," he said sharply. "I got no time for gossip. . . ."

A gun squinted in the starlight before him.

"Gimme them thirty seconds, with your hands right up in the air," said Harry Camden.

The sheriff made his hands fight their way up into the air, inch by inch, while he ground his teeth. He was a fighting man, this honest sheriff, but although he had faced death many a time for the sake of duty, something told him now that he was in a place where it would be foolish to take extra risks.

"What'll you have?" he asked sourly.

"My name's Harry Camden," said the latter. "I'm the gent that busted into the jail and took out Ned Manners."

"I'll have your hide for it," the sheriff said gravely. "You can lay to that, Harry Camden."

The fury of Camden burst out into words. "Sheriff," he said, "you're talkin' foolish. If it's a game between you and me, you'll be wishin' you was dead before you ever heard my name. Look yonder into the street."

The sheriff stared in the bidden direction, and then made out the magnificent form of a great black horse. "It's Crusader, and you've rode him into Twin Creeks!"

"I'll ride him out again," the other assured him. "Look me over, Sheriff, so's you'll know me the next time you see me. But Ned Manners is innocent . . . y'understand?"

"Innocent or not," said the sheriff furiously, "he's busted jail, and he'll come back and answer for that."

There was a little pause, and during it he heard the heavy breathing of the big man before him.

"I'm gonna do nothin' now," said the stranger at

length, "but if you lay a hand on young Manners, you'll hear from me ag'in, Sheriff, and you'll hear *pronto*. Now keep them hands stiff up 'n the air."

While the sheriff obeyed, Harry Camden went through his clothes. From beneath the armpits of the sheriff he extracted one pair of hidden weapons. From holsters he took two more. He threw them all far off into the brush.

"Now," he said, "I guess we've talked long enough to begin to know each other. So long, Younger!"

"Camden," said the sheriff, "maybe you've done a pile in your life, but you ain't never done a thing that was more fool than this here one. You can lay to that. You'll have the daylight let through you inside of a week . . . or else you'll get ten years in prison to think these here things over. Take my advice. Ride the devil out of Crusader, because he can't take you too far away from me to be safe!"

The last of this was spoken to Camden as he vaulted onto the back of the horse. A moment later the disappearing stallion was partly obscured by a sudden cloud of dust while the sheriff thundered an alarm call.

Yet Camden was in no haste. He was so desperately keen for action, now, that he lingered close to the town, until he heard the rushing of hoofs as the pursuers swept out of it. They were dividing and spurring up either valley of the two creeks. For his own part, he kept to the high rough ground in between and let Crusader work his way without haste.

Straight on until the gray of the morning he journeyed. Then, on a far distant upland, he loosed Crusader, tightened his own belt, and went to sleep. It was noon when he wakened, with a deep, bell-like baying far away in the air. Sometimes it died as the wind died; sometimes it increased in the wind and blew strongly to him. But there was no haste. They were long miles and miles away. Far down the valley there was no sign of them.

Every moment that Crusader could use grazing and resting was very much worthwhile. So Camden went to the spot where he had cached the remainder of the side of bacon. Who could eat plain strips of bacon, half roasted above a small fire? Harry Camden, at least, was one who could not only eat it but enjoy every mouthful of it.

He was half through that hasty meal when he saw the stallion coming toward him. Close and closer the deep-throated hounds were making their music. There could be no doubt at what target they were aimed, and the stallion seemed to know it, for he began to dance impatiently, tossing his head, and looking first down the valley, then toward his master.

Camden, however, continued to munch his half raw, half burned meat. When it was finished, he tossed the remnant of the side of bacon into the brush after he had rubbed it upon the hoofs of the horse. For the strong smell of the salt meat might kill the scent of the stallion. At least it would make the work of the dogs more difficult. After that, he went to a trickling little rill of spring water and drank, and still drank as the rout of hounds burst into view a scant quarter of a mile away and gave huge tongue at the sight of him.

There were fifty dogs. The whole countryside had contributed a dog here and a dog there to the good work. There were wise mongrels useful to solve trail problems and also useful to close and fight heroically. There were long-eared bloodhounds. There were gaunt-bellied wolfhounds, fast as the wind, tireless on the trail. If only their noses had been equal to the speed and to their sight.

These things Camden surveyed and took note of carefully while he tossed the blanket on the stallion and drew up the cinch. Ten seconds of work, but the pack was already closing with a rush. A great wolfhound, out-speeding the rest by many yards, came hurtling far in the lead, a scarred and savage veteran, useful on many a trail, strong as a wolf, wicked in fight as a bear. He came fast, silent, slavering with eagerness for the kill. Just at that moment the hunters themselves came into view, half a dozen of the leaders on the finest horses, with the sheriff at their head and, beside the sheriff, the aristocratic forms of Colonel Dinsmore himself and young Charles Mervin.

These people Camden saw, assured that they would not risk gunfire on him while fifty thousand dollars' worth of horseflesh stood so near to him. Then he faced the swift charge of the big dog, not a gun in hand, but with only that long knife. He stood very still, a little crouched, and, as the beast leaped for his throat, he dropped to the side and stabbed up and in. The hound lived long enough to utter one death screech, cut short by death itself. Then it fell and rolled away down the slope, followed by a shower of stones.

While the rest of the dogs raised their heads and slowed their pace before so terrible a foe that killed at a single touch, Camden leaped onto the black horse and was away—away with the ringing yells of the hunters pressing close behind him.

Up the remainder of the slope he let the stallion work at ease, although the hunt closed behind him fast, every moment. He could hear them shouting, some to the dogs, picking them out by name and urging them to close, and some to one another. Particularly he distinguished the trumpet tones of young Charles Mervin, who seemed to have a commanding part in the chase, owing to his friendship with the much-respected colonel, and owing, also, to his demonstrated ability as a rider and a shot, to say nothing of the fineness of his horse, which enabled him to keep constantly in the front rank, or a little in the lead.

He was at the top of the slope at last, however, and there lay before him a sheer descent—a gravel slide covered with broken rocks. They had tried to navigate that before, and it was dangerous work. The stallion, recognizing the place, tossed his head and snorted. But when the master threw himself off his back, black Crusader held back not for a single moment. He threw himself down the slope with braced legs. A small avalanche followed him. Great stones began to bound past him and behind. But when he struck the level far beneath, he leaped instantly to the side. A dozen boulders large enough to have dashed him to death sprang past. Camden, sore from a dozen bruises, was instantly on his back.

Behind them came the dogs streaming. But even dogs could not run fast down such a perilous place as this. They went cautiously, and some of them, halfway down, paused to raise their heads and wail out their rage and their hatred. As for the men, not one ventured it. Two or three raised their guns, but the sheriff, furious though he might be, commanded them not to shoot. There were too many thousands of dollars tied up in the horse that Harry Camden rode.

So, with a gesture of derision, Camden jogged black Crusader down the valley.

CRUSADER SPEAKS

He had something to contend with besides the speed of one band of horsemen, however. The wide-ranging voices of telegraph and telephone were calling on town after town along the plains and the hills to send forth their volunteers for the chase, and they responded willingly, as true Westerners will ever do for the chase of either man or beast.

Rounding the Sugar Loaf of that range, Harry Camden came upon a rush of horsemen straight in his face. He had to double back and shake them off by going straight up the sheer side of Sugar Loaf for some distance. Then he half circled it and dropped to a lower and smoother level again, where there was better footing for Crusader. But that detour cost him much, and cost Crusader still more. In addition, when he reached the foot of Mount Baldy, whose head was ever streaked with snow in the crevasses, another party came pouring out at him. On this occasion, he had merely to turn Crusader and flee swiftly down Squaw Creek, but the run told heavily on the tired horse. Where Squaw Creek narrowed to a gully, he encountered another climbing party in that mountain throat.

It was a desperate climb that took them out of the valley to the lip of the plateau above, and half an hour after they had gained it, there streamed into view those who had originally begun that wild day's hunting—Colonel Dinsmore and the sheriff and Charles Mervin, with a dozen other of the best-mounted men in the county at their backs.

It meant another hard run. Half exhausted as Crusader was, Camden dared not put him across the flat of the table-land. Instead, he drove the good horse at the rough country. There he dismounted. He himself led the way, and the horse, breathing through crimson, straining nostrils, followed through the brush, while the hounds yelled around them but dared not close, and the huntsmen cursed and raged far and farther behind.

He shot two impudent dogs. That made the rest keep back, and in the mid-afternoon he could let Crusader lie down like a tired man and sleep, while he himself stood by to keep guard. There was an hour of quiet. The eye of the stallion was bright once more and his ears pricking; all the time, sweeping around the verge of the horizon, rang the distant calling of the hounds. Five hundred dogs were working those hills, and a small army of hunters, and every hour saw the entry of new bodies of riders into the fray.

Camden listened as to an exquisite concert arranged in his behalf. The hunting yell of every dog he valued as a priceless thing of beauty. There were teeth ready for his flesh, a heart hungry for his destruction, and he folded his arms across his breast and listened with his amber eyes half closed and a strange, ugly smile.

It was the golden time of the late afternoon when a pack winded him again and came crashing into the thicket where he was hiding. He rode out onto the rolling hills beneath, and, looking back, he knew the dogs as they came, the same pack that had roused him that morning—the pack behind which the sheriff and Dinsmore were riding.

It seemed to Camden like a touch of fate that, out of so many bands, one should have come upon him so often. Perhaps a little touch of awe entered that wild heart of his. He gave Crusader his head. The stallion went off with a rush. That matchless lilt was back in his gallop after his rest, and, looking back at the tired pack, Camden smiled to see them falter and stagger under the pace.

But they came again, like the gallant animals they were, keen for their work that lay before them in full view.

Out of the hills they swept into badly broken ground. Here the dogs gained, as a matter of course, but no matter what the dogs did, so long as the riders lost ground. Through broken ground, he knew that he could rest Crusader while the other horses were punished by their masters to keep up with the pace. Through the jumble of tiny ravines, little spring-flood gulches, brambles and thickets, close-woven mats of second-growth timber intermixed with vines. Camden kept on his way on foot, and the stallion swept along behind him.

A full mile of that work left Harry Camden with

lungs wheezing and throat dry and choked with the dust that he had inhaled. He came out on the farther side with a comfortable sense that he had won again. He leaped onto the back of the stallion once more. They were flogging their horses behind him; those poor nags would come out into the open, beaten and staggering with weariness, groggy from the fierce pace, but Crusader would be merely breathing in comfort.

A narrow valley lay before him, and down this he turned the great horse at a moderate gallop—a moderate gallop for Crusader—a wild race for many a short-legged cow pony. But as he swung away around the first bend of the valley, he saw that they had tricked him at last. In that group of followers, there were some who knew this district—all strange to him—like a book. They had taken advantage of that knowledge. Cutting to the side, some of them had avoided the broken ground altogether and ranged easily into the lead, then broken into the valley lower down and were sweeping back to cut him off. The chosen men were here: old Dinsmore—his hat lost, his white hair blown by the evening wind that was rising—young Charles Mervin, the sheriff, and two others who were strangers to Camden.

He pressed ahead at a keenly maintained pace. They rushed behind him with shouts. Then pack and horsemen broke out from the thicket at his side, and the two currents, joining, came like a roar of waves behind him, horses snorting with fatigue and under the spur, dogs yelling, open-mouthed, wild for the kill and reeling with weariness, and the men, cheering one another hoarsely. They had not covered the ground over which black Crusader had fled this day. They had not covered the half of it. Besides, it is always easier to hunt than it is to be hunted. But still there was something left in the great stallion. If his muscles were weak, his heart was still strong, and that supported him until, rounding out behind the shoulder of a hill straight before them, came a full half dozen of furious riders. They must have been waiting there, fatigued by their work of the day, chatting and resting until they began their journey home through the cool of the dusk. Now they had the enemy given into their hands, and their wild shout of victory passed down the valley and spatted against the wall of the gorge like the spat of a gigantic hand.

Even the wild courage of Camden was daunted for the moment, but in an instant his heart returned, and then he felt Crusader weaken beneath him. The fighting soul of the great stallion could hardly stand up beneath that new discouragement. Camden, drawing his revolver, remembered that it was loaded with six shots, and that there were only six men before him.

That was the first furious impulse. Then, realizing that against certain daylight odds it is the purest folly to contend, he looked about him to see if by any miraculous chance, there might be another loophole for escape. There seemed none. He looked forward at six comparatively fresh men on six hard-running horses. He glanced behind him to the sheriff's own posse, exhausted, indeed, by the hunt that had lasted all the day but, being composed of chosen men, ready for anything—ready to keep on hunting through all the night, if need be. To his left, to fence him in, the wall of the cañon was flat and steep as a raised hand. On his right, Squaw Creek foamed and raged like a mad thing.

But Squaw Creek was his only chance, and, although he shuddered when he viewed the white-streaked rush of the stream, he scanned it more closely. If he were to find any escape, it must be from this direction. But the stream was too wide, by far, to be jumped, even by such a mighty fencer as black Crusader, and, as for swimming the current, there seemed force enough in the flying water to tear the clothes from a man's body.

Camden made those observations and those reflections in the first quick glance. Then, farther up the stream, he saw not a hope, to be sure, but a wild chance such as desperate men and hunted beasts may take. Here, far out across the river, was a small rocky island, a few scant rods across, and beyond this another water gap to the farther shore. Camden made up his mind at once, and, swinging Crusader to the right, he drove the stallion straight toward the jump.

There was no doubt that the big horse understood at once what was expected. The ears of Crusader flagged; the life went out of his gallop. He had lost all heart, and, without his best effort, he could never hope to clear that first long leap across the stream. So Camden, swinging low along the neck of the horse, like a jockey lifting a mount down the stretch in a race, called loudly on Crusader, and called again. The ears of the great horse pricked, and his gallop grew strong, and his head lifted a little as the head of a brave horse should.

All of this was seen by Colonel Dinsmore and young Charles Mervin, and they understood before the others. For to the cowpunchers the change of direction in the fugitive's flight meant little or nothing except an aberration of the mind. But the Colonel and Mervin were from hunting country, and they guessed the mind of Camden the moment he turned the head of Crusader. Mervin pulled the rifle out of the holster that ran along the side of his saddle, prepared to shoot. It was the colonel who knocked away his hand.

"If the wild devil can do that with Crusader half dead under him, by heavens, Charles, he deserves to have the horse and to keep him," said the colonel.

The sheriff had gone mightily excited as he saw this prize at last within his grip. He called an order that sent three men to the right to cut in close to the river, in case Harry Camden should attempt, desperately, to double back along the margin of the water. Then he shouted to the others and led them forward to close.

Meanwhile, black Crusader was gathering speed with every long bound that carried him down the slopes toward the margin of the stream. There was an eight-foot face of ragged stone, walling off the water at that point. But this gave all the better clearance for the jump, and, if Crusader winced when he first saw the peril and understood the mind of his rider, he gathered himself again desperately, and went at his work with a will.

There was no doubt about the destination of Camden now. Every man in both posses could tell what he planned. Already it was almost too late to check the fearful impetus of the big horse without rolling him into the stream. The 'punchers, drawing rein hard, fell into hopeless confusion, shouting vain protests about they knew not what, and staring at the horror to be. Then they saw Crusader plunge to the verge of the rock. They saw him rear. They saw him spurn lightly the edge of the bank and shoot away into the air. With the gap beneath him and the shooting white-streaked waters there so far below, he seemed to have taken wings and flung himself at the sky. The last of the golden setting sun flared along his wet sides, and his mane tossed up like the crest of a warrior, and the white foam flew back from his champed bit.

"Lord heavens!" cried the colonel, clutching the shoulder of Charles Mervin. "His ears are up . . . d'you mind that? He's dying like a brave horse, Charles!"

Charles Mervin, however, had clapped the back of his hand across his eyes and bowed his head to escape the sight of the thing to come, until he was rudely wrenched by the hand of the colonel, and the colonel's voice cried sharp and small at his ear: "He's over!"

It was announced by the wild uproar of the cowpunchers, too, and there Mervin saw horse and man, looking even more gigantic, leaping across the little island that half blocked the course of Squaw Creek. Once more Crusader soared into the air. They saw him strike heavily on the farthermost bank—they saw him slip far down the bank toward the curling, screaming waters—and then they saw the rider whip off the back of the horse and draw mightily at the bridle until Crusader, gathering himself, came staggering off the edge of the bank and away across country, head down, knees feeble, and his master running lightly before him, and the stallion following like an obedient dog.

The colonel and Mervin, who knew the horse so well, stared at one another incredulously. Even the cow waddies, with their rifles out and an easy shot before them, settled not a single gun butt into the steadying hollow of a shoulder. But they looked back to the colonel and read in his face that he did not want the robber harmed.

Still they watched and stared and said not a word to one another. The fugitive ran up the hills beyond the stream. He turned a little west. In another moment, on a top ridge, cleanly outlined against the red west, he stood and stared back at the others. It was a perfect rifle shot, but not a man raised his weapon. Not a man so much as spoke.

Black Crusader spoke the last word on the day of that historic hunt, as, indeed, was his right. No matter how exhausted he might be, he arched his crest before he disappeared, and raised his head, and presently his neigh, like a strong bugle call, rang back to them. Then horse and master dipped out of sight beyond the hill.

THE THOROUGHBRED IS RETURNED

It was a day of marvels to the men who rode in that chase. They returned wearily to their homes, and the colonel astonished Charles Mervin by actually showing a sort of high-hearted good nature as he made the journey back. But young Mervin dared not press him with questions or express surprise, because there was a great deal about the colonel that frightened Mervin nearly out of his wits.

It was during a late supper that the colonel disclosed the secret of his happiness.

"It was the way he ran and the way he jumped," said the colonel. "They called him a sullen dog and a quitter on the tracks. I wish to heaven that they could have seen him work today with a real rider. It's all he's needed . . . not a withered little runt of a fellow with no heart in him . . . like Joe Tracy. But a real man . . . a man's man! What do you think he weighs . . . this man-breaking, horse-charming, wild young devil?"

"Harry Camden?"

"Yes. Who else answers to that description?"

"Over two hundred pounds, I should say."

"Two-thirty, my lad, I say two-thirty, at the least. Crusader carried two hundred and thirty pounds over hill and dale, kept it up all day, and wound up his work by putting on wings and hopping himself and his rider over Squaw Creek as lightly as a sparrow. He was like a bird, wasn't he, Charlie?"

"He was, sir."

"And that rascal standing on the top of the hill and throwing me back a neigh to mock me . . . Charlie, I almost loved the horse for his impudence, eh?"

Charles Mervin could not exactly see the joy in the loss of a fifty-thousand-dollar horse in such short order. But before he could make an answer, and while the colonel's words were hardly more than spoken, there came ringing through the night and through the colonel's house a trumpet call that was very like that same neigh that had been blown back to them, early in the sunset time, from the ridge of the hill.

It made them both start. It brought the colonel out of his chair. "Listen!" he said.

"It couldn't be," said Charles Mervin, growing a little pale. "That devil wouldn't dare to come back to your house with his mischief."

"He's come back to murder me," breathed the colonel, "because I led the chase during so much of today. Call the servants together. Where did that sound seem to come from . . . ?"

Here there was a hurried entrance of the butler. "In

the paddock, sir . . . ," he began, stammering with eagerness and excitement.

"What's wrong?" barked out the colonel. "Call everyone in the house together and tell them to bring arms. Call in the men from the bunkhouse . . . there's a devil of a. . . ."

"They've just sent in the word, sir. Crusader. . . ."

"I know it! Has been seen with a man on his back. . . ."

"Has been seen in the paddock without any man near him. In the paddock with the blanket on his back!"

The colonel staggered a little as he rounded the table on the run for the door.

"Come on, Charlie!" he called. "Come on and let me see this affair before I go mad with it."

They hurried out together. It was all true. In a distant corner of the paddock, the light from many lanterns that the 'punchers had carried out glistened brightly over the great black body of Crusader. There he stood with his head down and a rear foot pointed, a very, very weary horse, indeed.

"Look in here, sir!" called one of the men.

The colonel and Mervin entered the box stall, and there was shown to them, by the lantern light, a message scrawled along the barn wall.

> Dere Colonel Dinsmore: You could of had them shoot me at Squaw Creek. You let me go free part because of Crusader and part because you liked the game. I don't take no charity, so I've brought back Crusader. That makes us quits. Now you keep that hoss if you can.
>
> H.C.
>
> P.S. You are a square shooter.

The colonel and Charles Mervin pored over this letter with bewilderment. It had been scrawled so raggedly that it was hard to read, and, once it had been made out, it was difficult to express the wonder and the concern that appeared in the face of the colonel. He passed out from the box stall again with Mervin.

"Charlie," he said as they stood together at the fence, looking at the perfect beauty of Crusader, "the point of this affair seems to be that this wild man, this Camden, is really a gentleman, after all!"

This remark rather amused Charles Mervin. Indeed, it seemed to him such a rare response and so typical of the eccentric old colonel that he could not help repeating it the next day, when he went to call on pretty Ruth Manners.

"An abysmal brute," Charles Mervin said, "but the colonel sees a good sport in the workings of a beastly, superstitious brain."

"You've got no right to say that!" cried the girl.

"Why not?"

"Because," she said, "I believe in him, too! And the colonel's right."

She was so angry, and she looked up to him with such fire in her eyes that he stepped close with his arms thrown out in a little gesture. This was what Camden saw as he came around the trunk of the pine on the hill. He saw a gesture that, it seemed to him, promised that the girl, the next moment, would be caught into the arms of Mr. Charles Mervin. It struck Camden blind and dumb. He cast up a hand before his eyes so that he might not see this thing, and then, whirling, he raced away through the trees and down the hillside.

In the hollow below he fell into a fit of brute passion. He caught up a young sapling and rent it up by the roots. He shattered its tough pole across a rock. He ripped the rock from its bed and smashed it to bits upon another.

After that he set his face for the heights, and for twenty-four hours he never ceased his journey until he lay, at last, with a drawn face but with a savage fire in his amber eyes, on a fragrant bed of balsam boughs on a mountain's side. The stars were coming. He watched them glimmering in the skies. Then he glanced deeper down into the valley. There were smaller, yellower stars scattered here and there, and every little golden spot of radiance meant a house and man. Camden started to his feet with a snarl and plunged deeper into the gloom of the woods.

III

CRUSADER TO BEAT FURY

There was a change in the manner of Crusader. In the old days he had been as content with his paddock and his big box stall as a king in a kingdom. He could loiter in the stall when he wished, or he could go to the trough for the purest of pure well water, or he could stand under the big tree in a corner of the corral through the heat of the day. Always his eye was calm.

Now there was a great difference. One would have thought him an exile from a happier place. In the night he rebelled against the box stall, and, when the door was locked upon him, he tried the stretch of the door itself with his hoofs and then tested the merits of the boards that walled him in with the same pile-driving blows. Twice the lock on the door was burst through and replaced. Then Crusader gave up the task of breaking a way out.

Still he was not any happier, and all night he could be heard stirring up and down in the stall, twisting and turning gloomily, here and there, like a child that has been told it must sit on one chair and stay there. When, in the morning, he was turned out into the paddock again, he would walk restlessly up and down the fence, like a wild beast in a cage, staring far away toward the mountain, blue in the morning and the evening and brown in the full flare of the sun.

This was not all, for the finest of hay and the choicest of oats no longer appealed to Crusader. He grew thin. His coat had lost its luster. His ribs were visible all up and down his sides; the long muscles could be seen the length of his neck.

"He needs room," said Colonel Dinsmore, and, at great expense, he had a forty-acre stretch of good pasture fenced to a height that even Crusader could not jump. But even with this ample range for exercise and diversion, Crusader improved no more. In fact, he seemed to be declining more than ever, for all day long he was trotting or galloping or restlessly walking up and down the fence that barred him from the mountains.

The colonel sent for the wisest man in horseflesh to be found in the whole range of the mountains. It was Jack Murran, who came on his bay stallion, Fury. The colonel went out with him, and they leaned together against the fence and peered through at Crusader.

"There," said the colonel, "is a fortune in horseflesh thrown away. What can I do to cheer up the rascal, Murran? You know the story. He's breaking his heart to get back to Harry Camden. How can I cheer him up?"

"Give him company," Murran responded.

"I've tried to. He does his best to kill the horses . . . he pays no attention to the mares, and they're so afraid of him that they daren't go near."

"That's the trouble," said Murran, "with a hoss like that. All nerves and fire. Wear themselves out. Damn it, man, what good is a horse of that size for real use?"

He gave his long scimitar-like mustaches a pull and stared at Dinsmore out of eyes that were a faded blue—sun faded, one might have said, from looking across the hot, shimmering face of the desert. As for the colonel, he could hardly believe his ears. He had been so accustomed to looking upon Crusader as the very greatest horse in the world that to hear his actual worth questioned shocked him. He felt that there must be a jest behind all this. But Murran was famous for a lack of humor.

"Tell me," he said, "what would you say that Crusader is good for, if anything, Mister Murran?"

"For winning races on a track that's shaved off smooth. For sprintin', he would do. But in this here country. . . ." He waved a hand toward the distant mountains, as though to call upon them to be a witness to the justice of his remarks.

"In this country?" prompted the colonel.

"I'd hitch him to a plow," said the curt Murran. "That's where he'd do the most good. That's where you could use the beef and the bone that he's got on him. Doggone me if I see any other way!" He went on to explain: "Suppose that you was to want a good cuttin' hoss that could foller a calf through a herd, dodgin' like a cat. Would those long legs of his be any good? He'd tie 'em into a knot, tryin' to keep up with the calf."

"I admit," the serious colonel said, "that Crusader would not be a very effective mount for the ordinary cowpuncher, granting even that the waddie could learn to ride and handle him. But there are other uses for a horse in this country."

"To go a distance," said Murran, "who'd want a hoss like that? He's got to have his water when he's thirsty. He's got to be groomed up fine as silk. And he's got to have that every day."

The colonel shook his head. "Environment is everything," he replied. "Crusader has been raised like a millionaire's child. That doesn't mean that he couldn't get on as a beggar. Give him his chance and you'd see him learnin' all the tricks just as any cow pony has learned them."

At this, Murran merely grunted. "Look yonder at Fury," he said, and pointed.

The colonel regarded the beautiful bay stallion with a tolerant eye. "Fury is a nice trick," he said. "For a child's pony, he'd do very well."

"A child's pony," echoed Murran, with wrath gathering in his face and in his eye.

"He's not an inch above fifteen hands, is he?" asked the colonel, still unable to control a smile.

"Size ain't what counts," Murran shot back, looking down approvingly over his own form, which was certainly far from Herculean. "Size ain't more'n half of it, partner. The way things is put together inside and out is what makes the difference. Look at that hoss, I say. Ain't he in shape?"

"As if he were in training," admitted the colonel. "Not too fine and not too fat. Just right, I should say."

"How did he get that way?" asked Murran. "I've been takin' a trip on him. He's had his shot of work every day. Work that'd about kill most hosses. But nothin' to Fury. And today I've rode him forty mile to this here place . . . and I'll ride him forty mile back ag'in, if I have to. And when he steps out tomorrow morning, he'll have his head just as high as he's got it now. Well, Colonel, could you say that much for your Crusader?"

With this, he grinned very broadly at the good colonel, who said gravely: "I rather think Crusader would hold up. He's no more of a show horse than he is a work horse, you know."

Murran flushed a little and then snapped his calloused fingers. "Talkin'," he said, "would never decide it."

"As for a test," the colonel responded, "I should be very happy to make one, if Crusader were in good condition, and if there were anyone who could handle him."

"How about that ex-jockey . . . that Tracy?"

The colonel smiled a little sadly. "Tracy is afraid to come within speaking distance of the horse," he admitted.

"There you are!" exclaimed Murran. "High-headed fool . . . excuse me for statin' the facts, Colonel . . . but that's what he is . . . too many nerves. All on the surface. Can't stand nothin'. *Won't* stand nothin'!"

The temper of the colonel had been put under a severe strain during this interview, and now his nerves snapped. But he held himself under a stiff control. "I really wish," he said, "that Crusader could have a chance to justify his existence . . . in your eyes. I suppose the other people hereabouts think of him very much as you do?"

Murran nodded. "A pretty fine picture hoss. A fine racer, of course. We know what his record is on the track. But we've seen these Thoroughbreds worked out before in endurance races. Take 'em across country, up and down, hot and cold, rough trail, poor feed . . . and they can't stand the gaff."

At this, the colonel cleared his throat and frowned. "I've heard somethin' about that," he said. "I know that some foolish men have sent out their fine horses . . . their best, even . . . and entered them in endurance tests here. They have put their horses into weather they were not accustomed to, terrain unfamiliar to them, different water, different food, and then expected them to do well."

"I've heard 'em talk the same way . . . after their hosses was beat," said Murran. "By my way of thinkin', a good hoss is a good hoss, come bad luck or good. He'll work his way out, and that's all there is to it! What's weather or food or water to Fury?"

He pointed triumphantly to the bay stallion, then he made a gesture implying some scorn toward the black in the corral—the lofty form of Crusader. But he had gone quite a bit too far. The colonel had endured a great deal more than he could stand, and now his temper got the best of him, although he was still able to smile.

"Murran," he said, "I should like to know what you would consider a conclusive proof of a horse's real ability."

"They ain't more'n one," said the other. "That's the Jericho race."

Even the colonel was taken a little aback by this. For the race over Mount Jericho, which took place every third year and was due to be run within six weeks, was a six-hundred-mile grind through terrible mountains and burning deserts, beginning and ending with the crossing of Mount Jericho itself, a terrible mountain that even a goat would have shunned. In that famous race, scores of the finest horses in the West were entered. Arabians were brought from across the seas to attempt the winning. But in the end, it was always some Western horse, built up with the blood of Thoroughbreds or Arabs, perhaps, but always with a liberal cross of the old Spanish mustang, that won—some hardy animal that was accustomed to the terrific mountain trails, the withering heat of the desert, the blighting winds that comb the bare rocks above timberline.

"Is Fury," asked the colonel, "entered in that race?"

"He is," Murran stated.

"Do you ride him?"

"Nobody else, sir!"

A thought had been born in the brain of the colonel, and his eye glinted with it. "Do you think, Murran, that Fury could beat Crusader in such a race?"

At this, Murran laughed frankly and openly. "Two like him! He'd beat two like Crusader!"

"That is easily said. . . ."

Murran was in possession of millions that far exceeded even the great wealth of the colonel. Copper and cattle told the tale of his success. Moreover, in his own way, he was just as proud of the horse breeding that had produced Fury as the colonel could be proud of the great Crusader himself. He grew a bit red in the face as he snapped out: "I'm willing to talk any way you say, sir! Five thousand that Fury beats Crusader. But who the devil will ride your hoss?"

"I'll attend to that. That's my risk."

"I'll give you odds, Colonel. Ten thousand to five."

"I never take odds in such propositions. Ten thousand, even, if you will."

"I hate to do this, Colonel," said Murran. But his pale blue eyes were shining.

"Naturally," said Dinsmore. "But an idea is an idea, and we have to suffer for them."

He called to a dapper young man who had just come out from the house toward the corral. "Charlie Mervin! Come here, will you? I want you to shake hands with Mister Murran. You are to witness that we have just wagered ten thousand apiece on the Jericho Mountain race. Crusader to beat Fury."

"But, Colonel," gasped the young Mervin, hurrying up, "who's to ride Crusader?"

"One man," said the colonel, "or no one."

THE CARDBOARD NOTICE

There was no doubt that the colonel regretted his bet ten minutes after it was made. He was heard to walk up and down in his room for a long time that night, before he went to bed. The next morning, early, he rode briskly to the town of Twin Creeks.

In Twin Creeks, he went straight to the house of Sheriff Tom Younger, that man of wisdom and of might.

"Sheriff," he said, "I see you are in health."

"You never seen me no other way," the sheriff assured him. "What might be wrong with you, Colonel Dinsmore?"

"Nothing. I've come to ask you a question."

"Set down and rest your feet, Colonel. What might it be?"

They sat down on the verandah of the old house, about which the huge cottonwoods made a semblance of coolness.

"I've come to talk about Harry Camden."

"It ain't the best thing I'd pick for talkin'," Younger observed.

"I know that. What I wish to know is . . . exactly what is there against Harry Camden?"

"You ask that?" shouted the sheriff. "Why, man, ain't it Harry Camden that stole Crusader?"

"He did," admitted the colonel, "but you know that Crusader is back in his corral."

"Because we made it so hot for the hound that he had to bring back your hoss!"

"Now, Sheriff, that's hardly logical. He proved that he could run away from everything in the countryside while he was on the back of Crusader."

"Him? Not at all! It was luck that saved him the day that he was hunted through the hills."

The colonel had not come to argue in this fashion, so he remained discreetly silent for the moment. Then he went on quietly: "That's the capital charge against him, then, the stealing of Crusader?"

"That? The devil, man . . . I should say not. Ain't it Harry Camden that come in and tried to wreck Twin Creeks?"

"When was that?"

The sheriff groaned at the mere recollection. "That jail was my pride," he said. "There never was a man that broke out or bought his way out. I had steel bars that I could trust. I had guards that I could trust. Then along comes this here Harry Camden. He makes a fool out of the best guard that ever stood over the jail. He busted in, he took out young Ned Manners, and he got clean away with him. Maybe you ain't heard about that more'n a dozen times?" he added sourly. "The boys'll never forget it, nor let me forget it. I ain't been able to mention the jail for months for fear of bein' laughed at."

"And yet," said the rancher, "the man whom Camden took out of the jail was innocent of any crime. He could never be put back into the prison, could he?"

"That ain't the point. We ain't talkin' about young Manners. We're talkin' about this Camden. He's guilty as the devil, partner!"

"And what else besides breaking into the jail?"

"A nacheral born thief. He's swiped stuff from twenty men!"

"I understand about that. When he needs ammunition, he rides to the nearest ranch and takes what he wants, but doesn't he always pay for it in his own way? If he takes food today, he comes down from the hills next week with a load of venison that will feed the whole ranch for three days. Isn't that the way he works it?"

"You can't take the stuff and then try to pay for it later," insisted the sheriff. "It ain't the law. A gent has to be willing to sell what he owns before you can out and buy it. And then pay your own price!"

"But Camden usually pays three times as much as it's worth."

"I dunno . . . I dunno," said the sheriff, frowning and shrugging his shoulders in a manner that very plainly indicated that he was tired of this conversation, or at least a good deal embarrassed by the direction that it was now taking. "The outstandin' fact is that young Harry Camden has made a pile of trouble. Folks don't feel safe ridin' through the mountains. That big devil might jump on 'em. Look at him, ridin' right into this here town and stickin' *me* up . . . right on this here porch, right. . . ." He choked with fury. "Yonder into them bushes he chucked the guns that he took from me." The sheriff drew out a long Colt .45. "And I says to myself then and I says to myself now that someday this here Colt will have a chance to talk right back to him, and say what it's got on its mind!"

"These various thefts," suggested the colonel, "might be compromised, I presume?"

"How d'you mean?"

"If people thought that Camden would pay back the value of any actual claims that they might have against him. . . ."

"I dunno," said the sheriff. "I never heard it put that way."

"How many?" asked the colonel. "How many actual complaints have been lodged against Camden by people who . . . ?"

"Complaints? I hear 'em near every day."

"They want him jailed?"

"Sure. I don't have to ask. He's a crook, ain't he?"

The colonel sighed. It was a difficult proposition to persuade the sheriff. Suddenly he said: "Sheriff Younger, there is preeminently only one thing in which you are interested."

"I dunno till you tell me what."

"The maintenance of the dignity of the law, sir."

"Sure, sure. Speakin' by and large, that's the thing."

"This affair of Camden in Twin Creeks . . . that is what troubles you most?"

"I dunno that I'd say that."

"Surely," said the colonel, "you would hold no malice against this fellow Camden because he liberated from jail a man who was in danger because he was accused of a crime that Camden himself had committed? And if he came to hold you up on this very porch, wasn't it to assure you that the guilt belonged on his own head and not on that of young Manners?"

"Looked at that way," said the sheriff more gently, "there's something in what you say. About him busting into the jail . . . or what he done to me . . . I guess that I ain't aimin' to hold that ag'in' him! Not at all. If the gents that have got claims ag'in' him would give them up . . . he could go free, for all of me."

It was a huge concession, and the colonel instantly took it up.

"I will pay every cent," he said, "of every claim that is made against Camden by any and all. You may publish that. Let people bring their charge and their proof to you, and I'll pay every cent of it without too much debate on the subject."

It staggered the sheriff. He sat for a moment as one dazed. Then he turned his head and examined the features of the colonel cautiously, as though fearing that the offer might be qualified with a smile. But there was no qualification. The colonel was perfectly serious.

"I dunno that I understand," muttered the sheriff. "He swiped your horse and now. . . ."

"He brought back Crusader. Will you do what I ask?"

After all, the sheriff was as generous a man as ever lived. He swore violently a few times. Then he shook hands with the colonel and vowed, with just as much additional profanity, that he would be glad to do as much as he could to give Camden another chance.

That was the reason that, the next day, a singular notice appeared in the *Twin Creeks News*. In a week it brought in merely half a dozen applications for relief. All these were trifling sums. The others who had been plundered by Camden seemed to be willing to let the matter drop, or perhaps they had been so generously repaid in kind that they would have welcomed another visit from the thief. All of those who made application received instantly the cash they demanded from the hand of the editor of the *Twin Creeks News* who asked them, in return, to renounce all legal claims against the criminal who was then at large. It was done.

The criminal record of Harry Camden was so securely purged that there remained against him only the voice of the colonel himself and the sheriff, and the sheriff and the colonel chose to hold their peace.

When the week had ended and the colonel and the sheriff decided that there would be no future applications, Dinsmore went into his room at his ranch and wrote out an announcement in large letters on a stiff piece of cardboard. It read as follows:

> Harry Camden:
> If you will trust yourself to an interview with me, you will find me any night after tonight, and beginning with tonight . . . Tuesday . . . alone in my room, unarmed. I shall be very glad to see you when you choose and will vouch for it that you will learn of matters which will be greatly to your satisfaction.
>
> Robert Oliver Dinsmore

This he carried to the corral fence and tacked it securely to the outer side of a post. Charles Mervin read the sign first and came hurrying into the house.

"Colonel," he said, "do you mean to tell me that you would trust yourself in the hands of that murderous villain . . . alone . . . and actually unarmed?"

"I mean exactly that," said the colonel, who disliked

explanations, and he refused to make further comment. He went to the open air and walked up and down to cool off and adjust his thoughts to this astonishing situation. He had only one desire, and that was to preserve the life of his friend.

PROTECTING THE COLONEL

Certain recollections decided Charles Mervin that it would be folly for him to await the coming of the big man and to try to check the onslaught of Harry Camden. Better, far better, to gather to his aid some man of known talent as a fighter and of unquestioned courage. The two of them, working together, might be able really to protect the rancher.

The person he sought out in the bunkhouse was Dan Johnson, long, freckled, silent, mighty of hand, and deadly with a gun. Dan Johnson listened to the strange story without saying a word, because words were never current coin with the big Swede. But when the story was ended, Dan Johnson took up his sombrero, clamped it hard on his head, girded his guns around his waist—for Dan was a true two-gun man—and then accompanied Charles Mervin to the house.

He agreed implicitly with Mervin that the only thing to do was to sit quietly near the room of the rancher and wait until the man from the mountains came. Then they would strike him down.

"Which it looks like settin' a trap for a lobo," stated Dan Johnson. "It looks sort of sneakin' work."

"What is he?" asked Mervin. "Very much worse than a wolf, in fact. Is he not?"

Dan Johnson was forced to agree. "After all," he said, "he's outlawed. We're safe."

"No longer outlawed," Mervin answered gloomily. "He was brought back inside the law today, because the colonel paid all his debts. And he persuaded the sheriff to drop his grudge. He's back inside the law."

"Suppose we drop him, then?"

"If we find him sneaking into the house? No jury in the country would ever find us guilty for that."

They sat down in the garden, close under the side of a strong hedge, commanding from their position the little balcony on which the two windows of the colonel's room opened. There seemed no reasonable doubt that the man from the mountains would approach the house from this direction, and, coming at them across the open lawn, they would be able to challenge him, and then pick him off as they chose.

It was careful work, however. They had to deal with one who carried with him the brain of a man and the sense equipment of an animal. Therefore, they could not drowse at their post. They had to sweep the lawn constantly and anxiously. They had to watch the road that twisted in a dim white course over the distant hill and into the next valley.

"The colonel believes that Camden is watching the horse pretty closely," said Mervin at last. "You would think that he was confident that Camden came down every night to see the horse."

"Maybe he does," murmured Dan Johnson.

"What?" exclaimed the other. "Comes down here to the ranch and risks his neck to see the horse?"

"We've found the print of his foot four times," said Dan. "Twice it was bare, and, by the size of it, I guess that it was Camden's, all right. Then, over by the watering trough, we seen what looked like the print of a pretty rough-made moccasin. I guess that was Camden again."

"You didn't tell the colonel?"

"What good would it do?"

"He'd double the guards on Crusader. Do you think that he can afford to lose that horse, Johnson?"

Johnson lighted a cigarette. "He's guarded enough. That fence is enough, and they's enough padlocks on the gate to break the heart of any crook that ever tries to get through 'em. No, sir, Camden ain't gonna sashay into that there corral and get away with the hoss. Not unless he had half an hour to cut his way through the fence and a plumb silent saw to do the work for him. Then he might take a chance to get Crusader out, but, just the same, he's been able to get in to the hoss. I guess half a dozen times he's been in to see him. That's why Crusader is dyin' on his feet."

Mervin started. "You think that he's poisoning the horse? Do you think that, Johnson?"

Johnson shook his head. "Seems," he said, "like it would please you a lot to have him turn out the worst skunk in the world. Well, sir, that ain't what I mean. Maybe he's bad, but I dunno that he's bad enough to kill a helpless hoss like Crusader. What I mean is that about the time when Crusader begins to get used to things in the corral and the stall, and about the time that he begins to walk up and down the fence a little bit less, and take a pile more notice of his chuck, along comes Camden again, and the next morning we find old Crusader out there in the corral, starin' at the mountains and neighin' at the hawks over his head, and bustin' his heart to get through that fence and away!"

To this Mervin listened, greatly impressed. "A very queer fellow," he said.

"If he could act like other folks," declared Dan Johnson, "there wouldn't be none better than this here Camden. You take it, by and large, it was pretty square of him to bring back Crusader after the colonel done him that good turn on the trail."

"I fail to see the point," Mervin objected stiffly. "He owed his life to the generosity of the colonel . . . the absurd generosity of the colonel, I think that I may call it. Naturally even the wildest man would wish to make some sort of a return. He could hardly have done otherwise."

At this, Dan Johnson smiled through the darkness. "Look here, Mister Mervin," he said, "I figger what the rest of the boys figger . . . that you got a reason for wanting to see this Camden put out of the way."

"I?" cried Mervin in the strongest protest. "By no means! What on earth could the fellow mean to me?"

"It's only hearsay," said the cowpuncher, and offered no more.

"Tell me what you're driving at," Mervin insisted. "I'd like to know . . . no matter whether or not there's anything in it . . . and, of course, there can't be."

"Of course," said the cowpuncher, "there ain't anything in it, but the boys have got to talk, you know.

There ain't very much else to do, Mister Mervin. What they say, I don't mind tellin', is that you see a good deal of pretty Ruth Manners. Which everybody else would like to, too, if they had the time."

"A lovely girl," admitted Charles Mervin at once. "But what on earth have my calls on Miss Manners to do with this brute, this cave man, Harry Camden?"

"Why," murmured Dan Johnson, with some embarrassment, and straining his eyes toward the other through the darkness of the night, "they say that Harry Camden is sort of interested in the same place, and that maybe you'd like to have him out of the way to get clearer sailin'. I've blurted it all out. There's what folks say. I guess that there ain't nothin' in it."

Mr. Charles Mervin felt very much like the ugly lady of the story who refused to have any mirrors in her house but could not help seeing herself in the water one day as she leaned to drink from the still waters of the pool. So it was with Mervin. He had been telling himself in such a convincing manner that he desired only the protection of the good rancher that he had almost persuaded himself that he had no ulterior motive whatever. Now, being brought up short and checked with the facts of the case, he could not help wincing. For he saw himself and the condition of his mind too clearly. He had never admitted before this moment, really, that he loved Ruth Manners. She had been merely a pretty picture that remained a vast deal of the time in his mind. But now she was something more. He could not avoid seeing that what the cowpunchers rumored among themselves was the truth, the whole truth, and nothing but the truth. He loved Ruth Manners. He dreaded the rivalry of that wild man, that singular will-o'-the-wisp, Harry Camden. How fortunate it would be if he could brush the thought of Camden from the mind of the girl forever—with a bullet!

He recovered from the brown study into which he had fallen. He looked to the cowpuncher. "Of course," said Mervin, "this is a very serious thing. Of course, there's nothing in it."

"Sure," said the good-natured companion. "I'm just telling you. Leave it go at that."

They became silent again, as they watched a lantern carried from the bunkhouse toward the corral, the immense, shadowy legs of the carrier swaying dimly across the fences and the barns as he strode like a giant. Then the lantern was swallowed in the black mouth of a barn. From the belly of the barn it cast forth only an occasional ray or sparkle. All the rest was darkness. In the darkness nothing lived, nothing stirred, except an occasional whispering of the wind in the big oak tree that grew on the farther side of the hedge and extended its strong branches across the place where they sat. They held their breath and waited.

"Could he get up to the house from the far side of the hedge?" Mervin asked of his companion in a sudden whisper.

"No chance of that. He'd have to get across the hedge before he could come at the house, I guess."

"Johnson!"

"Well?"

"Look sharp!"

"D'you hear something?"

"I *feel* something."

"What you mean?"

"There's a danger near us, Johnson. I can feel the chill of it in my bones."

"The devil, Mister Mervin," said the other sharply.

"What could there be that's wrong? Just look around you. There ain't a thing." He added: "I guess you been thinkin' about this till you got all wrought up and. . . ." Here, as he raised his head toward the tree, his voice ended in a gasp. He had no chance or time to cry out. There was only a brief gurgling sound that formed vaguely from the hollow of his throat.

Mervin glanced sharply up in the same direction, and he had scant time to glimpse a body descending from the limb of the tree that arched above them. The form struck Dan Johnson and crumpled the big cowpuncher against the ground as if he were a figure of brittle paper.

Mervin himself had barely time to snatch the revolver from his pocket, but he did not have time to press the trigger with his finger before the form of the assailant lifted himself from the helpless body of Johnson. Then there was revealed to the terrified Mervin no wild beast, but a thing in the shape of a man that sprang at him from all fours, like a very beast, indeed.

A hand whose fingers threatened to crush the bones of his wrist first fastened upon him, and the gun fell to the ground. Then a fist that struck, as a club strikes, landed with full force across the side of his jaw, and darkness dropped heavily across his brain.

When he recovered, he was dangling in mid-air, with the brightness of the stars swimming dizzily above his eyes. A moment later he had recovered enough of his senses to know that he was being carried through the balcony window and into the room of the rancher. Then he was caught by the nape of the neck, and thrust forward at arm's length by the big man who had captured him. Before him sat the colonel himself, staring wildly at this odd scene.

"I came along trustin' to your word, Colonel," said the deep rumbling voice of Harry Camden. "And this is part of what I found waitin' to murder me!"

CAMDEN TO RIDE CRUSADER

The surprise, the grief, the fury of the colonel made him half rise from his chair and then fall back into it. After this, he fastened his glance upon the white face of young Mervin and saw a great blue and red lump forming on the side of his jaw. Certainly that youth had received at least a partial punishment to reward him for his ill doing.

"Mervin," he said at last, "I am trying to believe that this thing is a dream. Do you mean to say that you attacked Camden when he came to the house upon my public and special invitation?"

"It was for the sake of your own safety, Colonel," stammered Mervin. "If Camden will stop choking me. . . ."

He was released, and sank into a chair where he fumbled at his throat and lay back breathing hard. He had received a shock far more severe mentally than physically.

"We were afraid, sir," he said at last, "that this man would do you some harm."

"Camden," said the colonel, turning his back on Mervin, "I hope you will believe me when I tell you that I had nothing to do with this . . . unhappy affair?"

The big man nodded. "There ain't any harm done," he said. "Let him run along and keep away from me, though. It sort of works me up, Colonel, to look at him."

"Mervin," the colonel said coldly, "I cannot help thinking that Mister Camden is very generous . . . and gives you very good advice. I'll talk with you later about this affair."

So Mervin, with a final glance of grief and rage at his conqueror, rose and left the room. The colonel had pointed out a chair that Camden took. Two hundred pounds of brawn and bone, he gave an impression of far greater size. He seemed a giant. His clothes, perhaps, helped toward that impression. They were primitive things. A flap of skin sewed roughly together served as moccasins. His trousers were frayed through at the knees. Undressed deerskin made his jacket. He carried no gun. There was only a long sheath knife at his belt, cased in a homemade scabbard of horsehide. His hat was a battered piece of old felt, faded from its original black to green. From under its short brim a brown, big-featured face and bright, steady eyes looked out at the colonel.

"Camden," said the colonel, "before I'm through talking, you will understand how greatly it would be to my disinterest to plan such an attack on you . . . to say nothing of what a man of honor would feel about such a matter."

Camden made a gesture that dismissed the entire story of the attack that had been planned against him. "Honest men," he said, "are like black foxes. You can tell 'em by a look. I wouldn't be here, Colonel, if I had any sort of a doubt about you."

At this, the colonel sighed with relief. "It's about Crusader," he said at last.

"You still got him," said the big man, snapping out the words. "That fence of yours is hard for me to beat. But I'll figger out a way, pretty soon."

"Perhaps," said the colonel, "you will not have to plan. I want to ask you, in the first place, if you think that with you on his back any horse in this country could beat Crusader on a cross-country ride?"

Camden smiled. "That ain't worth talkin' about," he declared. "I got no money to put up . . . otherwise, I'd make a bet. I mean, if I was on the real Crusader . . . not the skinny old black hoss that you got in your corral."

"Take Crusader with you," said the colonel bluntly. "Handle him as you please. Get him in shape. You still have five weeks. In the meantime, I'll enter his name in the Jericho Mountain race. Camden, will you ride him in that for me?"

"And afterward?" Camden asked sharply.

"Why, afterward . . . ," the voice of the colonel trailed away. It was what he had known must come into their discussion.

"I've arranged matters with the sheriff," he said. "You are now a citizen in good standing in the community, Camden. The law has no hold on you. I thought that, considering this small service, you might be willing to handle Crusader and ride him in the race for me. For that, plus a considerable sum of money, of course."

Camden shook his head. "The law don't bother me

none," he observed. "It's sort of a game to play with it, Colonel. What gents have done for me was never none too gentle. What the law has done for me ain't been none too gentle, either." He thrust out his great crag-like jaw as he spoke. "I don't ask no favors," said Camden. "I don't give none. I got no regrets about what I've done. I got no regrets about what others have done to me. It's a fight, and I like fightin'. I was made for it, and I was trained for it. And I ain't got the worst of the game yet. Now, what we're talkin' about is Crusader. I ride him in this race and win it for . . . *you!*" He put a solemn accent on the last word. "Me and Crusader walk around and get used to one another again," he continued. "And when we're pretty friendly, then I got to bring him back to your corral and put him up there? Colonel, I dunno that I'd better try it. I might do my best to get that hoss back into your corral, but it might be too hard for me to do it. Colonel, you been square with me, and I want to be square with you. Don't ask too much out of me."

It was perhaps the longest speech that Harry Camden had made before in his entire life; certainly never again, thereafter, did he say so much consecutively. Even the colonel was astonished.

"Crusader's disposition has changed," he said. "Do you think that you could still handle him?"

"I figger that I could, maybe," said the big man.

"Suppose we go out and see."

They left the house and went to the forty-acre run; the colonel unlocked the gate, and they entered. Before the first lock had been snapped behind them, a rush and a whir of hoofs sounded in their ears.

"Crusader's got my scent," Camden announced as the colonel shrank away for safety and even laid a hand on the rail of the fence to climb out of the enclosure.

The mighty hand of Camden fell upon his shoulder and drew him back. "There ain't nothin' to fear," said the man of the mountains. "Crusader won't do you any harm. He won't see nothin' but me." With this, he stepped boldly forward and met the charge of the black monster.

There was only enough starlight for the colonel to see what followed, but that starlight was enough. He watched Crusader dance and plunge and frolic around Camden. He saw the great stallion rear as though he would beat the man into the ground, but his fore hoofs descended gently. He saw the horse frolic like a dog that cannot show its joy except with its teeth on its master's hand.

When at last Crusader came to a pause, his head held high, the arch was back in his long neck and his eyes were glittering again. Magic had transformed him. Camden came slowly forward, with the horse following at his heels.

"It is a marvelous thing," said the colonel, with all of his heart in his voice. "It is a very great thing, my friend. Will you tell me how you managed it?"

"By never usin' a whip," Camden said. "And by lookin' at him the same way that you look at a man. When you look at a man, you figger on what is goin' on behind his eyes. When most folks look at a hoss, they don't figger on nothin' except how he's actin' . . . what he's doin' with his heels . . . his head, and all that. But a hoss has got a mind. A hoss has got a soul. If they's a heaven, Colonel, and I can get there, it'll be on Crusader's back. If they's a hell and I land there, Crusader, he'd come rarin' and tearin' down to hell and take me plumb out. That's about the way of it."

The colonel, although he was a hardheaded man, saw and watched and believed even those extravagant words. "In fact," he said, "Crusader is your horse, Camden. I've paid money for him. But you've made him know his master." He sighed bitterly. "I've never been able to touch that horse, Camden, unless at least two men were holding him."

"Colonel," said the wild man, "you can't hold no hoss like this with a rope. But you could walk around him and lay a hand on him where you pleased."

"Do you mean that?"

"I mean just that."

The colonel gathered his courage like a robe about him. He advanced. He stretched out a tentative hand. Crusader snorted and tossed his head. "He'd tear my arm off," breathed the colonel, stepping back.

"He won't touch you," insisted Camden. "Try him." He added to the horse a brief word—or perhaps it was a mere wordless murmur. At any rate, it made Crusader stand like a rock.

The colonel with fear and delight in his soul touched that fine head fairly between the nose and ran his fingers lightly down to the velvet of the muzzle. Crusader did not stir, nor did he move when the colonel slipped his hand down the silken neck of the stallion.

"Camden," he said, "if my heart were big enough to do such a thing, I'd give this horse to you. Because it's to you that he belongs. But I'll do something else, which is as generous as I can be. If you'll ride him in the Jericho race, I'll lend him to you for six months. If you win the race, you can have him for a year."

"And then?" asked Camden.

"Then we'll see."

There was a pause, during which Camden stared through the dim light at the face of the colonel.

"He's your hoss," he said. "And I'd go to hell and back for the sake of ridin' him only one day."

CAMDEN'S RESOLVE

The whole force of the big Dinsmore ranch stood about to see the famous Harry Camden ride famous Crusader away from the corral, but they were disappointed. He did not even mount the stallion. When the gate was unlocked, Camden entered and came out with Crusader behind him. Straight across the plains toward the mountains walked Camden, and just behind him jogged Crusader, his flanks a series of highlights and shadows, so deep were the hollows between his ribs.

Those who hunted for sensations followed the wild man across the plain for some time, until Harry Camden turned back on the riders and drew a long Winchester from the holster that ran diagonally down the blanket which he used in lieu of a saddle on the great horse. The view of that rifle served instead of a harangue. The followers observed, noted, and departed with haste.

Camden went on for the mountains. Crusader was lean and weak with leanness. The journey through the foothills was most exhausting, but Camden knew what he wanted, and he pressed relentlessly forward until he had climbed above the first range, and then journeyed laboriously on to the second. On the farther side of the crest he found the place. It was a narrow plateau, perhaps half a mile wide and eight or ten miles in length. It was fenced away from sheep and cattle or even the deer by the precipitous rocky slopes on either side. To be sure, the mountain sheep, those irresistible climbers, loved that airy pasture and were often near it, but they did not come in sufficient numbers to deplete its stores seriously. The bunch grass, that finest of all food for cattle, grew thick on this upland. The sun had cured it as well, and better than the finest haymakers in the world could have done. It was sweet to the tooth of Crusader.

There he ate his fill morning, noon, and night, and, when he cared for water, there was a rill that tumbled down from the eastern height and pooled itself in a little crystal lake at one end of the plateau. He had exercise, too, even during those days of the up-building of his strength. He was ridden at a gentle pace up and down the plateau with the weight of Harry Camden on his back, first walking, then trotting, then cantering, but, inside of a week, Camden let him gallop.

Another week and a third ended, before he was willing to loose the reins on Crusader, but, as the third week terminated, he would sometimes cry aloud to the big black stallion and send him winging over the rolling surface at breakneck speed. It was not running, it was flying, and the horse loved it as much as a man.

Once a week Colonel Dinsmore traveled up into the

foothills, and Camden brought the great stallion down. Every week, as he saw the changes in the big animal, the colonel marveled. The first seven days worked a great transformation. By the end of the first fortnight—the original and natural strength of Crusader showed through his shining coat, and the big ropy muscles working plainly.

"I am going back to bet against the field," Colonel Dinsmore said. "And the field is growing every moment, Camden. The entry fee is raised to a hundred dollars for every horse, and there are over sixty entries. Think of it, Camden! They have Thoroughbreds from England and from France. They have Arabs, Kentucky-bred. They have an Arabian mare that has been shipped all the way from the desert of Arabia. They have mustangs of the pure hell-fire breed. There are a few mongrels of the range . . . crosses of unknown blood, but every one a horse of tried endurance. Every one of them is being worked across the mountains now. They are growing used to the rocks and the steep places. There is only one devil that worries me, Camden. You are a big fellow . . . and Crusader is a big horse. Won't your own weight kill you? The best climbers ought in reason to be the small tough horses with the very light riders. What will Crusader do among the rocks?"

Camden opened his lips to speak, but apparently he decided that argument or illustration was useless. He merely stated a calm conviction: "Crusader will not be beaten," he said, and there let the matter rest.

After all, it is much easier to put faith in miracles than in common sense. There is in every man a desire to believe in the impossible. So it was with the colonel. He stared at the giant, formed a question in his mind, and then decided that it would be well enough to let matters stand unexamined. If this strange fellow, this child of nature, this unexplained mystery among men, was certain that he could win the race with Crusader, by all means let the thought be cherished in him. So felt the colonel, and, half an hour afterward, he was started for his ranch again.

He was gone some time before Harry Camden remembered that he had not yet asked a most important question concerning the course over which the race was to be run. For rocks and for mountains he would answer for the big stallion. But he must know the nature of that wide stretch of desert south of Jericho Mountain over which they must pass. If it were firm ground, let the heat and the distance be what it might, the confidence of Camden would not alter. But if it were soft sand, that was very different. For, in that case, Crusader must be given work in the same footing. He must be trained to plod patiently through sand, fetlock-deep, and learn the art of desert travel. For it *is* an art, and a horse that attempts to fight his way through will exhaust his strength quickly, whereas the horse that goes delicately, putting down the hoof flat and without a drive, gets on famously well. Camden had seen mustangs cross the desert sands with almost the ease of camels. This was the question for the answer to which he hastened after the colonel. He blanketed Crusader again, leaped onto his back, and presently was coursing down the side of the long mountain in pursuit.

The colonel, however, must have taken advantage of the fine spirits of his horse and loosed the reins on it, for it was nowhere to be seen, although Camden could see plainly the sign of its trail along the slope. He prepared himself for a longer chase, therefore, and he had just drawn back Crusader to a swinging, effortless long gallop, when he saw another rider had cut in and followed the same course.

Presently, in fact, he saw the horse and rider looming ahead of him, with the sun flashing on the sweating flanks of the animal. He recognized the horse at once. It was the fine mare of Charles Mervin, a beautiful brown mare with a white-stockinged left fore leg and another white-stockinged right hind leg. By that mark alone he could have recognized the animal, but, even without those marks, he felt that he would have known the rider. It was Mervin himself, and of all men in the world he was least welcome to the eye of Harry Camden, for this was the most ardent suitor of Ruth Manners; this was he who, as Camden had reason to believe, was the favored lover of the girl. Even now Mervin was changing the direction of his mare and turning her toward that point of the compass where the Manners' house lay.

It seemed odd to Camden. Here was a man from the household of Dinsmore who had ridden in the colonel's direction far up into the mountains; and yet he had not accompanied Dinsmore. Certainly he must have known that the colonel was riding, and where. Why, then, had Mervin chosen to go alone? Why was he not returning now in the company of the colonel? What had brought Mervin here among the highlands?

To see Crusader. There seemed no other object. Why, then, had he wished to see the stallion in secret, and spy upon the big horse from a distance?

Any one of these questions would have caused Camden to follow the other. He swung away from the trail of Dinsmore and followed close on the trail of

Mervin, keeping just out of sight, with always one range of hills between him and the other. They dipped out of the higher and steeper hills. They came into rolling ground in the dusk of the day, and at last, as he had surmised, Mervin came through the evening to the little hollow in which the Manners' house stood.

He reined Crusader into a clump of trees and stared gloomily down at the little shack; it brought back to him with a bitter vividness two great moments in his life—the happiest and the most tragic. Then the door of the house opened, and Mervin came out with the girl. Neither her father nor her brother was with them. It was another small touch that deepened the surety of Camden. For why should she wish to walk with young Mervin alone through the dusk of the day unless she loved him? So, with a swelling heart, Camden watched them walking up the hill. He feared, for a moment, that they were bound for the trees where he sat with Crusader, but they turned past him and strolled by so near that he could well nigh make out their faces through the shadows. All that they said was perfectly clear. They were talking of what most people in that district had in their minds most vividly at this time—the Jericho race.

"Ned has been to Twin Creeks to hear the talk," said the voice of Ruth. "Everyone is talking about the two Arabs . . . Ali and Musa. Have you seen them?"

"They may do well enough across the flat," Mervin said authoritatively. "But they'll never last in the mountains. That's where they'll fail. Is Ned betting?"

"Of course! Every man is. You can guess whom he picked out?"

"I can't imagine."

"Crusader!"

"Ah?" said the other. "It looks as though he'll have the most backing . . . at least from people around here. They've heard so much about him. But I don't think he'll ever start."

"Why not?"

"No one but Camden can ride him."

"Why shouldn't Camden ride him?"

"Too heavy, for one thing. But aside from that, he'll never get into the saddle to ride that race."

"What do you mean?"

"It's very simple. You know that all the horses and all the riders have to be in Jericho for a week before the race. That's arranged this year so that the crowds can look them over and make their choices, of course. Well, Ruth, can you imagine Camden living among other men for a whole week . . . among rough fellows such as will be in Jericho? He'll have a fistfight the first day and a gunfight the second, and, when the race begins, he'll be resting in jail. Sheriff Younger has sworn that if Camden so much as raises a hand, he'll take no further chances, but lock him up. And you can't blame the sheriff, can you?"

At this, she paused and faced Mervin. "You hate him, don't you?" she asked.

"Camden? Certainly not!"

"Well," she said, after a pause during which Camden hungered to hear her speak in his defense, "I suppose that you're right. He's nothing but a wild man. I suppose he'd kill a man with no more thought than most people would kill a chicken. Did you ever notice his eyes?"

"Yes."

"It makes me shiver just to think of them . . . but I hope he wins."

"Why?"

"Ned has followed a hunch. He's bet every cent he can put his hands on that Crusader will win. I don't know what we'll do if he fails."

In the darkness among the trees, as he passed on, the big man formed two solemn resolutions. The first was that Crusader should not lose if he ran the race; the second was that nothing under heaven should tempt him to any act of violence that would keep him from riding.

MERVIN DECIDES AGAINST CAMDEN

He waited to hear and see no more. He reined Crusader back into the night and fled softly back toward the mountains.

Having strolled to the rim of the hollow, the girl and Mervin came back again. They no longer talked of the race. It was quite another subject, quite another tone. Mervin was telling her plainly and forcefully that he was breaking his heart on her account, and that he would die without her. At this, the heartless girl laughed. Oh, that Camden could have been near to hear that laughter, for it would have taken a great burden from his mind.

That same mirth made Mervin stand very straight and stiff, and grow extremely red.

She explained at once, and without embarrassment. "I'm mighty flattered by all that you've been saying," she told him. "But, of course, I don't believe a word of it. You like me because I'm different. Not because you have to have me. I'm not the kind of girl that you're used to in the East. But suppose we were married. Do you think it would turn out well? Could you get along in country like this? Or could I get along in the city?"

"If you let me take the chance. . . ."

"That would be a wild gamble," Ruth Manners stated.

At this, he looked at her sharply, through the dark. In fact, he was immensely pleased by this mental acuteness. He was not one of those who care for a clinging vine as a wife. He liked cleverness, and she was very clever. She saw through him just far enough to make him nervous, although he still felt that the secrets of his nature were securely kept from her.

"If you really cared for a man," he said, "would you ask all of these questions, and have all of these doubts about East and West and city and country?"

"I guess not," Ruth answered with stunning frankness. "That's partly why I know that I don't care for you enough to marry you safely, Charles. My idea of love is a thing that will carry me off on wings. I won't be able to help myself."

"You'll never find a man in the world," Charles Mervin said with infinite conviction, "who'll be able to take you so far off your feet as that."

Her answer took his breath. "I've already met one who did . . . almost."

"What?" cried Mervin.

"I have only talked with him once, and that was the strangest talk any woman ever had with any man. He's the only man I was ever afraid of. If he wanted my love, I think he could take it, whether I wanted him or not."

Mervin could not believe his ears. "What man is that?" he asked finally.

"I couldn't tell you his name."

"Why not? If I know what you really like, perhaps I could make myself more after that pattern."

At this she laughed again, but with such an open frankness that he could not read malice into the sound.

"I laugh," she said, "because, if you knew his name, you'd be horrified. There's nobody in the world like him, Charles."

"By Jove," cried Mervin, "I think you're more than half in love with this man already, without knowing it!"

She was silent for a moment. He feared that he had offended her, until she spoke again, thoughtfully. "Perhaps I am," she said. "I don't know, really. Perhaps I am."

"I mean," he said, "that you may be caught by some foolish illusion. . . ." He corrected himself with haste. "I don't intend that as it sounds. But you see, sometimes even the strongest-minded people are taken off their balance by strange things. . . ."

"And what could be stranger than a wild man?" asked the girl, nodding in the night.

"A wild man?"

"Just that."

A chill of conviction darted through him. "Ruth," he cried, "you're talking about that inhuman devil . . . big Harry Camden!"

The words came out before he knew it—before he was prepared for them. He would have given a great deal to recall them after it was too late—after he realized the absurdity of what he had said. But the greatest shock of all was her answer.

"How did you guess that, Charles?"

"I'm right, then?" breathed Mervin. "It's Camden whom you prefer to me . . . I mean. . . ."

"Don't ask me," the girl advised. "I don't know. I can't think. My mind's all whirling. Charles, I'm going in."

He did not attempt to restrain her, but he watched the door open, saw her stand for an instant against the rectangle of yellow lamplight, then saw her disappear beyond the black wall of the house.

So Mervin went slowly to his horse, and mounted it, and began to ride hard through the night. He had made up his mind not ten seconds after the girl had spoken. What he decided was, first of all, that she was far more deeply attracted by Camden than she herself realized. In the second place, the form of Harry Camden loomed upon his eye again. He had always thought of him as a mere abysmal brute. He looked back into the picture of the man now and felt that he saw in it something that might prove attractive even to a woman—especially to a vigorous-minded girl like Ruth Manners. She had touched the huge fellow with the wand of romance and converted him, in a trice, into a hero. All that was strange about him helped the illusion. Charles Mervin, shuddering, nodded with a deeper conviction. If he desired her in the first place as his own wife, he desired her in the second place to save her from the terrible fate of becoming the bride of such a creature as Camden, that mighty-handed wild brute who happened to wear the form of a man.

Consequently, before the door had closed upon her, he had decided that the next step in his courtship of the lady should preferably be the removal of Camden from his path as a rival. He was a brisk young man, this

Charles Mervin. Now that he had made up his mind, he saw that two things could be accomplished in one mission.

He covered five miles of country until he came to the house that he had in mind. It was the remnant of what had once been a great ranch. The house itself had been a huge three-story affair, with four wooden turrets, each with a single hexagonal room in it, set off with six shuttered windows. The main part of the building was on an equal scale.

Even in the flourishing times of the ranch, there had never been a need for a house half of this size, and, since the fortunes of the Loring family had fallen into a decline, it had been a great white elephant on the hands of the descendants of that first Loring who had made fame and fortune raising cattle. Twin Creeks had known him as its first rich citizen. Now it knew Pete Loring, his descendant two generations removed, as one of its most penniless vagabonds.

For Pete was too filled with the greatness of his family in the past to be contented with any mere job as a rider on the range. He could ride and rope and shoot with the best of them, but the only accomplishment on which he prided himself and which he took pains to cultivate was his natural skill with a gun. For ability as a warrior was not out of key with the talents of a gentleman. Pete felt that the other accomplishments of a cowpuncher were rather to be frowned upon in himself. He had grown up in the last flush of the Loring prosperity, when they were still able to spend freely. He had as good an education as money was able to buy for him, and in a high-priced school he had picked up a taste for tailor-made cigarettes and wine. He had learned how to dress and how to talk as befitted a gentleman. His manners were smooth; his address could be ingratiating when he chose to make it so.

But, as a rule, he did not choose, for he felt that his neighbors about Twin Creeks were frankly below him. Moreover, he knew that the rough people in that vicinity were in the habit of smiling at his pride behind his back. They feared to affront him face to face because of his dreadful certainty with a gun. At the same time, among hard-working, careless-mannered cowpunchers and cowmen, he was considered in the light of a somber joke.

All of this, because he was a sensitive man, he realized perfectly. It deepened the hatred and contempt with which he repaid their scorn. It gave a darker shadow to his character. He still felt that all of those prosperous ranches that had been split off, morsel by morsel, from the great mass of the one-time Loring estate, were owned by people who had pirated their wealth from his ancestors. He considered himself their victim. When he saw their fine horses and their careless expenditures, he begrudged them all of their dollars.

Strange fancies grow up in an idle brain, and in the mind of young Peter Loring there was born a belief that, sooner or later, he was certain to have redress in some manner. The land that had once belonged to his forefathers, he felt should still be in the family, and he had a sort of sacred and inalienable right upon it. That this viewpoint might have been considered rather amusing by the men of the law never once occurred to him. In fact, he saw nothing amusing in himself. When he thought of himself, it was of a tragic figure, far above the pity of the world, but well worthy of its awe.

These were the things that Charles Mervin had learned soon after the first of his long visits to Colonel Dinsmore. The only man in the neighborhood who was of breeding and refinement enough to be a companion to him, outside of the colonel himself, was young Loring. But these were the details that made a meeting with Loring impossible. He remembered all of this, while he surveyed the romantic, dark outlines of the big house that towered above him, and listened to the banging of a ruined shutter in the rising wind.

Then a horse neighed loudly from the tangle of corrals that lay in the near distance, and the heart of Mervin grew stronger in him, for he was recalled to an identity of interest that he had with Loring, and the talking point on which he could open his call.

FACING PETE LORING

He dismounted at the hitching rack, tethered Flight, his mare, and advanced to the front door of the house, turning over in his mind the words with which he would introduce his subject. He was somewhat in trouble as he contemplated this thought. From what he had heard of young Peter Loring, that worthy might take it in mind to butcher his guest for daring to make the suggestions Mervin intended. Or else, he might decide to publish the proposals abroad and crush Mervin forever with the scorn of the world.

Mervin flushed hotly, and then turned quite cold. He was still pale, but resolved, when he gave his summons at the front door, which was opened after a considerable time by an old servant, his back bowed and his head thrust forth by the withering touch of time. His toothless mouth, pursed together as he stared at the stranger, seemed struggling to suppress a grin of malicious glee. But when he heard the name of the visitor, he nodded and asked Mervin in.

"Mister Loring," he said, "is resting after his dinner, sir, but I will tell him you have come . . . if you will sit down."

He hobbled away, and Mervin looked about him with a particular interest. Poverty was what he wanted to see. Poverty, that strong alembic in which the good of human nature is so often distilled away and only the dregs of evil remain behind. There was all that he could have wished. The lofty hall, whose arched ceiling was vaulted over with shadows two stories above, contained for furniture a mirror with a wretched little table standing beside it and a single tottering chair. Along the walls, the heavy woodwork had warped with the moisture of winters and the dry heat of summers; it stood out in gaping seams; it waved along the wall. Along the unpainted floor a pale path was worn by the passage of many feet from the front door to the next room.

Mervin noted these things and felt at the same time a chill of dread and of relief. The dread was inspired by the feeling that this man had been wronged by the world—that he must inevitably have been so, or else his condition could never have been like this. Those who have been wronged by society, repay society, in turn, with an unfailing, deathless passion for destruction.

The older servant was gone for some time, and, during his absence, Mervin heard certain stealthy sounds in the distance, as of furniture being quietly moved. He smiled, and the traces of the smile had not yet left his eyes when the old man returned and ushered him into an adjoining room.

It was bare as a tomb. The curtain rods were still rusting in their brackets, but the curtains were long since gone. A rag rug made a small patch on the wide, worn surface of the floor, and there were a few old chairs that had once been splendidly upholstered with leather. Rough usage had split away the leather here and there, and the contents were oozing forth—rolls of stiff padding.

The central piece was a table over the top of which, apparently, a cloth had been thrown—and thrown very recently and hastily, to judge by the wrinkles in it. An exposed corner of the surface of the table was notched with old brown and black marks where cigarette stubs had burned out, and in an easy chair beside the table sat Peter Loring himself, reading. The shaded oil lamp marked a path of light across his breast and over the slender, bony hands that supported the book. The rest of the man was in the dark. It was not until he had put aside the book and advanced to meet Mervin that the latter could make out his features. Then he recalled having seen the man before—riding a brown horse with two white legs—the same horse, in fact, whose description had in the first place inspired his visit this night.

Peter Loring was still known as Young Pete because in the background of the time behind him there loomed the grand form of Old Peter, gaunt, gray, taciturn, kindly. But he was well over thirty, and looked even older. He was a yellow-skinned, unhealthy-looking fellow with sunken black eyes and remarkably heavy black eyebrows that ran in a level, unbroken line across his forehead. On his coat were dim white spots—cigarette ashes that had recently been hastily brushed away, and the whole room was thick and rank with the heavy sweetness of the Egyptian tobacco.

"I am Charles Mervin," said the visitor.

"I'm very glad to know you," said Loring. "Will you take this chair?"

"I won't disturb you. . . ."

"If you please," said Loring, rather imperiously. "Because, as a matter of fact, the others cannot be offered to a guest."

He added this with a slight lifting of his chin and a flare of hostile light in his eyes, which Mervin avoided instinctively. But he took the chair that was pointed out to him with no further argument.

"You are staying with Colonel Dinsmore?" asked the other.

"The colonel has brought me out here a number of times. He knows that I love the open. And there's no open country in the East, you know. All too intimate. Little rolling hills . . . towns everywhere . . . a hand-made countryside. Very different from the West, you know."

To the majority of this speech, Loring replied with a gloomy nod, and all that he cared to say in answer was: "In the life of my father, sir, we saw a good deal of Colonel Dinsmore. I might even say that he was a family friend. But our fortunes have changed. Lately, the colonel, I may say, is a most infrequent visitor. A very rare pleasure to have a glimpse of him here." These last words came out in a drawling voice with a covered snarl of danger behind.

"The colonel," Mervin said defensively, "is such a gay fellow and has so many friends that I suppose we all see not half as much of him as we'd like to."

"Perhaps . . . perhaps," muttered Loring, with his habitual frown. "I haven't offered you a cigarette?" He lighted the smoke ceremoniously for Mervin.

"This is good stuff!" exclaimed the latter.

The dry tinder of Loring's temper instantly caught fire. "We have fallen very low, indeed," he said, "but still we can afford a bit of the best tobacco, Mister Mervin." He drew himself into a frozen silence, guarded with a mirthless smile.

Mervin was appalled. He had been prepared for a difficult interview, but this man was impossible of handling, it seemed. The high hopes that he had begun to build into the sky, he felt crumbling beneath his touch. He saw that he must strike into the nature of his business if he wished to make any headway whatever.

"You are riding a horse in the Jericho race?" he suggested at last.

"One must be amused," answered Loring. "I was able to rake together enough cash for the entry fee. As well that as to pay grocery bills, eh?" Once more his sour smile dared Mervin to show the slightest hint of surprise or even of amusement.

"You are a lover of horses, I see," Mervin said, trying another tack.

"Not at all," replied Loring. "Not at all. In fact, I frankly confess that I despise the sentimental bosh that a good many men of apparent sense talk about horseflesh. A horse is a dumb beast. If it was designed by God for any useful purpose, it was designed to be a slave to men, and any thing that is a slave is worth nothing but contempt. I have a truer respect for a mule than for a horse, Mister Mervin. I assure you that I respect a mule more because, though we may compel it to serve us, it serves us with frank hatred all the days of its life."

This cool doctrine he enunciated slowly, and his deep black eyes searched the face of Mervin slowly, carefully, for the faintest trace of dissent. As for Mervin, he was half inclined to think that the man was under the influence of liquor. He had never seen before so much wicked devil in any human. Perversity was the one controlling passion in the life of Loring, it seemed.

"A very sensible way of looking at it," Mervin stated, determined to be pleased in appearance. "As you say, there is a great deal of bosh talked at one time or another about horses. I understand, by the way, that the horse you ride greatly resembles mine."

"Perhaps," Loring said carelessly.

"In fact," insisted Mervin, making his point with some solemnity, "I understand that the resemblance is very great."

At this, Loring raised his brows, frowned as though he were hunting to find something offensive in this remark, and then shrugged his shoulders. "I suppose . . . ," he began, but before he had a chance to end the sentence, the door at the farther end of the room opened suddenly, and Mervin had a glimpse of a short, wide-shouldered man standing in the opening, with a broad, blunt-featured face. He had seen ugly men before, but never before one in whom the expression was so thoroughly evil as that of him who stood in the doorway, gave them a single glance, and then hastily and noiselessly closed the door again and was gone. Into the mind of Mervin ran certain odd tales that circulated now and again through the countryside to the effect that Loring, unable to gain a revenue in any other way, had confederated himself with a scattering of criminals and gave them refuge in times of stress in his big house.

"I suppose," Loring continued steadily, fixing those grim eyes of his upon Mervin, "that there are vague resemblances between horses as there are between people, eh?"

Mervin endured that stare very well. The danger in this man was stimulating as well as nerve straining. "I'd like to have you look at my horse. She's at the rack in front of your house now."

Loring hesitated for a long moment—long enough to allow Mervin to see that he had no desire to bestir himself. At length he rose, for courtesy could not permit him to refuse the invitation, particularly because of the pointed manner in which the other gave it. So they went out, carrying a lantern with them, and stood before the brown mare.

AN EXCELLENT ASSISTANT MURDERER

The first exclamation of Loring relieved the mind of Mervin of one anxiety.

"Why," he cried, "you have Sally Ann, here!" So striking was the resemblance between the two. But he added, raising the lantern and stepping closer to the head of the mare: "No, not Sally Ann. She's a shade smaller, I think. And . . . no . . . there's a barbed-wire nick in the left ear of Sally Ann. . . ."

"Hush," whispered Mervin. "Not so loud, if you please."

Loring whirled on him with a scowl. "I don't understand you, sir," he said stiffly.

"You shall, presently," answered Mervin. "But what I want you first to look to are the points of similarity. Would anyone other than yourself be able to tell the difference between the two? That is what I want to know."

Loring favored him with another stare in which, however, there was as much sheer curiosity as there was disapproval. Then, without a word, he went over the horse from head to heel. He came back and made a terse report.

"The stocking on the rear leg, there, is a bit longer than Sally Ann's. Otherwise . . . and I think I know the points of a horse fairly well . . . there's hardly a hair's difference between 'em. And, now, Mister Mervin?"

"I think that we could talk a trifle better in the house," said Mervin.

"This begins to become a mystery."

"I hope it will be one to your liking," Mervin said more pointedly than before.

At this, Loring paused abruptly on the way to the house and turned the light of the lantern into the eyes of Mervin. What he saw there was doubtless firm resolution and that shade of desperation that comes into the face of any man who has resolved beyond recall upon a dishonest action, or a criminal one of any nature.

"Well," said Loring, "it may be. . . ." He led on into the house and to the room that they had recently occupied. There he laid his hands upon the table and looked across it at his guest. "I like short talk," he said at last. "Now, Mervin, what do you want from me?"

"To begin with, I'm in need of money, Mister Loring," Mervin explained, growing a trifle red in spite of the long rehearsal of this speech. "I'm in need of money. . . ."

"And you presume, sir, that I am in need, also?"

"I presume nothing. I have come here to make a . . . business . . . proposal. No more."

"Very well. I'll hear you out."

"There are various ways of making money, and one

of the quickest and easiest ways, I understand, is to bet a small sum on a horse race."

Loring made a gesture. "I have lost money," he said, "in a great variety of fashions. I have lost money investing it in real estate. I have lost in mines and in cattle. All of these ways seem fairly expedite when one wishes to decrease a bank account. But I know of no way in which one can lose more money, or lose it faster, than by betting on horses."

"Exactly," Mervin said. "But if one could be more than reasonably sure. . . ."

"You have a system, I see," broke in Loring with an uncontrolled sneer. "A system? One system cost me ten thousand. I have never had any appetite to try out a second. Betting systems are short cuts to suicide, my friend."

Still Mervin endured and persisted. "This system of mine," he said, "has never been tried before. I want to ask you, in the first place, if you think that your horse has a good chance of winning the Jericho?"

"I have paid the entry fee," Loring said in his disagreeable way, "and I expect to ride the race myself. I suppose that's your answer. I would not make the effort if I did not think that I have a chance. Sally Ann is not the fastest thing on four feet, but she's one of the toughest . . . she has to be," he added grimly, "to suit my tastes . . . and I've ridden her two years without breaking her heart."

Mervin added slowly: "Flight, the mare you've just seen, was given to me by Colonel Dinsmore. He told me, when he made the present, that other horses might distance her at the beginning of a race, but that none would ever come in ahead of her in a long test. She's as gentle as a lamb and brave as a lion. She'll run her heart out and ask no questions. She'll go from morning to night, and, at the end of the day, she'll still have her ears pricking."

"Enter her in the Jericho, then, by all means," said Loring. "But may I inquire why you have come here . . . at night . . . to tell me the good points of your mare?"

Mervin gritted his teeth, but still his patience held. "I'll tell you this, sir. If your horse is half as good as you say she is, and mine is half as good as I think her to be, it will take a good deal of beating to get ahead of the pair of them."

"There will be several dozen entries. The odds are big against us. Is that what you mean? To enter them as a stable?"

"Not that. But suppose, Loring, that each horse ran half the race."

"What?"

"Loring, if you rode the first quarter of the race on Sally Ann, and then, in a secure meeting place, appointed beforehand, met Flight and mounted her and rode the next half of the race, on your return trip you could be met by Sally Ann again, mount her, and so you would start and end the race on the same horse, but a good half of the work would be done by another that could never be told from your own mare."

It was part of the pride of Loring never to be surprised, but he was plainly staggered now. He burst out: "By the heavens, Mervin, what a handsome scoundrel you are!"

Mervin was a fighter, and his nerve was of the best, but although he turned pale with fury, he held his temper. For, after all, he was more at home with his fists than with guns, when it came to fighting, and it would not be hard to guess how long it would take Loring to get a revolver in his fingers. So he ran on smoothly, as though he had not heard the last remark: "You understand, of course, that this race will be worth the winning. The actual stake and the added money will come to around fifteen thousand dollars."

"I know that, of course."

"Half of fifteen thousand would make seventy-five hundred apiece."

"I," Loring said coolly, "ride the horses and take the risk of detection, and you get half of the money?"

"Two parts to you, then, and one to me. Ten thousand to you and five thousand to me."

"Well?"

"There's more than the stake, however. Consider that before the time of the race, the crowd will have picked out its favorites, and among those favorites Sally Ann is not apt to be one."

"Not when they know that I am to ride. They would bet against me for the exquisite pleasure of seeing me lose, if for no other reason."

"Exactly! Very well, then. The odds against Sally Ann should go up to thirty to one. And there will be people on hand at Jericho who will be ready to back their opinions with hard cash. There are plenty of millions in this part of the country."

"Stolen, and otherwise," Loring said, sneering. "But stolen money will burn its way. . . ." He checked himself short. After all, the scheme they were even then contemplating would not brook too much moral contemplation.

"Twenty or thirty to one," he granted. "Well? What good would it do me? I have no money to bet."

"But I have, Loring. I have five thousand that I can get together. Five thousand at thirty to one would be a hundred and fifty thousand dollars. At twenty to one, it's forty thousand to me and sixty thousand to you. Am I wrong?"

The eyes of young Loring turned up to the high ceiling above him as though to note the cracks in the plaster and study the places where the laths were bared.

"Sixty thousand dollars?" he murmured at last. "Well, Mister Mervin, that would be worth some effort. They owe it to me, heaven knows. If I had what is my right, sixty thousand dollars would be a mere nothing. The very ground that Twin Creeks is built upon . . . however, let that go. The dogs owe me money. What difference how they pay it to me?"

"Very clear reasoning," Mervin agreed, grinning. "And certainly, Loring, it would be very strange if any horse should beat our pair?"

"Run such a distance and beat two such horses as ours? No animal in the world could manage that!"

"Certainly not. Flight will at least keep you close to the leaders. For the last quarter of the race, when all the men will be working hard on their ponies, you will have Sally Ann as fresh as a daisy under you. Certainly nothing could possibly beat you, Mister Loring. Nothing, I am sure."

"A thousand thanks. I am not a heavyweight, at least, and I shall fear nothing."

"Nothing," said Mervin, "except one man and one horse."

"And that?"

"The one that is sure to be the favorite."

"That will be one of the Arabs, I suppose."

"No, no! It can't be other than one horse . . . Crusader with Harry Camden riding him."

"Camden? Crusader?" Loring stated. "Why, man, no

one but a fool would bet on a pair of heavyweights like them to win any distance race of more than a mile or two."

Mervin shook his head, and there was a shade of thought in his eyes. "I've seen him," he said.

"With his ribs standing out?"

"As sleek as Flight, I give you my word. What Camden has done with the big horse is a miracle. If he can train Crusader in that fashion, why may he not work another miracle in the riding of the race? As for his weight, you have to remember that he does not ride in a heavy range saddle. He rides only on a light blanket, and he seems to know how to make himself a part of the horse."

"Perhaps he rides well. However, there is nothing that could beat the two mares, if your Flight is a tithe the animal that Sally Ann is!"

"You'll find her as good, or nearly so. But this Camden understands how to wring everything out of a horse. He is a part of Crusader, I tell you."

"Bah!" exclaimed Loring. "You will have to persuade me that a madman from the mountains can outride a gentleman. I only hope to heaven that you may be wrong."

"Not horsemanship . . . magic, Loring. That's what you'll have to contend with when you ride against Camden. I've seen him riding Crusader. He goes like the wind, and he manages the animal with his thinking, not with reins. They know one another better than two men."

Loring merely smiled.

"I tell you," Mervin said seriously, "that although I would bet freely against any other man riding in the race and any other horse than Crusader . . . I feel that even with our two horses against him we have no better than an even chance. And that chance must be improved, man, before I invest five thousand dollars."

"Improved?"

"Exactly that. I must have a better surety."

"Tell me how that can be managed?"

"Suppose, for instance, that Crusader never starts in that race?"

"Eh?"

"It could be managed."

"In what way?"

"Isn't it possible, say, that Camden should be incapacitated for riding . . . ?"

There was a gleam in the eyes of Loring now. He began to nod and smile in a wickedly gratified way at Mervin. "That's the way with the devil," he said. "He takes left-handed ways of getting at us. You start with a little crooked work in a horse race, which involves the loss of nothing saving honor"—and here he laughed, short and sharp—"but now you are coming on finely. You want a murder done, Mervin."

"Murder?" gasped out the other. "Certainly not. It was never in my mind. Never!" But, even as he spoke, the glitter was in his eye and flare was in his nostrils.

"You only mean that Camden should be incapacitated?"

"Only that, Loring. On my honor, only that. And the man's a mere brute. He doesn't deserve consideration as anything else. An animal, Loring, but no decency, no refinement, no. . . ."

"Honesty?" cut in Loring. Mervin was silent, and his host went on slowly and dryly: "Be anything, Mervin. Be a liar, be a villain, be a murderer, even, but don't be a hypocrite. Put your cards on the table. Face up! Let me see what's in your mind. Bah, man, you don't have to tell me, for I can see it too clearly in your eyes. You want him killed. You want it with your whole heart and your whole soul. You want the death of this Camden. Is that not so?"

Mervin blinked. Then, unable to speak aloud, he whispered: "I want him dead, Loring. I admit it. God knows it may be a guilty wish, but there's no need for such a man on the face of the world, and. . . ."

"You've said it, now. And now that I have your mind, I'm satisfied. Only, Mervin, I tell you frankly that I like my part of this deal better than you can possibly like yours. All that I have to do is to fight a man, and a strong one, and kill him. And that can be managed . . . oh, yes, that can be managed. But you, Mervin, have to sit in the background and pull the strings. You think you are master of the puppet show, but I tell you, my friend, that when I am in purgatory for this, you will be in hell for the mere thinking of the thing! However," he added, "that's apart from the point, which is . . . where am I to get at Camden, and how?"

"When he brings Crusader to Jericho."

"I must do it in the crowd?"

"Do you wish to do it alone, where there'll be no witnesses, and where'd they'd hang you for it? No, Loring. Do it in the open. They know that he's a killer. They don't know, a good many of them, that you could beat him with a gun. Because he's strong in his hands, they think that nothing can ever beat him in any sort of a fight."

Loring smiled. "You make," he said, "an excellent assistant murderer. My share is two-thirds, throughout all the profits?"

"Two-thirds, man. You stand to make a comfortable fortune."

"From this moment," said Loring, "never mention the money to me again."

TAKING WATER

When Camden was just two miles from Jericho, the sheriff met him—Tom Younger himself, riding on a strong gray gelding. He turned in at the side of the dancing black giant, and for a moment he watched the magnificent play of muscles over the satiny body of the stallion.

"You've trained him down fine, Camden," he said. "Not too fine, I guess?"

Camden smiled.

"You've never raced him before, you know," said the sheriff, "except when you were running for your life . . . with me behind you." He grinned at Camden, but there was no great store of friendliness in the smile.

"I was aimin' to free Manners," he said quietly. "I guess you ain't holdin' ag'in' me what I did to you, Sheriff?"

The sheriff twisted up his face into a sour grin. "I'll tell you this, Harry," he managed to say at last. "No matter what happens, I'll play with you fair and square. I won't make no trouble for you, and I won't hunt up no quarrels ag'in' you that the law might find. And I don't mind tellin' you, Camden, that they's some that would be plenty glad to see you jailed and kept there till the runnin' of the race is over. But all you'll get from me will be fair and square. Will you believe that?"

"I'll believe that, Sheriff," said the wild man. "No gent that is a fair fightin' man could ever want to step on a gent that was down."

"Down, Harry?"

"I'm down when I get inside of that there town. I hate towns. They ain't meant for me, I tell you. I hate 'em mighty bad. They crowd me. They don't give me no chance to get by myself or to think my own kind of thoughts, I tell you. No, sir, I'll be down so long as I'm in that there town of Jericho."

It amazed the sheriff to see the forlorn expression on his face, most like a child confronted by a great and baffling sorrow—a first day at school. He could not help smiling, but presently his smile darkened again.

"I don't mind tellin' you, Harry," he said, "that the law has been stretched till it's all plumb out of shape for the sake of what we've had to do for you. It was Colonel Dinsmore that saved your hash, young man. He come to me, and he talked pretty strong. And then he went along to the judge, and, finally, we decided that we'd give you one more chance. But understand, Camden, that you don't have to do no more'n lift a hand while you're in this here town, before I'll have you arrested if I got to call out every armed man in the town, which they's some considerable heap of men and guns in that town right now, young man."

"Maybe there is," sighed Camden. "But I ain't gonna bother them none."

"You'll watch yourself?"

"Every minute."

"Then, we'll all be happy in Jericho, Harry. I've been lookin' for hard times beginnin' when you come to town. But maybe I'm all wrong."

He turned off on a byroad. Camden went on into Jericho by himself, and for the first time saw that queer little town, which lies curled around the foot of Jericho Mountain as though clinging to the great slope for protection. Everywhere he found that the streets were crowded, for the race had brought throngs. Every cowpuncher who could afford to waste a week had left his job and ridden in scores, perhaps hundreds of miles to see the race and enjoy the excitement, and place his bets before the contest took place. Every rancher within a mile radius, every miner, every lumberman was there. Reporters and sportsmen had come from distant cities, and the tourists, wide-eyed, smiling, a little weary, were everywhere.

Through this crowd went Camden down the long, twisting street of the town. Beyond the double row of houses, and filling up the interstices between them, was every form of shack and lean-to and tent that could be imagined built or pitched for the convenience of the throng of visitors that, had Jericho been thrice its normal size, could never have been accommodated. He had not gone a block before he was recognized. In two blocks more the reporters were at him. They walked on either side of him, writing pads or cameras in hand. They shouted to him for statements.

"Do you expect to win?"

"Is Crusader in shape, do you think?"

"Got a picture of yourself?"

"What will Dinsmore pay you if you win?"

"Have you ridden over the course before?"

"Is Crusader too big for mountain work?"

Thus came the first of a rattling volley of questions that went on and on in gathering importance and gathering loudness until he said, at the last: "Lemme alone, gents. I'm not here to talk. I'm here to ride Crusader."

Even so they would not desist, and he paused in front of the hotel to the tune of clicking cameras on every side. People already had heard the rumor of his arrival. They were pouring out of the houses behind him. They were swarming up around the big horse. Crusader, standing like an ebony statue, merely flattened his ears against his neck, but otherwise paid not the slightest attention to them all. Camden tethered him and went inside. He found that his friend, Ned Manners, had succeeded in locating the room that had been reserved long in advance by Colonel Dinsmore. To it he conducted Harry Camden. They sat on the edge of the bed and ate a hurried lunch.

"The colonel doesn't expect you until tonight, at the quickest," Manners informed him, "and when. . . ."

There was a tap at the door, which opened before an invitation had been given. A short, thick-set man with a wide, ugly face stood in the doorway.

"Mister Peter Loring is downstairs asking for you, boy," said this ill-omened visitor. "I mean you, big boy!" He pointed to Camden.

Then, as he disappeared, Manners said: "D'you know Loring, Harry?"

"Never heard tell of him before. Who is he? One of these reporters?"

Manners grinned. "The most part of his talkin' he does with his guns. He's one of them busted-down gentlemen that ain't forgot what their grandfathers done. The only thing that he warms up about, they say, is how great all the Lorings have always been. What in the devil can *he* want with you? You ain't had no trouble with him, Harry?"

"I never heard his name before."

"He wants to get down a bet with you, maybe. But if he does, don't let him put up nothin' but cash. His word and his note ain't worth the time it takes to listen to 'em or read 'em. He's a deadbeat, Harry."

This warning reached Camden as he strode to the door and so down the creaking stairs to the verandah of the hotel, and there, leaning against one of the fluted wooden pillars that supported the roof that extended past the verandah, and far over the watering troughs where fifty horses could drink comfortably at the same time, stood a slender man with a yellow skin, and eyes lost in the deep shadow of his brows.

Camden, half a stride through the doorway, felt the stare of the other and knew that this was he who had sent for him, and that that errand was one of mischief. For there were instincts in Camden as keen as the scent is sharp in a loafer wolf. All of those instincts rose up in him to tell him that here was something foreign to his nature, something deadly dangerous. The stranger stood away from the pillar a little, thoughtfully smoking his cigarette and watching the big man.

But when he spoke, his remark was addressed to the nearest cowpuncher. "My friend," he said in his patronizing way that had earned him the hearty dislike of the entire countryside, "is that fellow Harry Camden?"

It was very much like asking if a roaring fire were warm, for Harry Camden was known, and known with fear. It is not for nothing that a man sticks up such a sheriff as Tom Younger and breaks open such a jail as that of Twin Creeks. Harry Camden was known and dreaded.

The cowpuncher gaped at the audacious questioner. "That's Camden," he muttered.

Loring turned still more toward the cow waddie and still more away from Camden, but the latter could see that, from the corner of his eye, Loring was still watching him closely. That Loring's right hand, carelessly resting on his right hip above the holster, surely had a meaning. Here was the very trouble that he had vowed he would avoid. Here was the very thing against which the honest sheriff had warned him. But what could he do? Could he advance? Could he retreat? He could only wait for the catastrophe to develop.

"He's Camden, is he?" said Loring. "Well, then, he's the man I want to see. Because I understand that he has been circulating remarks about me. Very ugly remarks, my friend. Perhaps you have heard them."

"No," gasped out the cowpuncher.

"You are too polite," Loring said. "Entirely too polite." He whirled suddenly back on Camden. "You know why I called you down here?" he asked.

"I dunno that I got any idea," muttered Camden.

"You haven't? Think it over, Camden. I tell you everything you have said has been reported to me. Everything! And what I require, Mister Camden, is a public apology, spoken so that all of these gentlemen will be able to hear you when you talk!" He smiled as he said it, and flicked the ashes from the end of his cigarette, which was fuming busily in his left hand. But the right was still poised at the hip, the fingers working a little, fiercely, greedy to be at the butt of the heavy Colt that hung in the black leather holster just below their tips.

A silence had followed the first speech of Loring. Now, hastily, softly, the spectators drew away from the line that ran from Loring to Camden, and packed in more closely on either side, making a human channel between the two men. To Harry Camden there came a passionate desire to take that slender form and break it in two. There was a still greater desire to whip out his own revolver. It might mean his own death, for he knew that in this quiet, composed man with the cold devil in his eyes, there was more danger than in all that he had ever encountered before. But there was his strong resolve; there was the recent warning of the sheriff. He drew a breath and then answered: "Stranger, I never seen you before. I got nothin' ag'in' you. What could make me want to spread any sort of lies about you?"

The breath that he had drawn was suddenly echoed on every side, and then a sort of groan from the doorway behind him, and the voice of his friend, Manners, saying hastily: "Harry, what in the name of heaven are you sayin'? He wants a fight, that's all he's askin' for."

"Yellow, I see," Loring said calmly, as before. "A very yellow dog, it seems. What I wonder at, Camden," he went on, sauntering toward the big man, "is that you have been able to impose upon all of these people during such a stretch of time. There are men all around us who wear guns. How have you been able to pull the wool over their eyes? Will you answer me that, my friend? What tricks have you used? And what lies?"

He came squarely before Camden. The difference in their sizes was more shockingly apparent. Now that he was close, Camden could see the waspish malignancy of the smaller man. He was fairly trembling with it.

"Stranger," Harry Camden said bitterly, "I dunno what I ought to say. It looks to me like you was hankerin' for a fight. But fightin' ain't in my line till after the Jericho race is over and done with. After that, gimme half a chance to find you and I'll talk this here thing out with you. But today is no time."

"No time for you," Loring said with a snarl. "No time for an underbred, overfed puppy to concern himself with such a trifle, but where the honor of a Loring is concerned, it is a very vital matter, I assure you. I ask you for the last time, Camden, if I am to have that apology?"

Harry Camden was silent. His face burned, and then grew white, for he heard a whisper on either side: "He's quittin'. He's bluffed down. He's takin' in water."

He, of all men. He who had been raised on battle, like any wolf.

"Very well," said Loring as cool as ever, "perhaps this will spur you on a bit and loosen your tongue." As he spoke, he raised his left hand, and with the flat of it struck Camden across the face so heavily that the sound was like the clapping of hands together. A white impress of the fingers stood out on Camden's cheek.

He hesitated for one instant, surveying the tensed, ready figure of Loring, whose hand was on the very butt of his revolver now. Then Camden turned on his heel and walked past the face of Manners, who stood at the door, in an agony of shame for his big friend. But Camden paid him no heed. He strode up the stairs and disappeared from view.

GRIM RESOLUTION

"On the whole," philosophized Loring, "one may divide people of this class into two categories . . . those who are bullies and will fight when they have to, and those who are bullies without having the courage to strike a blow when they are up against someone of their own strength. To the last category belongs this Camden. I suppose that you gentlemen will agree with me on that point?"

There was no answer, only a sick look of disgust and of horror on the face of every man, for in all the world the most fearful spectacle is that of a coward, and most cowardly, according to all their standards, had been the actions of Harry Camden upon this occasion.

Then a door slammed heavily in the upper part of the hotel, and that sound served to waken one man into action. It was Manners, who started suddenly forward from the doorway toward Peter Loring. He came directly up to that destroyer of men.

"Loring," he said, "I dunno what it was that kept my partner, Camden, from breakin' you in two, which it looks to me like he could of done it dead easy. But he had something else in his mind. And the way I look at it, partner, you and I are all fixed for an understandin' of just what it was that you claim that he said about you?"

Loring, as he looked at the other, surveyed him from head to heel with his usual consummate impudence. "Someone," he said, "has mixed trouble with this young man's gunpowder. Will some friend of his come and take him away?"

"All right," said Manners in a frenzy of shame and of rage at the disgrace that he had just received. "Maybe this here will waken you up." He flashed his open hand into the face of Loring—then he reached for his gun.

So vast was the difference between their speed that he had barely gripped the butt of his weapon when the other's Colt was exposed. His own gun was never drawn, for Loring's bullet ripped its way down the thigh of the younger man.

Manners, with an oath of rage rather than of mere pain or fear, toppled forward on his face, struck his forehead heavily against the boards of the verandah, and lay still.

There was a rush for him, in which half a dozen men even made so free as to elbow Loring in passing. For his part, he paid no heed to the fallen, but straightway approached one of those who had not been able to get in by Manners. He tapped the man whom he had selected—a substantial rancher of middle age—upon the shoulder and immediately copied down the name and the address of the other.

"Because," Loring said, "one never can tell. There

may be some legal action following even an affair like this, although you yourself will be able to testify for me, I presume, that I did not make a motion toward my guns except after I had been struck. I fired only in self-defense, to avoid a cruel beating at the hands of a man much larger and stronger than I . . . a fellow like a madman, who had rushed in upon me."

It happened that he had cornered the worst selection that he could have made. Now the man stared back at him gloomily and was brave enough to say: "Loring, I know you better'n you know me. Don't call me up on no witness stand, or else I'll tell how you tried to pick a fight with one gent and used him so damned bad that his partner had to step in between you."

"You, too," Loring said sneeringly, "seem remarkably interested in the affairs of Mister Harry Camden. Who is this other young idiot?"

"His name is Manners. He's a gent that Camden stood by. That's why he'd stand by Camden."

"And Camden, I suppose, is a friend of yours?"

"I ain't sayin' nothin' about Camden," said the cowman. "Maybe he's a yaller skunk. Maybe he ain't. He ain't like the rest of us. Maybe he's got special reasons for actin' the way he did. But the way I feel about it, I'd rather be a dead man first . . . I'd rather be a damned ghost!"

No doubt all who were in the town of Jericho felt the same way about it. There was universal pity for young Manners, stricken in the midst of an attempt to avenge the lost honor of a friend; there was universal detestation for the coward, Harry Camden; there was universal hatred for Loring, by whom the tragedy had been brought about.

Not that the tragedy was brought to its ultimate end. Loring had fired with a good deal too much precipitation to bring about any such happy end. His very spitefulness, his very surety that he had the younger man at his mercy, had made him strive with a double effort to murder the youth on the spot, and that venomous passion, perhaps, was the reason that his aim was bad and that the bullet went astray. As it was, the wound was terribly painful and accompanied by a great loss of blood, so that young Manners presently lay in one of the lower rooms of the hotel, very white of face, very set of jaw, while a surgeon probed and examined the wound, and told him that no bone had been broken. He would recover as fast as his strong young constitution permitted.

When the doctor spoke, there was kneeling by the bed of her brother none other than Ruth Manners herself, for she had come up with her father for the sake of the week before the race. People usually tried to manage the affair in this fashion. Time was dated according to the race of such and such a year. In the single week at Jericho, there were more engagements announced than in a twelve month on either side of that period. For it was a time of excitement, of gambling, of the taking of chances.

To the great social event, therefore, Ruth Manners had come up with both her father and her brother, and now, as she kneeled by his bed, almost as white of face as was he, she heard him pronounced in no danger and the first effect was a faint moan of joy.

Afterward she thought of another thing, and, starting up with word that she would instantly be back again, she hurried through the thinning group of strangers in the room and went straight into the upper part of the hotel to find the room of Harry Camden. It was pointed out to her at once, and her knock brought big Camden himself to the door. He regarded her with such a start and with such a smile of joy that even Ruth Manners half forgot the purpose for which she had come there, to wonder over him. Then she remembered what she had just seen, including the settled agony in the eyes of her brother as he had laid enduring the pain of his wound.

"Mister Camden," she said, "isn't this the proudest day of your life?"

He seemed so unused to the sound of her voice, and so delighted with that, and her nearness, that he hung over her for a time, still, before the smile faded from his face. He looked down at her with a bewildered face of sorrow.

"Something has gone wrong, I guess," he said in his mild, deep voice.

There was swift relenting in her heart of hearts, so swift that she hardened herself and became more cruel than she would have been otherwise. The storm of her anger broke out at him.

"Something has gone wrong? Not as far wrong as you'd like, I guess. You'd rather that poor dear Ned had been killed for you. For you! Oh, you great coward! They'll never let you rest after this. They'll hound you and work on you until they drive you to another name and another country. But, oh, you coward, you coward, to let him face that murderer . . . that Loring . . . that devil!"

Having flung out at him in this fashion, she relented with a quick falling of the heart, and, because she feared what she had done and wished to escape from looking it in the face, she turned and fled down the hall as fast as she could go.

Camden went slowly and heavily back into the room. He began to wander back and forth in the little chamber, touching the furniture with his hands, or standing at the window and staring across to Jericho Mountain with unseeing eyes of pain and of sorrow.

He was there for a long time until there came a rap at his door, a firm-handed rap. He looked up and found the sheriff and Colonel Dinsmore both before him. On their faces was the very thing from which he had fled. Surely these men should have understood that there was something remarkable. The sheriff, at least, having already threatened him with what would happen if he so much as raised a hand, must now have known that his threat had taken effect. No, there was no understanding. There was only blank confusion and distress in both of their faces, and there was shame—shame that another man should have exhibited such cowardice as had been seen in Harry Camden on that day.

Still, he endured. A big black vein swelled in his forehead. His heart thundered with a slow, tremendous pulse like a sea washed with a monstrous ground swell. But he said not a word.

"Camden," said the colonel, "what on earth has happened, my young friend? What has gone wrong?" Then he added, with an attempt at lightheartedness that only made the agony of the young man more acute: "Cheer up, Camden. We all have our blue days and our hard knocks."

Camden swallowed hard. It was difficult—it was very difficult. His whole nature cried out with a single voice and bade him destroy that detestable enemy, Peter Loring. But he kept himself firmly back. After the race, that would all be very well. But to repay brave and generous young Manners for the foolish and kind thing that he had done, he must make Crusader win and pay back to Ned a great sum of money for that small amount that he had invested in it, all in the blind confidence that the man whom he considered so great could not fail to win.

RUTH ENCOURAGES CAMDEN

He went downstairs again, at the last, wondering how he could face the townsfolk, even the children. Yes, the boys and girls worst of all, for they would not scruple to scream after him the ugly things that had been suggested by his conduct of that day.

He found where Manners was lying and tapped at the door, which was presently opened by the girl herself. "I thought," he said, "that I'd like to see Ned and have a word with him." He added: "If you think it wouldn't do no harm. . . ."

"He don't want . . . ," began the girl impulsively. Then, as she saw a look of horror flash into his brown eyes—the steady, amber eyes of a brute—she flushed in sympathy. "What I mean to say is that the doctor has given orders. Very few are to see him until he gets a little better."

He shrank from her. Again she was amazed. It had not seemed possible that so burly and huge a man should have such tender sensibilities, but he perceived the very first hint of her meaning, and now he was crushed by it. All at once, as he skulked down the hall, she was overwhelmed by impulse and ran suddenly after him and caught at his hand.

He paused and turned his white, strained face back to her.

"I'm sorry," she whispered, "for everything that I've said. I know that there's got to be some explanation. I know that you aren't a coward, Harry Camden." Then she fled back to the room. As she flashed through the door, she had an impression of Camden standing exactly as she had left him, in mid-stride, arrested like a statue. She whipped the door shut behind her and leaned against it, smiling, breathless, her heart racing she knew not why. Then she heard a very slow, immensely ponderous stride come back up the hall. She could trace its slow progress by the creaking of the flooring beneath it. It paused outside the door against which she leaned. There was then audible to the straining ears of the girl a long, heavy sigh. Then the creaking of the floor began again and diminished into the distance. But after that she knew, as plainly as if he had told her, that Harry Camden loved her.

But Harry Camden, poor devil, was beginning a week of the cruelest torment that any man on earth ever endured. It was not Loring, it seemed. He did not appear in the matter at all. But, having started the ball rolling by his exposing of the giant, the entire town, or rather, all the young hotheads and bullies in it, set upon Camden and began baiting him. He could not appear without receiving a volley of abuse. They thought of clever insults, and then cast themselves in his way in a public place in order to speak them. But to it he returned not a word. He went every day as early as possible to the stallion and stayed with him, exercising him through the meadows at the foot of Mount Jericho, according to the rules of the race that required that the horse should be conditioned in that fashion, under the eyes of competent judges. This was a provision wisely inserted, in order that no horse that was out of condition might be allowed to compete in the struggle, which had cost the life of more than one fine animal before this.

It was Crusader who pulled Camden through. Otherwise, he could never have endured a tithe of what he had to suffer, but the great horse was a comrade to him. There could be no insults from the stallion. There was always sure to be only the lifted head and the shining eye to greet the coming of the real master of Crusader's soul. That companionship kept the very heart of the man from going sour with grief and with weakness and with shame.

If he lay awake at nights, conjuring up again the vision of the arch-devil, Loring, then the thought of Crusader brought him sleep again.

Yet it was a changed Camden who sat on the back of Crusader on the day when the five-hundred-mile race began. His face was hollowed and seamed, and his eyes were sunken. However, the crowd saw nothing. Crowds never do, and of all the sixty-five horses that danced and pranced at the post upon that day, there was a shout of applause for every single horse, and there was a small cheer for every rider with the exception, sole and single, of Harry Camden. He felt it bitterly.

There he sat on the back of mighty Crusader and felt the greatness of his horse beneath him, and the warmth of the sun was welcome upon his shoulders. The clear air allowed his eye to pass up the great slope of Mount Jericho and detect every shrub to the very top. Here was a day, indeed, for the race.

There were literally thousands gathered at the start around the long, long line of the horses, and to each rider came separate friends, and eager admirers came in groups. Perhaps the largest number was gathered about the Arabs, and especially the chestnut, Ali. But there was a crowd, also, around Jack Murran's bay stallion, Fury. Even around Crusader, in spite of what they might think of the horse's rider, there was a continual group.

"If he only had another man up in his saddle, I'd double the bet that I put on him . . . but since Camden showed yaller, I wish that I hadn't put up a cent."

That was one of a hundred speeches that Camden heard and took care not to show upon his impassive face. For this must be endured as all else had been endured. The race was still to be run. But afterward? When he thought of what might come afterward, his heart swelled, and a sort of sweet pain came into his throat.

But here came someone to him at last. It was Colonel Dinsmore himself. He did not come near. He stood at a little distance. His face was as expressionless as stone as he bade Camden have good luck and take care of the stallion. But never since the day of the shaming of Camden had the colonel once looked fairly into his eyes, as though he feared lest such a glance would waken all that was savage in his nature and make him tell the giant all that he was in his mind about him.

The colonel was gone, and now, picking her way

quickly, into the very circle where the big black stallion stood, came a girl in white, very pretty, very trim, although the blurring eyes of Harry Camden refused to allow him to distinguish her features. She came straight on to him. He felt his hand taken by slim, cool fingers. He heard the voice of Ruth Manners come clear and strong.

"Good luck, Harry Camden,"—and then, more softly—"I'm mighty sorry. I know everything will be set right. I know it!"

THE RACE IS ON

The crack of the starter's gun left Harry Camden sitting stupidly in the saddle, staring at the place where the girl had stood. Then he was roused by a loud laughter.

"Damned if he ain't gone to sleep!"

"Nope . . . he's only cryin'!"

For tears, in fact, had rolled into the eyes of Harry Camden, and the sun glittered on them. Then he tossed the reins, and Crusader was away. The first mile was brisk running. It was always fast work. The tradition of the race was that the first mile should be well run out so that the spectators could see the lot off to a spectacular start. After that, they could pick their own pace, of course, and do exactly as they wished.

In that first mile, Camden tried the foot of the others in the contest and found it good. He passed all except three—three fine Thoroughbreds like Crusader, which, on account of the better start they had received, were well away in the lead. But outside of the Thoroughbreds, there was nothing to mention in the same breath at the end of the sprinted mile. For nothing that moves upon four feet can live with the Thoroughbred over a mile. The brilliant antelope, even, is left far, far behind. All other horses—the Arabians, the half-bloods, the mustangs—were left ridiculously far behind. However, that first wild mile was only the glass of wine that started the feast. The real work was still to do, and there was plenty of it—plenty of it.

It was like a whole army campaign contrasted with a battle; such was this cross-country run compared with an ordinary race. Five hundred miles of desert and mountain. Five hundred miles of spongy desert sand and of impossible rocks and cliffs among the mountains.

Camden had studied the whole matter out very carefully with Colonel Dinsmore as they sat beside the map. Every depression, every hollow on the course showed in that map, and they had decided between them what way Crusader must run. It was a beautiful problem, that course, for the shortest route was, of course, straight across the Jericho desert, and so, in the far distance, two hundred and fifty miles away, to circle the Corimba Peak and start back again. But, unfortunately, that straight line carried a rider over the worst of the mountains and through the deepest and the finest sand. Therefore, the whole task was to establish, first of all, just what going would be best for one's mount. The little, active horses were apt to select the straight line, because they would rather use up strength on obstacles than on great distance. The leggy, fragile animals, and mostly the Thoroughbreds and the nearly Thoroughbred horses that were entered in the race, took a wide sweep across the Corimba foothills and so added immensely to their mileage, but they found, in the long run, that it paid them to avoid the terrible friction of a more direct re-passage of the Corimba Mountains.

As for the black stallion, Camden had determined to avoid the very highest mountains and, yet, to keep close in, thus enabling him to avoid throwing away too many extra miles. That was not all the planning that he had done. He had worked out a thousand small schemes, figuring adroitly just how far it was best to take the stallion every day, and at what a rate he should proceed, and how that rate should be varied, lest the stallion grew stale to the work, and what effect too much food had on him, and when and where it was best to feed him, and on how much water he could make a march. These were some of the questions that merely began the doubts and the self-catechism of Harry Camden. But his labors were well rewarded.

Never once did he push the great horse, and yet as they crossed the desert and reached the foothills of the Corimba Mountains, the leaders were first a desert-bred mustang, a beautiful and hardy piece of horseflesh, then an Arab mare brought from Arabia specially for this contest, and third was the big stallion, Crusader. Beyond a shadow of a doubt, he had endured the desert going better than the other two. They looked at him sourly, the riders of those two horses, watching him move along with splendid ease and precision, never pressed, never urged by his master, but at the walk covering more ground than the average horse covers with a dog-trot.

"We'll get you when we hit the mountains," they assured Camden, and he listened and nodded and said not a word in reply. He had no use for speech until a certain day came, and then he would care to speak to one man only. Ah, if only that moment should be but five minutes hence.

Then, as they were laboring up through the foothills, a very strange thing happened, for a horse that had not ever been in sight an hour before, pressed up suddenly among them. It went straight on by them all, keeping up a smart trot. It was Peter Loring, riding erect in the saddle on a beautiful brown mare, marked with white. He gave Camden, as he went by, not so much as a haloo, but he said to the others: "Gentlemen, I hope you are not all of a feather up here."

The others growled after he had gone by, and they followed him with glances as black as the looks that they had given to Camden a little before.

He himself, on the stallion, did not attempt to pick up the difference between him and the flying mare at once. But he increased the pace of big Crusader, and, in the gray of the next morning, which was when he usually began his march of the day, he had sight, once more, of the two white stockings of the horse.

Twice that day the mare was out of sight. Twice she came back again. So they rounded the Corimba Mountains, and came down gradually into the white heat of the desert again.

There are degrees of heat, even on the desert. There is the cool north wind that brings a breath of relief, and there is also the burning south that shrivels whatever it touches. It was the south wind that blew now. It caught the horses and the riders weak from the labor and the nerve strain of that arduous crossing of the mountains. And it wrecked their nerves. They rode on through a smother of blown sand that sifted into the clothes and next to the skin of the riders and that kept the horses snooting to clear their nostrils of the grit.

Provisions had grown low in the scanty food packs of the men. The oats that they carried for their horses were exhausted. There was only the desert grass to keep them and the widely separated tanks and springs for water, all, however, well charted on the maps that they carried.

Here horses began to lag terribly behind. The whole body of horses had come over the mountains in a bunch, each pushing on resolutely behind the others, all afraid of being distanced, and, striking the desert below, the weak ones went to the wall at once and were forced to turn back toward the green foothills, glad to be out of the ruck.

That noon, Crusader forged to the lead. To his right, a mile away, was the glimmering form of the brown mare with that light and expert horseman, Loring, in the saddle. Then the brown mare was lost in the rolling ground, and Crusader went on alone—in the lead.

It was no grave satisfaction to big Harry Camden. He felt that he had the race in his lap. He was confident that none of those horses, once put to the rear, could ever pass him again. So he let Crusader go on at a walk, steadily, without pressing that willing worker, only soothing him, now and again, with the touch of his hand or his voice when the big animal began to grow nervous with the strain of the work.

That night they camped at the foot of that huge, shapeless mass—Jericho Mountain. It had been hard to climb the farther and smoother side even with fresh horses at the beginning of the contest. This far more sheer slope, with a weary horse beneath the saddle, was sure to be a heartbreaker.

But they found excellent bunch grass and a clear spring, so that they fared well enough, and, before darkness had thickened, he counted here and there across the hollows a dozen sparks of light—the fires that the other contestants had kindled as soon as they arrived at their last camping place.

The last camping place it would surely be, for Crusader, as the big man knew, could make the remaining distance on the morrow, weary though he might be.

In the first glimmer of the gray morning, he was riding again, letting Crusader trudge on up the slope. To the left, to the right, here and there, he made out other forms of horsemen, plodding through the dawn, but he had no fear. They were desperate. By the nodding, lowered heads of the horses he knew that they would have to pause time and again before the upper crest was reached.

But Crusader held upon his way undaunted. His ribs stood out, now, and his neck was growing lean, but he still carried his head well up. If some of the spring had gone out of his step, it was hardly noticeable. There was still ample strength in him to defeat any of the others who rode against him. Ample, indeed.

For, as the sun reddened the eastern rim of the horizon, and the rose bold and clear, he saw the competitors already falling back behind him, drawing together in a closer group, and then straggling in a long, drawn-out bunch. All falling back—no, yonder came one past the right flank of the others. From the top of a hill, Camden on Crusader saw the stranger drifting rapidly to the fore. Some cowpuncher making his last desperate bid on a failing horse? That must be it.

He plodded on for half an hour, and then he heard the crunching of gravel under hoofs behind him. He turned with a shock and a start in the saddle. There, behind him, he saw none other than Loring riding rapidly up at a dog-trot, for here the ground shelved into a level plateau.

On came Loring, and the brown mare beneath him seemed to go almost gaily. Certainly her ears were pricked sharply, and, if she were blackened with sweat, it was not the sweat of exhaustion. Up and up came the lighter rider, and then, miracle of all miracles, he began to pass Crusader!

AN ATTEMPT ON CAMDEN'S LIFE

Camden could not believe his eyes, but when he stared again at the mare, it was true. Marvelous, indeed, was the condition of the mare for one that had covered that five-hundred-mile cross-country race. Her ribs were a trifle gaunted, to be sure, but not more than was to be expected. Her head was carried lightly and high. She stepped firmly, lifted her feet well up. One might almost have thought that she was beginning the race, instead of starting the last long grind of the final day's march. With a chilling touch of gloom, Camden prefigured Crusader beaten. Crusader beaten, and all the nameless sacrifices that he had made were made in vain. The money of poor Ned Manners was gone. Beautiful Ruth Manners, whose courage and whose fine heart had made her come to him and give him one Godspeed in the hostile silence or the derision of the crowd—Ruth Manners would be struck down by the same club of defeat!

All of this was in the dread of Camden. He looked at Loring. The rider, to be sure, showed no more wear than his horse. His thin face was not attenuated, and a constant snarl was on his lips. Never had he seemed more wolfish, never more bitter and cruel. He sneered as he went by, and then pointed to the top of the slope far ahead and high above, with other summits rolling back and back beyond it—surely a heartbreaking prospect. But not a word was spoken as they passed each other, like ships by night. Only a glare of hatred and of rage, then they went on.

Still the mare was forging to the front. Camden, with his heart turned to lead, tried to comprehend, but it was incomprehensible. There was nothing to be made of it. Light though the weight was which rested in the saddle of Sally Ann, and skillful though the rider might be, yet there was a great voice in Camden that told him that, even with such a handicap, she could never have beaten Crusader. However, there was no use dwelling on possibilities. Here was an actual fact. She was pulling ahead, little by little, up the grueling slope of the mountain, picking her way lightly and neatly.

He had hope still. If he could come even within striking distance of the mare by the time she turned over the crest, Crusader would have more than a chance. Weary as he might be, and tireless as her energy seemed to be, yet on the long, smooth downslope on the farther side of the mountain and then across the long level at its foot to the starting point, the long legs and the tremendous stride of the stallion were sure to tell for his advantage. Even Loring must know this.

Camden had loosed the reins on the stallion and let him work his own way along, only heartening him and steadying him with a word now and again, or perhaps picking out a more roundabout, but less steep, route up among some difficult place among the rocks. The great horse worked like the giant that he was, heaving himself and his burden up and up the slope. Twice Camden saw the leader turn in his saddle and look back to mark the tireless progress of the stallion. After each backward glance, he urged the mare forward more fiercely.

He was afraid then, and, sensing the fear, Camden himself grew more confident, for he knew that fear is a load in the heart and a load in the saddle. Fear is the thing that turns flesh of man or beast into lead.

They had crossed the first and the sharpest of the rises of the mountainside, and on a little shelving plateau, with smoother ground ahead of him all the way to the round summit of Jericho Mountain, Camden halted the stallion to let the fine animal breathe. The stallion, letting his head fall as soon as his master was dismounted, propped his legs a little more firmly and panted with heaving sides. Camden listened anxiously. There was not a rattle; there was not a sign of roughness. All was well with the great black if only he could have a few moments to recover from this sudden exhaustion that the race had brought him.

But Loring, well above now, was still climbing like a madman, forcing his mare on and on, with never a pause or a breathing space. It was supreme folly for such a horseman to ride in such a way. Horseflesh could not stand it. But Camden, with a giddy beating heart, knew the reason. Fear was whipping Loring along, fear of defeat, fear of the loss of the prize that was so nearly won.

Camden looked beneath him. Far below, he caught

glimpses of the laggards—five, six, ten, or a dozen of them altogether. But half of them would never finish the race that day. Never! They were working as slowly as snails at the enormous mass of the mountainside. For the pace that Crusader had set in the march across the desert had been truly killing.

Now the final stage of the upward progress must begin. Far, far away now, was the brown mare, laboring along with the light form of Loring on her back. Would she ever come back to them?

At that, the heart of Camden leaped. He had to set his teeth, and then, leaping onto the blanket, he put the stallion up the slope. He would have burst into a gallop, even up that terrible angle, for the great heart of the horse could not brook a leader so far ahead as the mare. For well he knew, wise old racer that he was, that this was not a mere pleasure jaunt. This was the sort of work a victory in which brought extra oats and sweet apples, crushing deliciously under the teeth, and petting and fondling, and long days of delightful idleness in some green pasture. More than all, there was the mind of this man on his back, willing him on and pushing him on with a mental force, like a great controlling hand. The man's will was his hope, and the strength of the heart of Camden was the strength of the heart of the great stallion.

Yet he was reined in short and forced to take the upward way with short, mincing steps. Wise rider. For one upward leap was more exhausting than half a mile of such more careful travel. Now they were gaining, steadily, steadily, on the mare above them. Her head was down, she was plodding with a religious determination, but it was madness of the first degree to rush her up that great ascent with never a pause. Beyond a doubt, her master knew the folly he had committed and was cursing himself.

Across the ear of Harry Camden broke a sharp report, like the clangor of two sledge-hammers slung hard and brought face to face. Then a wicked humming, followed by a second hammer stroke.

The echoes rolled wildly around him. He did not know in what direction to take shelter, but one thing he did know, and this was that someone with a repeating rifle was firing point-blank at him. Another instant and then he was struck a rude blow on the left shoulder—a stunning shock, combined with a swift and searing pain.

NECK AND NECK

He looked straight above him. Yonder was Loring, struggling toward the summit. He had heard the shot, for he had turned in the saddle, waving a derisive arm. He could not have done the firing. Then Camden caught the glint of winking steel in the sun.

At such a time the mind acts, not the body. There was no volition in the lightning draw that snatched the revolver out of Camden's holster and made him fire. All that he saw was that one blink of light, and then a blur of shadow moving behind a shrub, but as he fired, he heard a scream, and a short, broad-shouldered man staggered out from the bush, dropped his rifle, and fell on his face.

Far, far above, Loring, turning again in the saddle at the last shot, saw what had happened and leaned suddenly over the horn of his saddle. But Camden, turning Crusader to the right, was instantly by the side of his victim.

It was the same man who had opened the door at the hotel and brought him word that Loring wished to see him. He was dead, or dying, for his face was a smear of red. The snap shot had gone home. As Camden, regardless of his own wound, dropped beside the fallen body, the eyes flashed open, scowled up at Camden, and then the lips mumbled: "Loring! He put me here. He was the one. . . ." That was all. The stare grew fixed. There was no struggle. Death came to him with no sting.

Camden closed his eyes to the glare of the sun. Then he lifted the body with his right arm and placed it in the shadow of the brush. But after that, he had his own wound to attend to. When he ripped his shirt open, he saw at once that it was no serious matter. It was a glancing cut off the bone of the upper arm. Terribly painful, bleeding fast, but easily bandaged. That bandage he made of his shirt, knotting it swiftly. Then he was back on the black stallion and heading once more up that endless slope. Not endless now.

Suddenly he was at the crest, and there was the brown mare, not so appallingly far in front. Astonishingly near, it seemed to Camden.

He spoke, and the great Crusader swung forward in his stride. Here was galloping ground, and what could the mare do to the gallop of Crusader? Yes, she did well enough. She was stretching well over the ground, running hard and true, with no sway or swerve to her pace—a wonderful feat, truly, for so small a horse after so long a ride.

The slope grew sharper; the galloping was discarded. Again the mare gained. Now they entered the rolling foothills, and galloping ground again.

But now the long, rolling canter of Crusader began

to tell. Slowly but steadily they pulled on Loring. Loring, turning in the saddle, saw behind him a wild vision of a man clad in a shirt rent half in pieces, blurred across with bright crimson, his left arm swinging in a helpless pendulum at his side, but with his right hand and with his voice controlling the stallion and riding wonderfully well, and with every stride gaining, gaining!

A yell of rage, and then almost of terror burst from Loring's lips, and he swung his quirt. The mare responded. She was true blue to the last bit of strength in her sturdy heart. But how could she stand against the racing legs of Crusader? He swept on and on, closer and closer. Darkness was spreading in the brain of Camden. Twice he felt himself falling forward, faint. Twice he rallied, and then, just before him, he saw the straining body of the mare, and a little way off a great semicircle of men and women and children standing, with the town behind them. It was not a roaring in his brain, then, that he had heard. It was the yelling of that wild crowd, seeing such a finish as the Jericho race had never before furnished and would never furnish again—a driving finish after five hundred miles of terrible labor across mountain and desert—two horses, side-by-side, then neck and neck.

There was a deep-throated shout from Harry Camden. It caught the stallion in mid-stride and flung him forward. The shining black head slid under the wire in front of the straining head of brown. Crusader had won.

That was what smote against the ears of Harry Camden as he turned the big black horse back to the starting point. The crowd washed about them, fearless of the terrible hoofs of the stallion. Here was Colonel Dinsmore. Here was a white, pretty face—Ruth Manners, making toward him. Here were volleyed questions—what had happened—had he fallen? But yonder sat Loring, crushed in the saddle, and that sight cleared the brain of Harry Camden.

"The race is over?" he asked hoarsely.

"All over, lad!" cried the delighted colonel. "Come down here and. . . ."

Camden came, but it was only to brush them aside with a sweep of his thick right arm, and from the grimness in his face they shrank back. He clove a way through the throng straight to the side of Loring. He reached up and with his one hand tore the man from the saddle and held him in a terrible grip. The man was helpless.

"Loring," they heard him say, "that gent on the mountain lived long enough to tell me that you put him there. And I've lived long enough to win this race, and now there's a thing between you and me, Loring . . . how will you want to talk?" As he spoke, he flung Loring from him.

There was no hesitation in that thin, yellow face. His revolver came out even before he had finished staggering. Twenty men could swear that the gun was clear of the sheath, or nearly clear, before Camden drew his own weapon. Yet when the two guns rang out, Camden stood erect, and Loring crumpled on his side.

The sheriff was there, one leap too late to stop the fight, but soon enough to snap his own gun into the ribs of Camden.

"Take my gun," he heard Camden say. "I'm sick of livin', I tell you, and so'll you be when you hear Loring talk . . . if he tells the truth before he dies. I wonder if he will."

That was exactly what Loring did. Perhaps conscience wakened in him as death drew near. Perhaps it was fear of a last Judge before whom he dreaded to stand with this stain on his heart.

He told the truth and the full truth that freed Harry Camden, and sent Mervin fleeing like a frightened rat for his life. He was never found. He disappeared from the face of the earth, and some said that the river must have caught him when he attempted to cross it with his horse.

Of that they never talked in the later days, Ned Manners and his sister, and his new-made brother, Camden. For one thing, they were too full of happiness to think of evil days. For another, they were too busy working the farm, which the money of Colonel Dinsmore had extended for them to twice its original bounds. But in a plot of the richest ground, near the house, so that he could come and put his head through the window whenever he heard the whistle of Camden, Crusader lived like a king. After all, as the colonel said, he was right royal.